MASTERS OF THE WILD
A Guidebook to Barbarians, Druids, and Rangers

Credits

Designers: **DAVID ECKELBERRY AND MIKE SELINKER**
Additional Design and Inspiration: **WOLFGANG BAUR, MICHAEL DONAIS, RICH REDMAN, JENNIFER CLARKE WILKES, TEEUWYNN WOODRUFF**
Editor: **PENNY WILLIAMS**
Creative Director: **ED STARK**
Art Director: **DAWN MURIN**
Cover Artist: **JEFF EASLEY**
Interior Artist: **DENNIS CRAMER, DAVID DAY, WAYNE REYNOLDS**
Typesetter: **ANGELIKA LOKOTZ**
Graphic Designer: **CYNTHIA FLIEGE**
Business Manager: **ANTHONY VALTERRA**
Project Managers: **JUSTIN ZIRAN, MARTIN DURHAM**
Production Manager: **CHAS DELONG**

Playtesters: Rich Baker, Tim Beach, Andy Collins, Michael Donais, Dale Donovan, Jeff Grubb, Robert Gutschera, Gwendolyn FM Kestrel, Jessica Lawson, Duane Maxwell, Angel McCoy, David Noonan, Jonathan Tweet, JD Wiker, Jennifer Clarke Wilkes, Skip Williams, Teeuwynn Woodruff, Warren Wyman, Justin Ziran

Based on the original DUNGEONS & DRAGONS® rules created by Gary Gygax and Dave Arneson and the new DUNGEONS & DRAGONS game designed by Jonathan Tweet, Monte Cook, Skip Williams, Richard Baker, and Peter Adkison.

Resources: Some of the material in this book originally appeared in the FORGOTTEN REALMS® Campaign Setting, Magic of Faerûn, Defenders of the Faith: A Guidebook to Clerics and Paladins, Sword and Fist: A Guidebook to Fighters and Monks, and Song and Silence: A Guidebook to Bards and Rogues.

This Wizards of the Coast game product contains no Open Game Content. No portion of this work may be reproduced in any form without written permission. To learn more about the Open Gaming License and the d20 System License, please visit www.wizards.com/d20.

U.S., CANADA, ASIA,
PACIFIC, & LATIN AMERICA
Wizards of the Coast, Inc.
P.O. Box 707
Renton WA 98057–0707
(Questions?) 1–800–324–6496

EUROPEAN HEADQUARTERS
Wizards of the Coast, Belgium
P.B. 2033
2600 Berchem
Belgium
+32–70–23–32–77

620-88164-001
9 8 7 6 5 4 3 2 1

TABLE OF CONTENTS

TABLES

Introduction

"Feel the green."

—Vadania

For all its magic, its fearsome dragons, and its powerful wizards, the world of the Dungeons & Dragons® game is still predominantly a natural one. Animals, plants, and weather patterns form the basis of its ecology, and the strength of nature is never in doubt. The characters who most closely embrace this wild, natural world are fully equipped to deal with its down-to-earth realities. These characters aren't consumed in far-flung extraplanar experiments, worship of distant immortal deities, or abstract systems of ethics. They don't withdraw from the natural world into monasteries or cities. Druids, rangers, and barbarians belong to their world in a way that no other characters can. The barbarian fills his existence with a zest for living and possesses indomitable strength. The ranger combines knowledge of nature with mystical grace. The druid welcomes into herself all the wonders of land, sea, and sky.

Despite their power, these "masters of the wild" are at heart humble people. Because they adapt to their world and seek to protect it, fools may consider them weaker than warlords and rulers who force their wills upon the land. While barbarians, druids, and rangers approach life differently than people who band together in walled cities do, these characters nonetheless make formidable opponents. This book examines the masters of the wild in detail and provides you with new tools that you can use to maximize their adventuring potential.

WHAT THIS BOOK IS AND IS NOT

The material presented herein pertains to the new edition of the Dungeons & Dragons game. You'll find new feats, spells, and prestige classes, as well as useful advice for getting the most out of your barbarian, druid, or ranger character.

Nothing here supersedes or replaces the rules and information presented in the core rulebooks, except as noted. This supplement is designed to mesh with the rules system presented in the *Player's Handbook*, the *Dungeon Master's Guide*, and the *Monster Manual*.

This book presents options, not restrictions, for playing the D&D® game. However, players should ask their Dungeon Masters (DMs) about incorporating elements of this book before making changes to their characters. DMs can also make good use of the new feats, spells, and prestige classes presented here for designing nonplayer characters. Use what you wish and change or ignore the rest. Have at it, and enjoy!

HOW TO USE THIS BOOK

This book's primary goal is to help you customize your barbarian, druid, or ranger player character. With the material presented here, you can personalize your character and broaden his or her capabilities.

Chapter 1 discusses the advantages of playing a barbarian, druid, or ranger. Here you'll find advice on how to take advantage of your character's class abilities and minimize any potential weaknesses. Explanations of, advice on, and expansions to topics that are already part of the game, such as choosing favored enemies are also here.

Chapter 2 offers special feats, such as Fast *Wild Shape* and Dragon's Toughness, with which to enhance your character's abilities. In addition, there is an extensive discussion of skills, with notes on new and interesting uses of class skills for barbarians, druids, and rangers.

Chapter 3 presents items of interest to both spellcasting and nonspellcasting characters.

Chapter 4 offers advice on how to play alongside animal companions. It also includes statistics for new dire animals as well as for members of a new subtype of animal—legendary animals.

Chapter 5 takes your character in exciting new directions with the animal lord, the blighter, the frenzied berserker, and many other prestige classes.

Chapter 6 expands the selection of divine spells available at all spell levels.

CHAPTER 1: NATURE'S LORE

"Time flows like a river. All our sufferings, these are just pebbles in the riverbed."

—Vadania

This chapter examines the roles of the barbarian, the ranger, and the druid in the campaign. Such characters might appear to be loners, cut off from civilization and stuck in the cycle of nature. Fundamentally, though, the DUNGEONS & DRAGONS game isn't about solo play; it's about team dynamics in an unpredictable world. Thus, barbarians, druids, and rangers must somehow find ways to work harmoniously with other classes, using their particular talents to advance the group's goals. This section discusses how to integrate these "outsiders" into a campaign so that they can use their strengths to the fullest.

THE BARBARIAN IN PERSPECTIVE

"There's a logic to chaos. Hit 'em with everything you've got. Hit 'em fast, hit 'em hard, hit 'em till they stop moving. That's logic."

—Krusk

The barbarian's road is the path to power. Without the combat tricks of the fighter, the holy energy of the paladin, or the lithe grace of the ranger, the barbarian still more than holds his own in combat. How? He's tougher and stronger than everyone else, and that makes all the difference.

Many melee-oriented characters profit from an obvious versatility. The ranger and the paladin balance their combat prowess with spellcasting and other special abilities. The rogue has a wide range of skills, the fighter a selection of bonus feats, and the monk a palette of special abilities. The bard is the very definition of flexibility. So why does the barbarian fare so well in comparison with them? Because he has focus. He won't try to trick or deceive you. He won't try to do anything but overcome you by force. That devotion to a single methodology makes the barbarian an unusually effective war machine. After all, during any given round of combat, the two actions that most characters perform are attacking and avoiding the attacks of others. So why not be good at it?

Of course, a barbarian must be able to take hits at least as well as he can dish them out. Survivability is of paramount importance to a character who relies primarily on combat. While it's good to have the might to strike down foes, it's also important to live long enough to see the next fight. The barbarian has more hit points, on average, than a character of any other class, and his damage reduction ability effectively increases that total. Even rage, his signature offensive ability, gives him extra hit points that may allow him to survive an extra round or two of combat. In addition, the barbarian's uncanny dodge ability minimizes his exposure to surprise, flanking, and

traps. Finally, many high-level barbarians don suits of mithral full plate (medium armor) to preserve their fast movement while gaining the best Armor Class possible. This same reasoning also explains the popularity of *rings of evasion* and *cloaks of displacement* among barbarian characters. In addition, the barbarian's rage, damage reduction, and uncanny dodge abilities improve as he rises in level, making him even more formidable.

All that obvious power and toughness can make a barbarian forget about some of his other advantages. His class skills are diverse enough to allow for considerable variation, and it is the choice of skills more than anything else that differentiates one barbarian from another. One may concentrate his skill ranks in Intimidate to become a swaggering warrior; another may choose to know the outdoors through Intuit Direction, Swim, and Wilderness Lore.

Other adventurers tend to view the barbarian as an unsophisticated, ignorant, and unintelligent thug. In fact, more than a few barbarians do fit that stereotype, but plenty of others are clever—if not brilliant—warriors. They may not be worldly, but neither are they gullible. Nor are they necessarily violent, except when the situation calls for judicious use of might.

Race and the Barbarian

Human and humanoid societies exist at all levels of cultural development, from primitive to advanced, so the barbarian class is open to all races. Social restrictions make some races more likely than others to embrace the barbarian way of life, but concrete disadvantages to adopting the class are few.

Humans: Lacking the fighter's bonus feats, a barbarian can profit greatly from the bonus feat and the bonus skills that the human race offers. Humans are also the most likely humanoids to descend into—or fail to rise above—a primitive culture. While that may be a regrettable trait for humanity in general, it makes human barbarians the most common and the most accepted members of that class.

Dwarves: Barbarians generally don't flourish in highly regimented societies, so it's no surprise that dwarves training for warcraft tend to become soldiers (fighters) rather than barbarians. Where the normally orderly dwarven society is absent for some reason, dwarven barbarians can arise. For example, a dwarf who grew up among primitive humans would be a perfect candidate for the class, as would one whose keep was overrun and left in chaos. Dwarves make good barbarians for many reasons. Not only does the dwarf's +2 bonus to Constitution enhance the barbarian's already high average hit points, it also extends his rages. In addition, the barbarian's fast movement ability offsets the dwarf's normally slow movement rate. Finally, the dwarven racial bonus on saving throws to resist spells fits in nicely with the distrust of wizardry that some barbarians exhibit.

Elves: Most elven societies do not accept barbarians, perhaps because elves do not make especially good ones. The elf's penalty to Constitution devalues the barbarian's natural strengths, and although he is known for his carefree nature, the typical elf finds the primitive and sometimes savage ways of the barbarian repellent. A noteworthy exception is the wild elf (grugach), who takes up the barbarian's path with pleasure, despite his Constitution penalty.

Gnomes: Gnome barbarians are as rare as elven ones, though the reasons for this are primarily social. Gnomes do not separate themselves from the natural world, but they do tend to prefer sophisticated professions such as alchemy, engineering, and skilled trades. The average gnome enjoys his own cleverness too much to adopt the boldly direct approach of the barbarian. That's unfortunate, because the gnome doesn't perform poorly in that role. His size bonus to AC and attacks and his racial Constitution bonus offset his Strength penalty most of the time, and the barbarian's fast movement can compensate for the gnome's slow speed.

Half-Elves: Most barbarians are either humans or half-orcs, but half-elves run a close third. Since the half-elf has all the capriciousness of both his human and his elven sides, the requirement for a nonlawful alignment is easy to meet. Half-elves who find themselves cast aside by human and elven communities may find the barbarian's path an especially inviting one. Becoming a barbarian may even lead to a form of acceptance for the half-elf—although tribal societies are not known for welcoming outsiders, they readily accept a strong sword-arm in times of trouble.

Half-Orcs: Orcs are savages, it's true. So, it's no real surprise that many half-orc heroes are barbarians. All orcs can feel the battle rage pounding in their hearts, but only those who are also barbarians can harness their blood frenzy to best effect. The half-orc's bonus to Strength, the prime statistic for the combat-focused, is worth the sacrifice of Charisma and Intelligence. (After all, how often must the barbarian try to woo or outwit someone?) Count the number of times the fighter swings his sword, and remember that not only does the half-orc barbarian typically do more damage than the fighter with each hit, he also hits more often. If you're looking for the most powerful barbarian, and you can live with a bit of social stigma, then half-orc is the right choice.

Halflings: For the barbarian, high Constitution is usually better than high Dexterity, so gnome tends to be a better choice than halfling. Moreover, primitive or savage halfling communities are quite rare. Halflings are creatures of comfort, and their communities are strong. While their athleticism and bravery do them credit, and their racial bonus to Listen checks falls right in line with the barbarian's class skills, the penalty to Strength is too great a drawback to overlook.

Monsters: Among the monstrous races, grimlocks, lizardfolk, locathahs, and orcs are the most likely to adopt the barbarian way of life.

Grimlocks are xenophobic, subterranean creatures. Though they are blind, they can still sense their foes through blindsight. Grimlocks charge into combat wielding battleaxes, and that trait in itself seems barbaric. Grimlocks are strong, tough, and formidable enough to make fine barbarians. Because of the grimlock's various advantages, his level equivalent is his class levels +5.

Lizardfolk make ideal barbarians, both because their societies tend to be primitive and because their livelihood depends primarily on hunting and raiding. Fast movement provides them with a speed advantage over members of most other races. Rage greatly enhances a lizardfolk's already above-average Strength and Constitution scores, which can provide a significant bonus on their weapon and natural attacks. Because of these advantages, the lizardfolk's level equivalent is his class levels +4.

Locathahs are an exotic but reasonable choice for barbarian player characters. They tend toward neutrality in alignment, and while they don't trust outsiders, they aren't as aggressive as grimlocks. Perhaps that's because locathahs are unusually intelligent and wise (+2 racial bonus to Intelligence, Wisdom, and Dexterity) for humanoids who favor the barbarian class. Locathahs have a terrible land speed (10 feet) that even the barbarian's fast movement can't fully compensate for. Because of his advantageous ability modifiers, formidable natural armor, and ability to breathe water, however, the locathah's level equivalent is his class levels +3.

The orc is another common choice for barbarian, and his +2 racial bonus to Strength is a good selling point for the class. The DUNGEON MASTER'S Guide provides rules for playing an orc, which is basically a more extreme version of the half-orc. Many of the same considerations noted for half-orcs (above) apply to the orc as well.

The Barbarian and Other Classes

Barbarians can be very opinionated, so it's not surprising that they provoke strong reactions from other characters. In most cases, though, these differences in approach are just hooks for good roleplaying.

The barbarian makes an excellent addition to adventuring parties in need of more muscle. If you're playing a barbarian, you may find some good advice in the following paragraphs about getting along with your fellow adventurers.

Bards: There's nothing like a good skald to inspire your battle rage or while away the downtime between adventures with songs and stories. You don't really understand his spellcasting, but you can appreciate it more than that of the wizard or sorcerer—after all, the bard's magic can heal. Best of all, though, he can help you achieve immortality by making up songs and legends about your exploits. So what if he tends to get the party into trouble with his boasting and tomfoolery occasionally? What's life without a little conflict?

Clerics: You can certainly appreciate a good healer, but the typical cleric spends a lot of time talking about the afterlife and trying to convert others to his faith. You don't worry all that much about the next life—you have to focus on the here and now if you want to survive. Cler-

---

Level Equivalent

Some monsters are innately more powerful than members of the common races (human, elf, dwarf, and so on). When one of those monsters gains levels in a class, some number is added to its class levels to determine its effective level. The total of its class levels and this number (which varies according to creature type) is its level equivalent.

For example, a grimlock's level equivalent is equal to its class levels +3. This means that a 1st-level grimlock barbarian is effectively a 4th-level character—in other words, roughly equal in power to a 4th-level player character of one of the common races. (What gives a grimlock this advantage is its blindsight, coupled with its immunity to attacks that rely on the target having a visual sense.)

An ordinary member of a monster race (one without class levels, such as the grimlock described in the *Monster Manual*) does not have a level equivalent.

In addition to grimlocks, creatures discussed in this book that have level equivalents are lizardfolk, locathahs, centaurs, dryads, nymphs, gnolls, sahuagin, and yuan-ti.

For more on level equivalent, see Monsters as Races in Chapter 2 of the DUNGEON MASTER'S Guide.

ics who follow nature deities (including nonhuman deities such as Corellon Larethian) are another matter. They have their feet on the ground, so to speak, even if their heads are in the sky, and you welcome their presence. It's wise not to offend any cleric if you can help it; you can't deny the power of deities in the world.

Druids: You get along with the druid just fine. She has healing powers, but she doesn't proselytize the way the typical cleric does. Maybe that's because both of you are committed to nature, or because you share many skills, or because she simply prefers to follow her own path. Whatever her philosophy, the druid is the sage of your world—her knowledge of nature outstrips even your own. Although you may never adore nature the way she does, you both walk the same trails and drink from the same springs.

Fighters: You can't help but appreciate the company of a fighter, since his approach to life is so much like yours. He is a staunch ally in battle and a friendly rival outside it. The fighter has more options and tricks than you do in combat, but you're often the more formidable foe, especially while you're raging. In addition, you have a wider array of skills than he does, so you have the advantage over him in wilderness exploration. None of this hurts your friendship, though. A little competition is a good thing, after all.

Monks: If you have an opposite number, it has to be the monk. Your zest for life and focus on reality are diametrically opposed to her philosophy of withdrawal from the world. You have no trouble expressing your opinions, but she's terribly reserved—she must either be afraid of something or be too stifled to show her feelings. Other people claim that your approach to life and hers are both valid, but you think she's simply wrong. You don't worry much about her choices, though, as long as she doesn't try to impose them on you.

Paladins: The paladin is a welcome ally in combat, but off the battlefield, the two of you seldom see eye-to-eye. You hate restrictions, and she, of course, is rigidly lawful as well as good. You tend to set aside social niceties and get right to the heart of a situation; she wastes time with platitudes and negotiation. Even in combat, the two of you sometimes differ in your approaches. Whereas the paladin considers her foes' actions in a moral sense and tries to protect the weak, you simply want to crush your enemies and to see them driven before you. Nevertheless, the two of you can work together quite effectively as long as your overall goals coincide.

Rangers: In melee, the ranger is your polar opposite. Light and graceful, he often wields two weapons while you typically fight with a single large one. You're mightier than he is, but he dabbles in divine spells. Look past those superficial differences, though, and it's obvious that the two of you have a lot in common. You share more than a few class skills, including Wilderness Lore. You both embrace the outdoors, and you're both uncomfortable in heavy armor. The ranger is better at tracking foes than you are, but you're happy to throw in your muscle against his favored enemies.

Rogues: Some people dislike rogues, but you can see the advantage of having one around. Without her, you're likely to bear the brunt of a lot more traps. And not even

you can ignore the impressive damage she can inflict when you're helping her flank a foe. Rogues and barbarians often achieve a profound respect for one another that eventually deepens into genuine friendship.

Sorcerers: Here's a fellow who can fire off some very flashy spells, but his power doesn't come from gods, or even from books, like the wizard's does. He says his spellcasting ability is natural, and maybe that's true—he does wield his power with an easy grace, as though it were part of him. As long as he's honest with you about his abilities and treats you with respect, there's no reason the two of you can't become close friends. But if he tries to forge an air of mystery about himself, as some sorcerers do, he's likely to earn your antipathy instead.

Wizards: You don't understand the wizard, and you don't trust what you don't understand. How can just reading a book give her such incredible powers? For all you know, she could be in league with some dark deity, so her ability to toss around *fireballs* won't earn her any respect from you until she takes the time to explain how she does it. At that point, maybe you can move beyond your basic mistrust of the unknown and begin to form a personal connection with her.

Choosing When to Rage

"Sometimes my mind just gets in the way. Sometimes not."
—Krusk

The barbarian's rage is limited in both duration and frequency, so the question of when to activate it is an important tactical decision. But the considerations change as the barbarian gains levels and has more opportunities to rage.

The low-level barbarian can rage only once or twice per day, so he must use the ability wisely. One option is to save his rage for the combat that he guesses to be the big showdown of the day. In the typical dungeon, it's often obvious when the party is facing or about to face the toughest villain. In this case, it makes sense to rage as soon as the battle begins. The faster the enemies can be eliminated, the less damage they do, and the fewer party resources must be expended in the battle. Unless the barbarian's Constitution score is especially low, his rage should last long enough to finish even the toughest fight of the day.

It sometimes makes sense for a low-level barbarian to rage when he's low on hit points. The extra hit points that rage grants may keep him on his feet long enough to finish off his foe, and a rage opportunity left unused is no good to an unconscious or dead barbarian. However, this tactic can be problematical. The bonuses last until the rage ends. At that point, the barbarian immediately loses those extra hit points—and if he's already severely in-

jured or unconscious, he might die from that additional loss. In fact, a barbarian who uses this tactic frequently is more likely to end up dead after a fight than anyone else in his party.

As the barbarian gains levels, deciding when to rage becomes easier. The mid-level barbarian, who can rage three or more times per day, might want to use the ability whenever he faces spellcasting enemies. It grants him a +2 morale bonus on Will saves and a +2 bonus on Fortitude saves (through increased Constitution). Given that Will saves can be something of an Achilles' heel for the barbarian, anything that minimizes his chance of falling victim to fear or mental domination is a good thing—not just for him, but for everyone in his party. The same reasoning applies when he's facing opponents who use poison or a draining ability that requires a saving throw—the barbarian should rage to try to prevent any negative effects he knows are coming. He might also consider raging to gain the Strength bonus he needs to open an especially stubborn door or overcome a physical obstacle, or to gain the saving throw bonuses when he fears setting off a troublesome trap.

At 20th level, when he can rage five or more times per day, the barbarian should simply use the ability at the start of every significant encounter. Against obviously weaker foes, he can withhold his power just as the wizard or spellcaster conserves spells, but whenever the outcome is worth worrying about, he should rage.

THE DRUID IN PERSPECTIVE

"Nature is by definition uncontrollable. At best you can attempt a momentary influence, but even that is subject to the whims of nature."

—Vadania

The druid's home is more spacious, and possibly more beautiful, than that of any other character. Tall oaks, pines, and elms form the roof over her world—a canopy more vibrant and interesting than any ceiling fresco. The grasses and leaves provide her with a floor and a soft bed. Where are the walls? The druid laughs, for she knows no walls—no boundaries to her never-ending natural world.

Within her home or outside it, the druid is never without friends. That wolf hiding in the grass, the hawk flying above, and the mighty bear—these make loyal traveling companions as well as fearsome opponents for uninvited guests. Should she need clever scouts to prowl the bushes or soar through the sky in search of enemies, or strong warriors to protect her from harm, her friends can be at her side in a moment. If their aid isn't enough,

she can become one of nature's creatures and either defeat her foes with claw and tooth or take wing and escape. Woe to the cretin who thinks the druid powerless outside her wood, for even in the darkest dungeon, she is never without friends, spells, or powers.

Unlike many adventurers, the druid is fully prepared to go it alone. The fighter, wizard, and rogue depend on the cleric to heal them, and the cleric depends on the fighter to keep enemies at bay. The druid, on the other hand, can defeat her enemies with fiery spellcasting nearly as powerful as the sorcerer's, take the form of a tiger or a lion to gain the upper hand in melee, then heal herself when the battle is done.

Because of this versatility, the druid has much to offer a group of adventurers. She can take on any role that's required. Need a healer for the barbarian? Can do. Need a little more firepower to strike down foes from a distance? No problem. Need some spells to make the party tougher? Sure thing. How about reasonable combat skills, allies that can be summoned at a moment's notice, and the ability to bring down the rain or clear away the clouds? The druid is your choice. With all these options, hundreds of druids can share the same world and still be nothing alike. One may concentrate on healing, another on the creation of magic items, another on animal companions, and yet another on assuming other shapes.

Race and the Druid

Druids can emerge from any natural environment. Where they are rarest is where cobbled stones and the noisy advance of civilization have replaced a carpet of leaves and the gentle song of the lark. Some races are more likely than others to take up the druid's path for cultural reasons, but in game terms there's no race that makes for an especially bad druid. Since Wisdom is the primary ability score for the class and no race has a bonus or penalty to this score, no obvious racial choice exists for druid characters.

Humans: Though humans lack the special abilities of other races, the bonus skill points and feat they gain at 1st level make them excellent candidates for the druid class. After all, a druid who knows more of the forest's secrets (though extra ranks in Wilderness Lore) is by definition a more powerful druid. The human druid also has the acceptance of her peers, especially if she is from a savage or primitive background. The one glaring human weakness, poor night vision, is problematical for druids, but they can eventually compensate for it through spells, magic items, or *wild shape*.

Dwarves: Dwarven druids, as the *Player's Handbook* notes, are rare. Since dwarves often exhibit fierce loyalty to clan or keep, placing nature first doesn't come easily for most of them. Nor does it help that many dwarves spend their lives working underground, carving up rock and stripping precious resources from the earth. Nevertheless, a dwarf who leaves that life behind can be a formidable defender of nature, tough beyond measure. The extra hit points a dwarf gets from her racial Constitution bonus are invaluable to a druid who spends a lot of time in battle. The druid's ability to take other forms though *wild shape* compensates nicely for the dwarf's slow movement rate, and darkvision is a real blessing.

Elves: Elves are the archetypal druids, with good reason. From birth, children of this race learn to love the woodlands and the natural world in general. Elven druids have several racial advantages, not the least of which is their improved vision—low-light vision and bonuses to Spot and Search checks. Sadly, they must set aside their racial training in the longsword, rapier, and bow; a druid who uses any of those weapons loses all her druid powers for 24 hours. The physical frailty of an elf (–2 penalty to Constitution) is a slight disadvantage, but one that most elven druids are willing to accept. Best of all, an elven druid can return to the woodland home of her youth and find acceptance and even honor among her kind. Not many cultures are so accepting of the druid, and in few other settlements can she feel truly comfortable.

Gnomes: Though many do not realize it, the gnomes' bond with the natural world is nearly as strong as the elves'. Gnomes live simply, in wooded hills and warm burrows. Unlike members of other races, they can converse with burrowing creatures through an innate *speak with animals* ability. Whether it is a blessing of the deities or a trick the gnomes learned over time, this ability bonds them with animals in a way that few others understand. Add in the gnome's low-light vision and natural hardiness, and the gnome druid has many of the dwarf's physical advantages as well as the social acceptance that the elf enjoys. Though her small size makes the gnome druid physically weaker than a human, *wild shape* allows her to take the form of an animal with great strength, such as a bear or leopard. Humble, playful people that they are, gnomes make talented and steadfast druids.

Half-Elves: Lost and looking for her place in the world, many a half-elf finds solace in serving nature. Perhaps it's a way of accepting her elven half or appeasing elven kin—or perhaps the half-elf whom society has cast aside finds a certain appeal in the sometimes lonely path of the druid. Whatever her reasons for taking up the class, the half-elven druid benefits from her elven heritage through her improved vision. Half-elves may also have an easier time getting along in a human-dominated world than elves do.

Half-Orcs: It's unfortunate that so few half-orcs take up the druidic path. Like their orc parents, many half-orcs live in wild frontiers, often far away from settled and well-defended towns. Those same frontiers are often home to druids. Half-orc characters have two significant advantages: darkvision and a a +2 racial bonus to Strength. Moreover, although some may mock the half-orc for her lack of intelligence and her crudeness, a druid can live without great intelligence and charisma. Like the half-elf, the half-orc must live with a degree of social stigma, so she may find a solitary existence in the woods preferable to dealing with those who can't accept her for what she is. Nature, after all, embraces all living beings and brings peace to the tormented soul.

Halflings: Halflings make good druids. Their natural athleticism and sensitive ears are ideal for outdoor survival, and their general good luck and bravery serve them well too. The primary reason that so few halflings take up the sickle and mistletoe is the strength of the halfling community. Their predilection for comfortable beds, fine food, and ample drink tends to discourage them from choosing more challenging lives in service to nature. The few who do take up the druid's path find that their size is no impediment to excellence.

Monsters: Among the monstrous races, two stand out as likely druids: centaurs and lizardfolk. Both races generally have tribal societies, and both live in harmony with their environments. It is not uncommon in either culture to find druids in positions of leadership.

A centaur makes an excellent druid because of her +3 racial bonus to Wisdom, her natural familiarity with the outdoors, and her skill with horticulture. Her level equivalent is her class levels +7, so a 1st-level centaur druid would be appropriate for a 6th-level party.

Lizardfolk druids are easier to integrate with the average game than are their centaur counterparts—if nothing else, it's easier to take a lizardfolk than a centaur into a dungeon. Since the lizardfolk's level equivalent is her class levels +4, a 1st-level lizardfolk druid can join a campaign when the average character level is only 3rd. Unlike centaurs, lizardfolk druids have no racial adjustment to their Wisdom scores, but they do have respectable natural attacks at their disposal. As aquatic creatures, they're the only druidically inclined race that can also breathe water.

An enterprising player might also consider the dryad (class levels +4) and the nymph (class levels +12) as choices for a druid character. Both have strong ties to nature, and abilities that benefit from the addition of the druid class.

The Druid and Other Classes

The druid's defense of the natural world is neither short-sighted nor provincial. She is, in some sense, a living extension of nature's will. Therefore, when evil threatens the land, she's likely to enlist in the fight, even if it takes place far outside her grove. On other occasions, the druid may become involved in adventures out of loyalty to friends, or out of curiosity about some aspect of nature.

As noted above, the druid has no difficulty fitting into most adventuring parties. If you're playing a druid, you may find some good advice in the following paragraphs about getting along with your fellow adventurers.

Barbarians: Though the barbarian may rush headlong into combat, your relationship with him tends to be a good one. Both of you have woodland skills, and while you may not share the same view of the world, you do traverse the same hills and valleys.

Bards: You can understand the traveling lifestyle of the bard, but you don't envy it. Bards tend to stir up nearly as much trouble as rogues do in their wanderings, but bards at least make charming and versatile adventuring companions. Their wide range of skills, their spellcasting talent, and their combat ability make them suitable backups for nearly any other character class. Add to that their incredible musical effects, and what's not to like? The bard reminds you that zest for living is a good thing, and that whatever duties you take on, life is a precious gift that should be enjoyed, not merely spent.

Clerics: You and the cleric share many spells and some similar obligations, but you certainly don't share the same viewpoint on life. Your mind is focused on the earth, while he contemplates the heavens. This difference does not necessarily make for poor relations; indeed, you and he can develop a healthy respect for one another's abilities and come up with some highly useful spell combinations. True friendship is rare, however, unless the cleric has chosen the Animal, Plant, or Sun domain.

Fighters: It's always handy to have a fighter around when there's trouble. Through the barbarian may be tougher overall, the fighter is incredibly skilled in the art of war, which means he usually knows a lot of fighting tricks that can help his group defeat sophisticated and powerful adversaries. On the other hand, it seems that he devotes his entire life to combat—and what sort of attitude is that? It's that mindset—concentrating on petty squabbles instead of more important issues—that encourages ever-increasing conflict in the world. All things considered, you get along fine with the fighter when your goals coincide with his, but you would rather spend time with the ranger or the barbarian.

Monks: The monk seeks enlightenment through an ascetic lifestyle, which ultimately amounts to a denial of the self. To you, that seems utter folly. While there may be other planes of existence and a state beyond the "mortal realm," people should live in the present—in this world. You can sympathize with that lonely figure who came out of a monastery, but you have trouble embracing her outlook on life. As long as she's content to let others pursue their own paths, though, the two of you might be able to forge a bond of friendship.

Paladins: Your relationship with the paladin is often strained because the two of you have different outlooks on life and devote yourselves to different goals. The two things you have in common are a sense of moral duty and a desire to protect something in this world. You're both champions of your causes, and at those times when your interests overlap—when confronted by an overwhelming evil, for instance—you can form an alliance that few foes can withstand. Lasting friendship between the two of you is rare, however.

Rangers: As might be expected, you and the ranger get along well. You share an understanding of the natural world, and though your means may vary, you see the need for each other. The one thing that disturbs you about the ranger is his vengeful dislike of certain creatures. You can understand the desire to hunt—that's a natural instinct—but you don't understand the desire to eradicate a certain type of being. Though your skills tend to overlap, the two of you together with your animal companions can greatly increase the capabilities (and sheer numbers) of an adventuring party.

Rogues: You appreciate rogues for their unique talents, but your lifestyle rarely brings you into contact with them. For the most part, that suits you just fine. The fact that civilized society considers rogues to be miscreants, thieves, and assassins doesn't concern you, since you care little for society's strictures anyway. But some rogues think of life as a game, and too many others think of nothing but worldly goods. This leaves you little in common with the party's rogue, though you respect her skills.

Sorcerers: You may not fully understand the sorcerer or his origin, but you do respect innate gifts. The sorcerer, through some quirk of fate or bloodline, has a talent for magic, and unlike the wizard, he doesn't cloister his body inside a moldy tower or his mind inside an equally moldy tome. Most sorcerers are charismatic people who don't hide from the world or hold themselves above it. Those attributes make it easy for you to get along with them.

Wizards: There's a place for learning and a place for academic study. Wizards spend far too much time with their noses in books and not enough time getting exercise in the fresh air. But despite their typical lack of physical prowess, they often make pleasant companions and able adventurers, and their spells complement yours nicely. From your perspective, the only real flaw in the wizard's magic is that she draws her power from unnatural sources, calling in energy from places not of this world. Thus, while you are wise enough to befriend the wizard in your own adventuring group, you often take some small pleasure in fighting a villainous wizard.

Rules Update: Using *Wild Shape*

"They tickle and itch, but you get used to feathers. Never quite get used to the eggs, though."
— The druid Kelliana of Blue Tribe

Wild shape is one of the druid's most useful and flexible class features. The following version of this ability supersedes the one presented in the *Player's Handbook*.

Wild Shape

At 5th level, a druid gains the spell-like ability to turn herself into a Small or Medium-size animal (but not a dire animal or a legendary animal) and back again once per day. The druid may adopt only one animal form per use of this ability.

The creatures available as *wild shape* forms include some giant animals (as described in Appendix I of the *Monster Manual*) but not beasts, magical beasts, or anything with a type other than animal. The druid may use *wild shape* to become a dog or a giant lizard, for example, but not an owlbear. The form chosen must be that of an animal she is familiar with. For example, a druid who has never been outside a temperate forest could not become a polar bear.

The druid can freely designate the new form's minor physical qualities (such as fur, feather, or skin color and texture) within the normal ranges for an animal of that kind. The new form's significant physical qualities (such as height, weight, and gender) are also under her control but must fall within the norms for the animal's species. The druid is effectively disguised as an average member of the new form's species, gaining a +10 bonus on her Disguise checks as long as she maintains the form.

This change of form never disorients the druid. Upon changing to an animal form, she regains lost hit points as if she had rested for a day, though this healing does not restore temporary ability damage or provide any other benefits of resting for a day, and changing back does not heal her further. If slain, the druid reverts to her original form, though she remains dead.

When the change occurs, the druid's equipment, if any, melds into her new form and becomes nonfunctional. Material components and focuses melded in this way cannot be used to cast spells. When the druid reverts to her true form, any objects previously melded into the animal form reappear in the same locations they previously were and are once again functional. Any new items the druid wore in animal form (such as a saddle, rider, or halter) fall off and land at her feet; any that she carried in a body part common to both forms (mouth, hands, or the like) at the time of reversion are still held in the same way.

The druid acquires the physical and natural abilities of the creature whose form she has taken while retaining her own mind. Physical abilities include size as well as Strength, Dexterity, and Constitution scores. Natural abilities include armor, natural weapons (such as claws, bite, or gore), sensory abilities (such as low-light vision), and similar gross physical qualities (presence or absence of wings or gills, number of extremities, and so forth). Natural abilities also include mundane movement capabilities, such as walking, swimming, and flying with wings. The druid also gains all the racial bonuses and feats of the animal form selected. She does not gain any supernatural or spell-like abilities (such as breath weapons or gaze attacks) of her new form, but does gain all the form's extraordinary abilities. All these alterations last until the *wild shape* ends.

The druid's new scores and faculties are average ones for the species into which she has transformed. She cannot, for example, turn herself into a wolf with a Strength of 20. Likewise, she cannot change into a bigger or more powerful version of a creature (or a smaller or weaker version).

The druid retains her own Intelligence, Wisdom, and Charisma scores, level and classes, hit points (despite any change in her Constitution score), alignment, base attack bonus, and base save bonuses. (New Strength, Dexterity, and Constitution scores may affect final attack and save bonuses.) The druid also retains her own type (for example, humanoid), extraordinary abilities, and spell-like abilities, but not her supernatural abilities. She loses her ability to speak while in animal form because she is limited to the sounds that a normal, untrained animal can make. (The normal sound a wild parrot makes is a squawk, so changing to this form does not permit speech.)

Though the druid retains any spells she previously carried, her new form may not permit her to use them. Unless the chosen form is one with prehensile hands (such as a monkey or an ape) or some other manipulative appendage, the druid may not be able to manipulate material components and focuses for spells—even if those are not melded into her new form. Likewise, her lack of a humanlike voice means she cannot cast spells with verbal components or activate command word items. In the same manner, the lack of appropriate appendages may prevent her from using manufactured weapons and magic items. If the usability of a particular spell or item is in doubt, the DM makes the decision.

The druid can use this ability more times per day at 6th, 7th, 10th, 14th, and 18th level, as noted on Table 3–8 in the *Player's Handbook*. In addition, she gains the ability to take the shape of a Large animal at 8th level, a Tiny animal at 11th level, and a Huge animal at 15th level. At 12th level and beyond, she can take the form of a dire animal.

At 16th level, the druid may use *wild shape* to change into a Small, Medium-size, or Large elemental (air, earth,

fire, or water) once per day. She gains all the elemental's special attacks and special qualities when she does so, regardless of ability type (that is, she gains the supernatural and spell-like abilities of the elemental as well as extraordinary ones). She also gains the elemental's feats and racial skill bonuses for as long as she maintains the *wild shape* while retaining her own creature type (humanoid in most cases). At 18th level, she can assume elemental form three times per day.

Choosing a Wild Shape

Beginning at 5th level, the druid gains the ability to use *wild shape*. During her career, a variety of choices present themselves as she masters larger and smaller forms, and eventually she can assume the form of a dire animal or an elemental. The array of options can be downright bewildering.

The primary consideration in selecting an animal form is what you want it for. Here are some factors a druid should consider when approaching this decision.

Detecting: Because the druid can use the extraordinary abilities of the form chosen, she can gain blindsight as a dire bat or a porpoise. Most animals have low-light vision, and a few (such as the snake and the owl) also have racial Spot or Listen bonuses.

Escaping: The one of the best way to escape a troubling situation through *wild shape* is to take to wing as a hawk or an eagle. The fly speeds of those creatures are 80 and 60 feet respectively, and that's usually fast enough to escape from an advancing army or a land-bound monster. The owl, despite its popularity, doesn't fly especially fast (only 40 feet). In a dungeon, or against some airborne foes, the cheetah or horse may be a more appropriate choice. A light horse has a respectable land speed of 60 feet; the cheetah moves only 50 feet normally but can also travel 500 feet in a sprint (see the cheetah entry in the *Monster Manual*). Escape doesn't always require fast movement, though—a high-level druid can use *wild shape* to take the form of a Tiny animal and use the Hide skill to avoid enemies.

Fighting: *Wild shape* can make the druid a formidable opponent. Until 8th level, when she can use *wild shape* to become a Large animal, her best choices are the wolverine, black bear, or leopard, with three attacks each. Of these, the black bear offers the highest Strength score and the leopard the highest AC. The wolverine's rage ability grants it the same Strength bonus as the black bear, plus a few additional hit points. The form of a constrictor snake might also prove very useful, especially against enemy spellcasters.

For an 8th-level druid, the polar bear reigns supreme with its Strength score of 27. The heavy horse is weaker in combat but a lot less conspicuous, if that's a concern. The only other options worth considering are the big cats—lions and tigers—whose pounce and rake abilities are a fair trade for the polar bear's higher strength. The tiger is uniformly tougher than the lion, but both can hold their own in combat. Finally, reach provides a significant advantage in a fight, and the druid can gain that in the form of a Large viper.

At 12th level, the druid can use *wild shape* to become a dire animal. As a dire bear with a Strength of 31, she can

do 30 or more points of damage in a single round. The dire lion is her second-best choice.

When the druid reaches 15th level, the dire tiger becomes available, but the dire bear may still be a better decision. The dire tiger's Huge size makes it easier to hit than the dire bear, and the addition of pounce and rake attacks may not entirely compensate for that disadvantage.

At 16th level, the druid gains a significant new option—elemental form. This allows the druid access to all the special abilities of the chosen elemental, including whirlwind, drench, vortex, push, and burn. Because of its high Strength score, the earth elemental is probably the best choice, though the water elemental has a better AC. If AC is not a factor, however, the dire bear is still a better fighter than any elemental simply because of its higher strength.

Impressing Foes: Bears, lions, and elementals impress the local populace and frighten even veteran mercenaries. A DM may allow a +2 circumstance bonus on Intimidate checks for a druid using an impressive form.

Impressing Other Animals: The druid usually relies on her Animal Empathy skill to calm hostile or hungry animals and reassure them that violence is not necessary. The druid who takes the time to use *wild shape* to assume the target animal's form often has an easier time in this negotiation, even though she doesn't gain the ability to speak with the creature directly. To represent this advantage, the DM may allow the druid a +4 circumstance bonus on Animal Empathy checks made against an animal whose form she has assumed.

Scouting: Avian forms are good for scouting, but don't overlook subterfuge as an option. An old story tells of a druid who learned all her enemies' plans when she assumed the form of a heavy horse and served a day as the steed for the commander of the evil army. Most people pay little attention to horses, livestock, or passing frogs, and the druid can profit from that.

Training Animals: The training process becomes much easier if the druid can simply assume the animal's form and demonstrate the behavior or action she wants. The DM may allow the druid a +4 circumstance bonus on her Handle Animal checks when she uses *wild shape* in this fashion.

Traveling: Because of their good fly speeds, birds are the obvious choices for travel. Should travel by ocean, sea, or river be an option, the dire shark moves at an impressive speed (90 feet) that even the eagle cannot match. At 15th level and higher, the druid should seriously consider the form of an air elemental for travel because of its incredible fly speed (100 feet).

THE RANGER IN PERSPECTIVE

"You could just as easily get a shark to give up swimming as you could get a ranger to stay at home."

—Soveliss

Despite his association with the forest, the ranger cannot be described as "rooted." Too great an attachment to places, material possessions, and traditions is unhealthy from his point of view. After all, change is a fundamental aspect of nature, and it doesn't pay to fight that.

In fact, the ranger is among the most versatile of all characters. Yes, he wears armor, but it's never as clunky as the paladin's. Yes, he casts spells, but he never relies solely on them for survival as the wizard does. Yes, he moves like the breeze, but never with the blatant fear of straight-on confrontation that so many rogues display. Though the bard claims to be a jack-of-all-trades, it is the ranger who quietly proves himself the perfect balance of disciplines.

The ranger's versatility makes him more of a generalist than most other characters, and that can be as much a hindrance as a boon. He can't deal as much damage with a single blow as a greatsword-wielding fighter with Weapon Specialization or a wizard with a maximized *fireball*. What he can do is mete out a wild flurry of damage from multiple sources, then retreat before his opponent can return the favor. A ranger of moderate level might unleash three unerring arrows in one round, switch weapons and close in the next round, then lay his opponent low with four blows from his two weapons in the third round. If that opponent is a favored enemy, the second and third rounds might not even be necessary.

In many ways, the ranger's greatest strength is leadership. Like the rogue, he often scouts ahead of fellow party members, where he can make the best use of his Track feat and sense-oriented class skills. Unlike the rogue, however, he feels physically outmatched by the challenges that those talents reveal. As the first to spot an enemy, he must decide whether to close or sneak back, and his friend's lives may depend on the wisdom of his decision.

Race and the Ranger

Every humanoid race has spawned rangers, and each offers its own set of advantages. As with the druid, no obvious racial choice exists for a ranger.

Humans: Most rangers are human. Dividing a human ranger's initial skill points evenly between Bluff, Listen, Sense Motive, Spot, and Wilderness Lore gives the 1st-level human ranger a +5 bonus on those checks against favored enemies, in addition to any other bonuses he may have. Moreover, he doesn't have to choose between Weapon Focus and Alertness to augment his best attributes; he can get them both right away. Of course, the human's biggest advantage is that he is a member of the dominant race on the planet.

Dwarves: Like most of their race, dwarven rangers tend to live underground. Such "cavers" need not worry much about maintaining relations with fey creatures or protecting the trees, but that doesn't mean they should skimp on ranks in the Wilderness Lore skill. It's a necessity for tracking foes, especially since dungeon floors count as hard ground (see the Track feat description in the *Player's Handbook*). The Listen skill is also vital in a dungeon environment, and the ranger gets a bonus on Listen checks against favored enemies. The dwarven ranger's racial combat bonuses already let him shine against three categories of foes (orcs, goblinoids, and giants), so those are excellent first, second, and third

choices for favored enemy. Choosing giants first might well pay off when that first ogre comes charging down the dungeon corridor.

Elves: The elf is the ranger incarnate. He has bonuses on two skills for which the ranger gets also favored enemy bonuses: Listen and Spot. That means a 5th-level elven ranger gets a +4 bonus on Spot checks against his first favored enemy, on top of his skill ranks and any other bonuses he has. Most fey creatures favor elves, so the elven ranger can create a strong network of allies during his travels through the forest. In addition, his need for but 4 hours of meditation and 4 hours of rest rather than 8 hours of sleep means he is almost always on watch at night, when his low-light vision and high Spot bonus are the most useful.

Gnomes: Like the dwarf, the gnome ranger starts out with solid bonuses against some very common favored enemies: goblinoids, kobolds, and giants. Like the elf, he gets a racial bonus on Listen checks. Like the halfling, he gains bonuses on attack rolls and AC for being Small. Unlike anyone else, the gnome ranger with an Intelligence score of 10 or higher has both arcane spells and divine spells at 4th level, plus the best possible base attack bonus. All this makes the ranger class an excellent fit for the gnome. However, gnome rangers rarely leave their homelands—a loss to adventuring parties everywhere.

Half-Elves: The half-elf is already an outsider, so the ranger lifestyle is second nature for him. Nearly everything said above about the elf (racial bonuses on Spot and Listen checks, low-light vision, and so on) applies to the half-elf as well, though not always to the same degree. Socially, however, the half-elf is a better bridge between the

natural and the civilized worlds than either the elf or the human is.

Half-Orcs: Though many half-orcs consider barbarian and fighter to be better class choices, the half-orc ranger is a true monster against his favored enemies. A racial bonus to Strength, the best possible attack progression, and favored enemy bonuses mean that a 10th-level half-orc ranger with a Strength score of 22 and Weapon Focus (battleaxe) has a +20 attack bonus against his first favored enemy, not including the bonus of the magic battleaxe he has in each hand. A half-orc going this route must try to compensate for his Intelligence penalty, since the ranger's strength lies not only in combat but also in skills. Probably the biggest disadvantage for the half-orc ranger is that few believe he is a friend of the forest. Still, he has his ways of persuading people.

Halflings: The *Player's Handbook* notes that halfling rangers aren't encountered often, but that's primarily because they can choose when encounters occur. The halfling's Strength penalty undercuts his ranger bonuses, but consider the 9th-level halfling ranger with Weapon Finesse and a through-the-roof Dexterity score. He's tossing thrown weapons and wielding pairs of melee weapons, as well as moving silently and hiding better than anyone else through frequent use of the *pass without trace* spell. In addition, his exceptional bonus on Listen checks lets him know that his foe is coming long before he has to decide whether to fight or flee.

Monsters: Members of several monstrous races also make particularly good rangers. Among these are centaurs, gnolls, grimlocks, sahuagin, and yuan-ti (pureblood and halfblood).

All these creatures have racial bonuses to Strength, and each has one or more advantages all its own. The sahuagin's ability to breathe water and its blood frenzy are significant advantages, though they are effectively limited to underwater environments. The yuan-ti halfblood has several interesting options—scales for a natural Armor Class bonus, snakes instead of arms for natural attacks, or even a snake head with a poisonous bite. Add to this the spell-like abilities and psionic powers that all yuan-ti have, and either creature is a formidable foe.

The level equivalents of these creatures vary widely. The gnoll's level equivalent is class levels +3, the grimlock's is class levels +5, the sahuagin's is class levels +5, the centaur's is class levels +7, the yuan-ti pureblood's is class levels +12, and the yuan-ti halfblood's is class levels +13.

One final note about nonhuman rangers: All of them can select human as a favored enemy, and they should strongly consider doing so. Humans are the most frequently encountered foe in almost every D&D game, so favored enemy bonuses against them come into play often.

The Ranger and Other Classes

The ranger's single-minded pursuit of a favored enemy often provides the impetus for a quest. For example, if orcs occupy the hinterlands, it's the orc-hunting ranger who gets a group together to chase them out.

When selecting companions for his missions, the ranger should consider how his skills and attitudes fit with theirs. If you're playing a ranger, you may find some good advice in the following paragraphs about getting along with your fellow adventurers.

Barbarians: You and the barbarian make a terrific one-two punch, since you can both inflict tons of damage. Working together, you can also avoid nasty surprises—you watch for foes coming out of the woodwork and he ignores sneak attacks and avoids traps. A party with the pair of you doesn't have as much need for a rogue as one not so doubly blessed. The only issue between you and the barbarian is that you may want to leave combat long before he does.

Bards: The bard seems like such a dilettante. Both of you are extraordinarily versatile, but you're versatile with a purpose (at least in your mind). Nonetheless, you're both favorites of elves, so you tend to get along. On a good day, you're cool toward him (like you are to everyone else), and he's superficial toward you (like he is to everyone else).

Clerics: Though you might get along with a druid more easily, you rarely turn down an alliance with a cleric. Of course, the extent of the friendship always depends on his domains. A cleric with Animal, Healing, Sun, or other domains relating to nature is always a welcome companion, but you're less likely to enjoy the company of one who specializes in Death, Destruction, or Trickery—unless of course you're an evil ranger who doesn't care much about the cycle of life.

Druids: You and the druid are natural partners, in both senses of the term. You appreciate guidance in the ways of the wild, so you're willing to help out the druid in return for some of her knowledge. She's a better divine spellcaster than you are, but this works for both of you, if you plan accordingly. You carry the standby spells such as *protection from elements* so that she can focus on healing and controlling animals. Though your skills are similar, a party with both of you benefits from the many animals and summoned allies you both tend to have in tow, which can deliver a swarm of attacks against your foes.

Fighters: The fighter is a demonstration of everything that's wrong with society—he's clanky, monomaniacal, and graceless. You're almost as good at fighting as he is (considering that he gets bonus feats), but you have other abilities as well. When you're in a party with him, the monsters tend to consider you (with your light armor) as the lesser of the two threats—at least until you hit four times in a round.

Monks: The monk's ascetic lifestyle is very similar to the sort of self-exile you embrace. Both of you are nimble and silent, and you both have the ability to make extra attacks each round. Best of all, each of you respects the other's need for solitude. You and she could live in the same woods for years and never say a word to each other—except the occasional "Help!" When you do join forces, you make a powerful combination.

Paladins: If the fighter is rigid and loud, the paladin is even more so. Even if you're both of good alignment, you may be so far apart on the law and chaos axis that you can't have a civil conversation. Even her warhorse is a sticking point, since at any moment it can command your mount, and you're not about to stand for that. Still, the two of you do have one thing in common: If something goes against your code, you're unshakable in your fervor to set things right. When you both agree on something, it's not a good idea to get in your way.

Rogues: You have a lot in common with the party rogue because your skill sets overlap but don't compete. When the two of you move down a hallway together, you can back each other up in ways a paladin and wizard couldn't begin to understand. You may live in different environments, but you respect each other's abilities and attitudes.

Sorcerers: Sorcerers are what rangers would be if they were arcane spellcasters—fast, focused, and uncluttered by tomes and universities. You and the sorcerer work well together because you can depend on him to do what you expect and do it well.

Wizards: Wizards can be maddeningly unpredictable. You want maximum versatility in combat, and so does she—mostly for staying out of melee. But just when you decide to wade in for two-weapon battery, you discover that she's targeting the area for a *fireball*. Still, any arcane spellcaster is better than none, since she's bound to have lots of useful spells.

Variant: Urban Rangers

The *Player's Handbook* describes rangers as forest denizens who can use the natural camouflage of the woods to advantage. Soveliss, girded in his tree-trunk-brown studded leather, is ready at a moment's notice to disappear among the trees. This is a fine lifestyle for the majority of

rangers, but some prefer to stalk foes through other terrain. The urban ranger is the king of the streets, capable of tracking a foe through a marketplace or across a castle parapet.

To play an urban ranger, use the rules from the ranger class description in Chapter 3 of the *Player's Handbook*. Every rule mentioned there also applies to an urban ranger. With your DM's permission, however, you can adopt a few modifications designed to make your character more effective in the unorthodox urban terrain.

- Make the following class skill switches: Animal Empathy for Gather Information and Knowledge (nature) for Knowledge (local). Saying goodbye to an exclusive class skill is hard, but you need as many ranks in Gather Information and Knowledge (local) as you can get.
- Trade the Track feat for the Shadow feat (see Chapter 2). This gives you an edge in following someone through city streets. Also, you might want to adopt the special use of the Hide skill called Tail Someone, as described in Chapter 2.
- Take an organization or culture rather than a creature type as a favored enemy. For example, you might choose the Knights of the Hart, which would allow you to use your favored enemy bonuses against elves and humans who belong to that organization, but not against other elves and humans. Be sure to make such a choice in concert with your DM, or you could end up with a favored enemy you never encounter.
- Swap out a few ranger spells for bard spells of equal level. Here are some trades to consider: *detect snares and pits* for *detect secret doors*, *speak with animals* for *message*, *speak with plants* for *detect thoughts*, *plant growth* for *phantom steed*, and *tree stride* for *dimension door*. You might want to see if your DM would let you trade for spells from different class lists as well, though you're unlikely to get *chain lightning* out of the deal.

An urban ranger who wants to adopt a prestige class might consider the watch detective, the foe hunter, or the bloodhound (see Chapter 5). All those focus on improving the ranger's best attributes without advancing the naturalistic aspect of the class.

Below are statistics for an urban ranger created with these variant rules: the dwarven constable Sergeant Reginald Fitz-Louis and his trusty mastiff, Baskerville.

Sergeant Reginald Fitz-Louis: Male dwarf Rgr12; CR 12; Medium-size humanoid; HD 12d10+36; hp 102; Init +1; Spd. 20 ft.; AC 17 (touch 11, flat-footed 16); Atk +14/+9/+4 melee (1d8+3/19–20, +1 *ghost touch longsword*) and +13/+8 melee (1d6+2/×3, +1 *handaxe*) or +15 ranged (1d8+1/19–20, masterwork light crossbow with +1 *crossbow bolts*); SQ Dwarf traits, favored enemies (cult of Vecna +3, goblinoids +2, giants +1); AL LN; SV Fort +11, Ref +5, Will +7; Str 15, Dex 12, Con 17, Int 14, Wis 17, Cha 15.

Skills and Feats: Appraise +4, Bluff +7, Concentration +6, Craft (metalworking) +4, Craft (stoneworking) +4, Diplomacy +4, Disguise +4, Gather

Information +19, Hide +11, Intimidate +4, Knowledge (local) +12, Listen +11, Move Silently +6, Perform +4, Ride (horse) +6, Search +17, Spot +18; Alertness, Expertise, Improved Two-Weapon Fighting, Shadow, Skill Focus (Gather Information), Weapon Focus (longsword).

Dwarf Traits: +1 racial bonus on attack rolls against orcs and goblinoids; +2 racial bonus on Will saves against spells and spell-like abilities; +2 racial bonus on Fortitude saves against all poisons; +4 dodge bonus against giants; darkvision 60 ft.; stonecunning (+2 racial bonus on checks to notice unusual stonework; can make a check for unusual stonework as though actively searching when within 10 ft. and use the Search skill to find stonework traps as a rogue can; intuit depth); +2 racial bonus on Appraise checks and Craft or Profession checks related to stone or metal (figured into the statistics above).

Favored Enemies: Reginald has selected the cult of Vecna as his first favored enemy, goblinoids as his second, and giants as his third. He gains a +3, +2, and +1 bonus, respectively, on melee damage rolls and on his Bluff, Listen, Sense Motive, Spot, and Wilderness Lore checks against these creature types.

Spells Prepared (2/2/2; base DC = 13 + spell level): 1st—*detect secret doors, message;* 2nd—*cure light wounds, detect thoughts;* 3rd—*neutralize poison, phantom steed.*

Possessions: +3 *studded leather armor,* +1 *ghost touch longsword,* +1 *handaxe,* masterwork light crossbow, 25 +1 *crossbow bolts, circlet of persuasion, figurine of wondrous power* (onyx dog), *potion of sneaking, potion of cure moderate wounds.*

Baskerville: Male onyx dog; CR 1; Medium-size animal; HD 2d8+4; hp 13; Init +2; Spd. 40 ft.; AC 16 (touch 12, flat-footed 14); Atk +3 melee (1d6+3, bite); SA Trip; SQ Darkvision 60 ft., low-light vision, scent, *see invisible,* speaks Common; AL N; SV Fort +5, Ref +5, Will +1; Str 15, Dex 15, Con 15, Int 8, Wis 12, Cha 6.

Skills and Feats: Listen +5, Search +3, Spot +9, Swim +5, Wilderness Lore +1 (+5 when tracking by scent).

Choosing a Favored Enemy
"Do unto others as they seek to do unto you."
—Soveliss

Over the course of twenty levels, the ranger chooses five favored enemies. Many factors can come into play here, including the player's choice of background ("I chose my path when orcs devastated my homeland"), campaign environment ("Here in the snowy northlands, we live to fight the remorhaz"), and game utility ("What are we going to fight in the near future?").

Once the ranger makes a choice, he can't later change his mind. That means the player must bet on what kind of creatures the character is likely to meet most often. The Dungeon Master can help with this, since he or she knows what's out there in the campaign world.

Against his favored enemy, a ranger gets a bonus on Bluff, Listen, Sense Motive, Spot, and Wilderness Lore checks, as well as damage rolls with melee weapons and with ranged weapons fired from no more than 30 feet away. (This damage bonus does not apply against creatures immune to critical hits.) The value of the bonus is

+1 when the ranger first designates that creature type as a favored enemy, and it rises by an additional +1 at 5th, 10th, 15th, and 20th levels. He chooses his first favored enemy at 1st level, the second at 5th level, the third at 10th, the fourth at 15th, and the fifth at 20th.

There's a tradeoff involved in making these choices. Should the ranger's first favored enemy be a low-CR or a high-CR creature? Remember, the first favored enemy chosen is the one against which he has the highest bonus throughout his career, and the last is the one against which he has the lowest bonus. Is it better to gain an early advantage or to forego the immediate benefit and work toward the long term? In fact, both are perfectly valid choices. For example, suppose you choose orcs first. That gives your ranger a useful bonus against orcs when he's likely to see them most—when he's low level. When he's 20th level, though, he has a +5 bonus against orcs (which he may rarely see at that point) and a lower bonus against the more powerful creatures that he's likely to meet more often. Conversely, if you choose demons as your ranger's first favored enemy, he's not likely to get much benefit out of his bonus for a long time because he probably won't meet many demons until he has several levels under his belt. But when he does meet them, he immediately has a substantial bonus against them.

Aberrations: This category is a rich choice for favored enemy. Aberrations include beholders, carrion crawlers, driders, gibbering mouthers, mimics, mind flayers, nagas, otyughs, rust monsters, skum, umber hulks, will-o'-wisps, and many others. Of these, skum are the lowest-powered at CR 2. Thus, if you want an early advantage, aberrations may not be a good first choice. However, there's a clump of them in the CR 6–8 range, and even more beyond that, so this category is a fine choice for a second, third, or fourth enemy. If you don't mind waiting a while to reap the benefit, go ahead and take aberrations as your first choice.

Animals: Animals are among the best choices for first favored enemy. Your ranger should meet a lot of them at low levels, but he'll continue to meet tougher ones as he advances. Dire animals range all the way up to CR 9 (the dire shark).

Beasts: This surprisingly small category of foes includes odd creatures such as ankhegs, griffons, hippogriffs, hydras, owlbears, purple worms, and stirges, as well as dinosaurs, rocs, and sea lions. The CRs in this grouping range from 1 (stirge) to 12 (purple worm), so beasts are a good choice for a ranger's first, second, or maybe even third favored enemy.

Constructs: These creatures are immune to critical hits (and thus to the ranger's favored enemy damage bonus), so this is a suboptimal choice unless you're using the variant favored enemy rules, below. Bluff and Sense Motive are useless against constructs. The bonuses on Spot, Listen, and Wilderness Lore checks still apply, but since constructs frequently just sit in place until disturbed, these benefits aren't much help either.

Dragons: This category is a great choice at any level. A ranger can meet a wyrmling white dragon right out of the gate and still be fighting dragons when he reaches 20th level. This is one of the few categories that scales up as the ranger advances, since dragons advance as well.

The bonus is also effective against dragon turtles, half-dragons, pseudodragons, wyverns, and anything else with the dragon type. Pay special attention to those Bluff and Sense Motive bonuses—often the best way to deal with a dragon is by skillfully playing on its desire for treasure and fame.

Elementals: Unless you use the variant favored enemy rules below, your favored enemy damage bonuses don't work against elementals because they are immune to critical hits. The other bonuses still apply, but what good is a Spot or Listen check against a creature that anyone can see and hear from a quarter-mile away?

Fey: This category is an excellent choice for evil rangers, but good rangers tend to ally with these creatures rather than fight them. Dryads, nymphs, satyrs, and sprites fall into this grouping. Nymphs are the toughest at CR 6, so if you're going to take fey as a favored enemy, you might want to do so early.

Giants: Giants make great favored enemies for dwarves and gnomes, who already have racial bonuses against them. In addition to the six giants, this category includes ettins, ogres, ogre mages, and trolls. Since your ranger is likely to meet ogres early in his career, consider giants as a first or second favored enemy choice. That way, when he meets storm giants later on, he'll have a significant bonus against them.

Humanoids: This category requires the choice of a specific humanoid subtype, but only an evil ranger can choose his own subtype. Some choices here are better than others.

Humans: This is easily the best choice in the game for everyone except the nonevil human ranger, who can't select it. In almost any D&D game, player characters must fight many human foes. Even a ranger allied with humans should consider taking this option early.

Dwarves, Elves, Gnomes, Halflings: All four of these choices are much more limited than humans. If you think your ranger would be surprised to find a tyrannical halfling warlord trampling life and liberty across the campaign world, avoid these groups.

Orcs: This is an excellent choice for dwarves (who already get a +1 bonus on attacks against orcs) and a pretty good choice for others as well. Since the bonuses work against both orcs and half-orcs, this can be a good option to take early, when your ranger is fighting orcs and their leaders in abundance. And even though he's not as likely to meet orcs at higher levels, he may still have to deal with the occasional orc army or high-level half-orc NPC.

Gnolls: This is not as versatile a choice as orcs in most campaigns. The typical ranger is less likely to meet advanced gnolls than advanced half-orcs as he rises in level.

Goblinoids: This is a fine choice, particularly at low levels. A dwarven or gnome ranger already has a +1 racial bonus on attack rolls against these creatures and is likely to fight them for living space regularly. This category also includes bugbears, goblins, and hobgoblins (CR 2, 1/4, and 1/2, respectively). It's a good choice for first favored enemy, but it isn't too useful later.

Reptilians: This is a surprisingly good choice for a gnome ranger, who already has a +1 bonus on attack rolls against kobolds. Lizardfolk and troglodytes are also reptilians. Again, this is a good choice for a first favored enemy but less useful thereafter.

Aquatic: Speaking of lizardfolk, this category includes that race as well as locathah, merfolk, and sahuagin. If you expect your ranger to go to sea a lot, consider this option for his first or second favored enemy.

Magical Beasts: In a campaign with lots of bizarre creatures, you probably can't do better for a favored enemy than this. The list is enormous, and it includes most of the traditional D&D foes, such as basilisks, chimeras, cockatrices, displacer beasts, krakens, manticores, phase spiders, remorhazes, ropers, sphinxes, and the tarrasque. There's at least one magical beast at every CR from 1 to 15, so your ranger gains value from the choice at every level. Moreover, he gains bonuses against all the celestial and fiendish creatures summoned by his arcane foes. Consider taking magical beasts as a first or second favored enemy.

Monstrous Humanoids: This category includes such creatures as centaurs, grimlocks, hags, harpies, kuo-toa, medusas, minotaurs, and yuan-ti. Since there is little commonality about where and when a ranger might meet these creatures, it is a very versatile option. All the creatures noted above are CR 7 or lower, so this category is a decent choice for a second or third favored enemy.

Oozes: These mindless, formless creatures aren't subject to critical hits, so favored enemy damage bonuses don't work against them unless you're using the variant rules below. You won't get bonuses on damage rolls, Bluff checks, or Sense Motive checks, and you probably won't hear them coming. Still, a high Spot bonus is very helpful against a gelatinous cube.

Outsiders: This category is among the few appropriate choices for a ranger's fifth favored enemy, but since you must choose a specific kind of outsider, you have to guess what sort your ranger is likely to fight. The list of options includes nearly all creatures native to planes other than the Material Plane. Of these, only celestials, demons, devils, formians, and slaadi have enough CR variation to justify them as good choices over the long haul—and of those, only demons and devils are commonly encountered foes. See the variant rules below for another way to approach rangers' favored enemy bonuses against outsiders.

Plants: There's something quite odd about the concept of hunting plants. They're immune to critical hits and thus to favored enemy damage bonuses, and Bluff and Sense Motive checks are generally useless against them. In addition, most of them don't move enough for your bonuses on Listen and Wilderness Lore checks to be useful. A Spot bonus might be nice, but you gain much more utility out of choosing another favored enemy unless you use the variant favored enemy rules below.

Shapechangers: Even though only a few creatures have this type, lycanthropes alone have enough variation to make this category an excellent choice. A lycanthrope can have any CR above 1, so a ranger can benefit from this choice at any time in his career.

Undead: When your ranger runs into skeletons and zombies in his first few adventures, you might be tempted to choose undead as a favored enemy. Resist the temptation. All undead are immune to critical hits and mind-influencing effects, and some are also incorporeal, so they don't make noise. Thus, favored enemy bonuses are all but useless against undead unless you're using the variant rules below.

Vermin: This category is a moderately good choice. A lot of monstrous spiders and centipedes live out there, and even though your ranger won't be bluffing them, every bit of extra damage helps.

Variant Favored Enemy Rules

Some favored enemy choices have significantly less utility than others—namely outsiders and those types that are immune to critical hits. The variant rules presented here make these choices more appealing. As with all variant rules, a player wishing to utilize these must first get the DM's consent.

Favoring Subtypes of Outsiders: In this variant, the ranger can choose a subtype of outsider as a favored enemy. The available options are air, chaotic, earth, evil, fire, good, lawful, water, and no subtype. A ranger who chooses chaotic outsiders, for example, gains favored enemy bonuses against chaos beasts, demons, djinn, ghaeles (a type of celestial), lillends, slaadi, and titans, whereas one who chooses outsiders with no subtype gains bonuses against aasimars, half-celestials, half-fiends, jann, ravids, and tieflings. When choosing among these options, consider your ranger's alignment and the conditions in which he normally adventures.

Favoring Subraces of Your Own Race: A good or neutral ranger cannot select his own race as a favored enemy, but his enemies can, which is disconcerting. In this variant, a ranger can select a subrace of his own race as a favored enemy. Generally, the DM should allow this only when it corresponds to deep divisions within that race. For example, a high elf could select drow, but not gray elves. Similarly, hill dwarves might select derro or duergar, but not deep dwarves. Half-orcs (especially if raised among humans) could choose orcs. This variant also allows the ranger to choose others of his own race who come from a hostile country as a favored enemy.

Defensive Favored Enemy Bonuses: A ranger using this variant gains his favored enemy bonus on Hide and Move Silently checks instead of on damage, Bluff checks, and Sense Motive checks against a particular favored enemy. Also, he can use his favored enemy bonus as a dodge bonus as if using the Dodge feat. (That is, each round he must designate one favored enemy opponent against whom the AC bonus applies, and he gains no bonus when flat-footed.) The ranger retains his other bonuses on Listen, Spot, and Wilderness Lore checks. Once you choose this option for a particular favored enemy, you may not reverse the decision. This variant is recommended for rangers who choose constructs, elementals, oozes, plants, or undead as favored enemies, though other members of the class may find it useful as well.

Variant Intimidation Rules

It's an unfortunate fact that the barbarian, regardless of his might, can still fail to intimidate foes who are cowed by the stylish bard or the magnetic sorcerer. The two optional rules presented here are designed to make the barbarian a bit more frightening. These rules work whether the barbarian is raging or not, though rage does increase their effectiveness.

Raging Intimidation: A raging barbarian gains a +4 bonus to both his Strength and his Constitution scores. This variant also grants him a +4 morale bonus on his Intimidate checks. After all, when a barbarian begins to scream and froth at the mouth, just about anyone is a little more likely to do what he says.

Intimidation through Strength: Sometimes it's appropriate to change the key ability score of a particular skill. While Intimidation is usually a function of Charisma, this rule allows the barbarian to apply his Strength modifier rather than his Charisma modifier to Intimidate checks. This assumes, of course, that he accompanies such attempts with appropriate displays of might, such as breaking objects or showing off impressive muscles. A barbarian who is raging is even better at intimidation because of his increased Strength score.

CHAPTER 2: SKILLS AND FEATS

"He just sat there, downing poison pepper after poison pepper. Each of his challengers would pop one pepper and then leave on a stretcher."

—A town crier's description of Krusk

The first section of this chapter details new ways of using some of the skills listed in the *Player's Handbook*. The second section presents a number of new feats designed with barbarians, druids, and rangers in mind—though, of course, any character who qualifies can take them.

NEW WAYS TO USE SKILLS

New ways to use the Handle Animal, Hide, and Wilderness Lore skills are discussed below, as well as variant rules for using the Intimidate skill.

Handle Animal

Once you have befriended an animal, you might want to train it before taking it into dangerous adventuring situations with you. Teaching an animal a trick requires two months and a successful Handle Animal check (DC 15). If the creature is your animal companion, a +2 circumstance bonus applies to the check. This represents the animal's unusual degree of loyalty and willingness to cooperate.

New Tricks

See the Animal Companions sidebar in Chapter 2 of the *Dungeon Master's Guide* for the basic list of tricks animals can learn. Several additional tricks are detailed below.

Armor: The animal is willing to accept the burden of armor.

Assist Attack: The animal aids your attack or that of another creature as a standard action. You must designate both the recipient of the aid and a specific opponent. The animal makes one attack roll per round it is assisting. If it hits AC 10, the creature it is aiding gains a +2 circumstance bonus on attack rolls against the designated opponent until the animal's next turn.

Assist Defend: The animal aids your defense or that of another creature as a standard action. You must designate both the recipient of the aid and a specific opponent. The animal makes one attack roll per round it is assisting. If it hits AC 10, the creature it is aiding gains a +2 circumstance bonus to AC against the designated opponent until the animal's next turn.

Assist Track: The animal aids your attempt to track. If its Wilderness Lore check (DC 10) succeeds, you gain a +2 circumstance bonus on Wilderness Lore checks made for tracking.

Calm: This trick lets an animal deal with dungeon environments. It becomes willing to move through or rest quietly in darkness, to skirt ledges around pits, and to climb up slanted passages and staircases. When the situation requires it, the animal even allows itself to be harnessed for travel over vertical surfaces.

Hold: The animal initiates a grapple attack and attempts to hold a designated enemy in its arms, claws, or teeth. An animal with the improved grab ability uses that in the attempt; otherwise, the attack provokes an attack of opportunity.

Home: The animal returns to a preset location, traveling overland as required.

Hunt: The animal attempts to hunt food for you (and any others you designate) and bring it back through the use of Wilderness Lore. While an animal automatically knows how to hunt for its own needs, this trick causes it to return with food rather than simply eating its fill of what it finds.

Subdue: The animal attacks a designated target creature to subdue it, suffering a –4 penalty on its attack roll. The attack trick (above) is a prerequisite for this one.

Stalk: The animal follows a designated target, doing its best to remain undetected, until the target is wounded or resting, and then attacks.

Steal: In this variation on the fetch command, the animal grabs an object in the possession of a target creature, wrests it away, and brings it to you. If multiple objects are available, the animal attempts to steal a random one.

Hide

The Hide skill is as useful in the wild as it is in a city. Sometimes, however, rangers and druids must adapt their skills to city situations (see Urban Ranger, in Chapter 1). This section describes how to use the Hide skill to track someone surreptitiously.

Tail Someone

Since the Hide skill allows for movement, you can use it as a move-equivalent action or part of a move action if desired. This means you can try to follow someone while making periodic Hide checks to remain unseen. How often you need to make a Hide check depends on the distance at which you follow. If you stay at least 60 feet away from your quarry, you can get by with a Hide check once every 10 minutes, provided that your quarry doesn't suspect you're following and that you do nothing but maintain the tail. At distances of less than 60 feet, you must make a Hide check each round.

Of course, you still need appropriate concealment to succeed at Hide checks while tailing, but many options are often available. In a forest, of course, there are plenty of convenient trees to hide behind. If you're trying to tail someone on a city street, you can duck behind passersby—though in that case, you wouldn't be hidden from the people you're using for cover, just from your quarry. If the street is fairly crowded, using passersby as concealment imposes no penalty on your Hide check, though you might still suffer a penalty for your movement (see the Hide skill description in the *Player's Handbook*).

If you don't have moving people to hide behind, you can instead move from one hiding place to another as

you follow your quarry. Distance is a factor, though—this option works only as long as your next hiding place is within 1 foot per Hide rank you possess of your current one. (If you have a magic item that helps you hide, such as a *cloak of elevenkind* or a *robe of blending*, add 1 foot to that limit per point of Hide bonus it provides.) If you try to move any greater distance than that between hiding places, your quarry spots you. A movement penalty may apply to your Hide check if you dash from one hiding place to the next at more than half your normal speed.

Even if you fail a Hide check while tailing someone or are spotted while moving too great a distance between hiding places, you can attempt a Bluff check opposed by your quarry's Sense Motive check to look innocuous. Success means your quarry sees you but doesn't realize you're tailing; failure alerts him or her that you're actually following. A modifier may apply to the Sense Motive check, depending on how suspicious your quarry is. The table below gives Sense Motive modifiers for particular situations.

Your Quarry . . .	Sense Motive Modifier
Is sure nobody is following	–5
Has no reason to suspect anybody is following	+0
Is worried about being followed	+10
Is worried about being followed and knows you're an enemy	+20

Wilderness Lore

The description of the Track feat in the *Player's Handbook* notes that with a successful Wilderness Lore check, you can track someone for a mile or until the tracks become hard to follow. But what if you're following someone who really knows how to hide a trail? In that case, the quarry may make a Wilderness Lore check to hide his or her trail. This is opposed by your Wilderness Lore check for tracking. The DC modifiers listed in the Track feat description in the *Player's Handbook* apply to the quarry's check.

FEATS

Feats provide characters with new capabilities or improve those that the heroes already have. This section offers a variety of new feats designed specifically for barbarians, druids, and rangers—though, of course any character who qualifies can take them. Many of these new feats have at least one prerequisite, such as a minimum ability score or base attack bonus. Asterisked feats on Table 2–1 are available as fighter bonus feats.

Virtual Feats

If a character has a class feature or special ability that exactly duplicates the effects of a feat, then he or she can use that "virtual feat" as a prerequisite for other feats, as well as prestige classes, and so forth. For example, a ranger can fight with two weapons as if he had the feats Ambidexterity and Two-Weapon Fighting, so he is considered to have those feats for the purpose of acquiring the Greater Two-Weapon Fighting feat detailed in this section. If the character ever loses the virtual prerequisite, he or she also loses access to any feats or other benefits acquired through its existence. For example, a ranger who wears armor heavier than light loses access to the virtual feats noted above, and thereby to Greater Two-Weapon Fighting as well. Acquiring a virtual feat does not give a character access to its prerequisites.

Wild Feats

The feats in this new category relate to the *wild shape* ability, and all require it as a prerequisite. Any class feature or ability that has the words "*wild shape*" in its name (such as *lesser wild shape*, *greater wild shape*, and *undead wild shape*; see Chapter 5) counts as *wild shape* for meeting prerequisites. Wild feats apply to any version of *wild shape*.

New Feats

"I smell blood and bones and the whiff of fear."

—Soveliss

Animal Control [General]

You can channel the power of nature to gain mastery over animal creatures.

Prerequisites: Animal Defiance, ability to cast *speak with animals* and *animal friendship*.

Benefit: You can rebuke or command animals as an evil cleric rebukes undead. To command an animal, you must be able to speak with it via a *speak with animals* effect, though you may issue your commands mentally if desired. The number of times per day that you can use this ability is equal to 3 + your Charisma modifier. Your highest divine caster level is the level at which you rebuke animals.

Special: Animals you command through this ability count against the HD limit of animals you can befriend through *animal friendship*.

Animal Defiance [General]

You can channel the power of nature to drive off animals.

Prerequisite: Ability to cast *detect animals or plants*.

Benefit: You can turn (but not destroy) animals as a good cleric turns undead. The number of

Table 2–1: Feats

General Feats	Prerequisites
Animal Defiance	Ability to cast *detect animals or plants*
Animal Control	Animal Defiance, ability to cast *speak with animals* and *animal friendship*
Brachiation	Climb 6 ranks, Jump 6 ranks, Str 13
Clever Wrestling	Improved Unarmed Strike, Small or Medium-size
Destructive Rage	Ability to rage
*Dragon's Toughness	Base Fort save bonus +11
*Dwarf's Toughness	Base Fort save bonus +5
Extended Rage	Ability to rage
Extra Favored Enemy	Base attack bonus +5, at least one favored enemy
Extra Rage	Ability to rage
Faster Healing	Base Fort save bonus +5
Favored Critical	Base attack bonus +5, at least one favored enemy
Flyby Attack	Ability to fly, either naturally or through shapechanging
*Giant's Toughness	Base Fort save bonus +8 or higher
Greater Resiliency	Damage reduction as a class feature or innate ability
*Greater Two-Weapon Fighting	Improved Two-Weapon Fighting, Two Weapon Fighting, Ambidexterity, base attack bonus +15
Improved Flight	Ability to fly (naturally, magically, or through shapechanging)
Improved Swimming	Swim 6 ranks
Instantaneous Rage	Ability to rage
Intimidating Rage	Ability to rage
Multiattack	Access to a form with three or more natural weapons
*Multidexterity	Access to a form with three or more arms, Dex 15
*Off-Hand Parry	Ambidexterity, Dex 13, Two-Weapon Fighting, base attack bonus +3, proficiency with weapon
Plant Defiance	Ability to cast *detect animals or plants*
Plant Control	Plant Defiance, ability to cast *speak with plants*
*Power Critical	Improved Critical, base attack bonus +12, proficiency with weapon
Remain Conscious	Base attack bonus +2, Endurance, Iron Will, Toughness
Resist Disease	—
Resist Poison	—
Resistance to Energy	Base Fort save bonus +8
Shadow	—
Snatch	Access to a form with either claws or bite as natural weapons
Supernatural Critical	Favored enemy that is immune to critical hits, base attack bonus +7
Wingover	Ability to fly (naturally, magically, or through shapechanging)

Item Creation Feats	Prerequisite
Create Infusion	Wilderness Lore 4 ranks, spellcaster level 3rd

Wild Feats	Prerequisite
Blindsight	Ability to use *wild shape* to become a dire bat
Extra *Wild Shape*	Ability to use *wild shape*
Fast *Wild Shape*	Ability to use *wild shape* to become a dire animal, Dex 13
Natural Spell	Ability to use *wild shape*, Wis 13
Proportionate *Wild Shape*	Ability to use *wild shape*, natural form neither Small nor Medium-size
Scent	Ability to use *wild shape* to become a wolf, Wis 11
Speaking *Wild Shape*	Ability to use *wild shape*, Int 13

times per day that you can use this ability is equal to 3 + your Charisma modifier. Your highest divine caster level is the level at which you turn animals.

Blindsight [Wild]

Your senses are as keen as the bat's.

Prerequisite: Ability to use *wild shape* to become a dire bat.

Benefit: You gain the extraordinary ability blindsight (as described in Chapter 3 of the DUNGEON MASTER'S *Guide*), which operates regardless of your form. Like the dire bat, you emit high-frequency sounds, inaudible to most creatures, as a form of "sonar" that allows you to locate objects and creatures within 120 feet. Since this ability relies on hearing, any circumstance that deprives you of that sense also negates your blindsight.

Brachiation [General]

You move through trees like a monkey.

Prerequisites: Climb 6 ranks, Jump 6 ranks, Str 13.

Benefit: You move through trees at your normal land speed by using your arms to swing from one branch to another. To allow brachiation, the area through which you are moving must be at least lightly wooded, with trees no farther apart than 15 feet. You may not use this ability while holding an item in either hand, or while wearing armor heavier than medium.

Create Infusion [Item Creation]

You store a divine spell within a specially prepared herb (see Chapter 3 for details on infusions).

Prerequisites: Wilderness Lore 4 ranks, spellcaster level 3rd.

Benefit: You create an infusion of any divine spell available to you. Infusing an herb with a spell takes one day. When you create an infusion, you set the caster level, which must be sufficient to cast the spell in question but not higher than your own level. The base price of an infusion is its spell level times its caster level times 50 gp. To create an infusion, you must spend 1/25 of this base price in XP and use up raw materials costing one-half this base price.

Any infusion that stores a spell with a costly material component or an XP cost also carries a commensurate cost. In addition to the costs derived from the base price, you must also expend the material component or pay the XP when creating the infusion.

Clever Wrestling [General]

You have a better than normal chance to escape or wriggle free from a big creature's grapple or pin.

Prerequisites: Improved Unarmed Strike, Small or Medium-size.

Benefit: When your opponent is larger than Medium-size, you gain a circumstance bonus on your grapple check to escape a grapple or pin. The size of the bonus depends on your opponent's size, according to the following table.

Opponent Is . . .	Bonus
Colossal	+8
Gargantuan	+6
Huge	+4
Large	+2

Destructive Rage [General]

You shatter barriers and objects when enraged.

Prerequisite: Ability to rage.

Benefit: While you're raging, you gain a +8 bonus on any Strength checks you make to break open doors or break inanimate, immobile objects.

*Dragon's Toughness [General]

You are incredibly tough.

Prerequisite: Base Fort save bonus +11.
Benefit: You gain +12 hit points.
Special: You can gain this feat multiple times.

*Dwarf's Toughness [General]

You are tougher than you were before.

Prerequisite: Base Fort save bonus +5.
Benefit: You gain +6 hit points.
Special: You can gain this feat multiple times.

Extended Rage [General]

Your rage lasts longer than it normally would.

Prerequisite: Ability to rage.

Benefit: Each of your rages lasts an additional 5 rounds beyond its normal duration.

Special: You can take this feat multiple times, and the additional rounds stack.

Extra Favored Enemy [General]

You select an additional favored enemy.

Prerequisites: Base attack bonus +5, at least one favored enemy.

Benefit: You add an extra favored enemy to your list (see Table 3–14 in the *Player's Handbook*) beyond your normal allotment. Initially, you gain the standard +1 bonus on damage and the usual skill checks against this new favored enemy. When you advance beyond the level at which you gained Extra Favored Enemy, this bonus increases in the same way other favored enemy bonuses do. For example, suppose you select goblinoids as your first favored enemy when you are a 1st-level ranger and magical beasts as your second when you reach 5th level. Then you take Extra Favored Enemy as your feat at 6th level and select aberrations. At this point, you have a +2 bonus against goblinoids and a +1 bonus against both magical beasts and aberrations. When you reach 10th level, your bonuses rise to +3 against goblinoids and +2 against magical beasts and aberrations.

Extra Rage [General]

You rage more frequently than you normally could.

Prerequisite: Ability to rage.

Benefit: You rage two more times per day than you otherwise could.

Special: You can take this feat multiple times, gaining two additional rages per day each time.

Extra *Wild Shape* [Wild]

You use *wild shape* more frequently than you normally could.

Prerequisite: Ability to use *wild shape*.

Benefit: You use your *wild shape* ability two more times per day than you otherwise could. If you are able to use *wild shape* to become an elemental, you also gain one additional elemental *wild shape* use per day.

Special: You can take this feat multiple times, gaining two additional *wild shapes* of your usual type and one additional elemental *wild shape* (if you have this capability) each time.

Fast *Wild Shape* [Wild]

You assume your *wild shape* faster and more easily than you otherwise could.

Prerequisites: Ability to use *wild shape* to become a dire animal, Dex 13.

Benefit: You gain the ability to use *wild shape* as a move-equivalent action.

Normal: A druid uses *wild shape* as a standard action.

Faster Healing [General]

You recover faster than others do.

Prerequisite: Base Fort save bonus +5.

Benefit: You recover lost hit points and ability score points faster than you normally would, according to the table on the next page.

Hit Points Recovered per Character Level per Day

	With Faster Healing	With Faster Healing and Long-Term Care from a Successful Heal Check	Normal	Normal and Long-Term Care from a Successful Heal Check
Strenuous Activity	1	2	0	0
Light Activity	1.5	3	1	2
Complete Bed Rest	2	4	1.5	3

Ability Score Points Recovered per Day

	With Faster Healing	With Faster Healing and Long-Term Care from a Successful Heal Check	Normal	Normal and Long-Term Care from a Successful Heal Check
Strenuous Activity	2	3	0	0
Light Activity	2	3	1	2
Complete Bed Rest	2	3	2	4

Favored Critical [General]

You know how to hit your favored enemies where it hurts.

Prerequisites: Base attack bonus +5, at least one favored enemy.

Benefit: Select one of your favored enemies that is normally subject to critical hits. Whenever you attack this type of creature, the threat range of whatever weapon you are using is doubled. For example, a longsword usually threatens a critical hit on a die roll of 19 or 20 (two numbers). In the hands of a character with Favored Critical using it against a favored enemy, its threat range becomes 17 through 20 (four numbers). If it is also a *keen longsword*, its threat range becomes 15 through 20 (six numbers: 2 for being a longsword, 2 for being doubled as a *keen* weapon, and 2 for being doubled again by Favored Critical).

Special: You can take this feat multiple times. Each time you do, it applies to a new favored enemy. The effects of this feat do not stack with those of Improved Critical.

Flyby Attack [General]

You attack while on the wing.

Prerequisites: Ability to fly, either naturally or through shapechanging.

Benefit: When flying, you take a move action (including a dive) plus another partial action at any point during that move. You cannot take a second move action during a round in which you make a flyby attack. You can use this feat only while you are in a form that allows natural flight; it cannot be used in conjunction with magical flight (such as a *fly* spell).

Normal: Without this feat, you can take a partial action either before or after your move.

*Giant's Toughness [General]

You are amazingly tough.

Prerequisite: Base Fort save bonus +8.

Benefit: You gain +9 hit points.

Special: You can gain this feat multiple times.

Greater Resiliency [General]

Your extraordinary resilience to damage increases.

Prerequisite: Damage reduction as a class feature or innate ability.

Benefit: Your damage reduction increases by +1/−. If it would normally rise thereafter with level, it does so at its previous rate. For example, a 15th-level barbarian has damage reduction 2/−. By taking this feat, he raises it to 3/−. Thereafter, it continues to rise by +1/− at the designated intervals: to 4/− at 17th level, and to 5/− at 20th level. You may not take this feat more than once.

*Greater Two-Weapon Fighting [General]

You are a master at fighting two-handed.

Prerequisites: Improved Two-Weapon Fighting, Two-Weapon Fighting, Ambidexterity, base attack bonus +15.

Benefit: You get a third attack with your off-hand weapon, albeit at a −10 penalty.

Improved Flight [General]

You gain greater maneuverability when flying than you would normally have.

Prerequisite: Ability to fly (naturally, magically, or through shapechanging).

Benefit: Your maneuverability while flying improves by one grade. For example, if your normal maneuverability is poor, it becomes average.

Improved Swimming [General]

You swim faster than you normally could.

Prerequisite: Swim 6 ranks.

Benefit: You swim at one-half of your land speed as a move-equivalent action or at three-quarters of your land speed as a full-round action.

Normal: You swim at one-quarter of your land speed as a move-equivalent action or at one-half of your land speed as a full-round action.

Instantaneous Rage [General]

You activate your rage instantly.

Prerequisite: Ability to rage.

Benefit: Your rage begins at any time you wish, even when it's not your turn or when you're surprised. You can activate your rage in response to another's action after learning the result but before it takes effect. Thus, you can gain the benefits of rage in time to prevent or ameliorate an undesirable event. For example, you can gain the additional hit points that rage grants just before a blow that would otherwise cause you to fall unconscious, or better your chances of making a successful saving throw against an incoming spell.

Normal: You enter a rage only during your turn.

Intimidating Rage [General]

Your rage engenders fear in your opponents.

Prerequisites: Ability to rage.

Benefit: While you are raging, you designate a single foe within 30 feet of you who must make a Will save (DC = 10 + one-half your character level + your Charisma modifier) or become shaken for as long as you continue to rage and the target can see you. (A shaken creature suffers a −2 morale penalty on attack rolls, saves, and checks.) A target who makes the save remains immune to the intimidating effect of your rage for one day. Creatures immune to fear and those with no visual senses are immune to this effect.

Multiattack [General]

You are adept at using all your natural weapons at once.

Prerequisite: Access to a form that has three or more natural weapons, either naturally or through shapechanging.

Benefit: Your secondary attacks with natural weapons suffer only a −2 penalty.

Normal: Without this feat, your secondary natural attacks suffer a −5 penalty.

*Multidexterity [General]

You are skilled at utilizing all your hands in combat.

Prerequisites: Dex 15, access to a form with three or more arms.

Benefit: You ignore all penalties for using your off hands. (A creature has one primary hand, and all the others are off hands; for example, a four-armed creature has one primary hand and three off hands.)

Normal: Without this feat, a creature suffers a −4 penalty on attack rolls, ability checks, and skill checks made with an off hand.

Special: This feat is the same as the Ambidexterity feat for creatures with three or more arms.

Natural Spell [Wild]

You cast spells while in a *wild shape*.

Prerequisite: Ability to use *wild shape*, Wis 13.

Benefit: You complete the verbal and somatic components of spells while in a *wild shape*. For example, while in the form of a hawk, you could substitute screeches and gestures with your talons for the normal verbal and somatic components of a spell. You can use any material components or focuses that you can hold with an appendage of your current form, but you cannot make use of any such items that are melded within that form. This feat does not permit the use of magic items while in a form that could not ordinarily use them, and you do not gain the ability to speak while in a *wild shape*.

*Off-Hand Parry [General]

You use your off-hand weapon to defend against melee attacks.

Prerequisites: Ambidexterity, Dex 13, Two-Weapon

Fighting, base attack bonus +3, proficiency with weapon.

Benefit: When fighting with two weapons and using the full attack option, you can on your action decide to attack normally or to sacrifice all your off-hand attacks for that round in exchange for a +2 dodge bonus to your AC. If you take this option, you also suffer penalties on your attacks as if you were fighting with two weapons. If you are also using a buckler, its AC bonus stacks with the dodge bonus. You can use only bladed or hafted weapons of a size category smaller than your own with this feat.

Plant Control [General]

You channel the power of nature to gain mastery over plant creatures.

Prerequisites: Plant Defiance, ability to cast *speak with plants*.

Benefit: You rebuke or command plants as an evil cleric rebukes undead. To command a plant, you must be able to speak with it via a *speak with plants* effect, though you may issue your commands mentally if desired. The number of times per day that you can use this ability is equal to 3 + your Charisma modifier. Your highest divine caster level is the level at which you rebuke plants.

Plant Defiance [General]

You channel the power of nature to drive off plant creatures.

Prerequisite: Ability to cast *detect animals or plants*.

Benefit: You turn (but not destroy) plants as a good cleric turns undead. Treat immobile plant creatures as creatures unable to flee. The number of times per day that you can use this ability is equal to 3 + your Charisma modifier. Your highest divine caster level is the level at which you turn plants.

*Power Critical [General]

Choose one weapon, such as a longsword or a greataxe. With that weapon, you know how to hit where it hurts.

Prerequisites: Improved Critical with weapon, base attack bonus +12, proficiency with weapon.

Benefit: Once per day, you can declare a single melee attack with your chosen kind of weapon to be an automatic threat before you make the attack roll. If the attack is successful, you roll to confirm the critical, regardless of whether the actual attack roll was a threat.

Special: You can take this feat multiple times. Each time you do, it applies to a new kind of weapon. You may use this ability only once per day per kind of weapon to which it applies.

Proportionate *Wild Shape* [Wild]

You use *wild shape* to become animals of your own size, even if your *wild shape* ability would normally exclude that size category.

Prerequisites: Ability to use *wild shape*, natural form neither Small or Medium-size.

Benefit: You use your *wild shape* ability to take the form of an animal whose normal size category matches your own. For example, a cloud giant druid (size Huge) with this feat could use *wild shape* to become a Huge shark or a giant squid.

Normal: The size of the animal form you can assume through *wild shape* is limited by the parameters of the ability, regardless of your original size.

Remain Conscious [General]

You have a tenacity of will that supports you even when things look bleak.

Prerequisites: Base attack bonus +2, Endurance, Iron Will, Toughness.

Benefit: After your hit points are reduced to 0 or below, you may take one partial action on your turn every round until you reach –10 hit points.

Resist Disease [General]

You have developed a natural resistance to diseases.

Benefit: You gain a +4 bonus on Fortitude saves against disease.

Resist Poison [General]

You have built up an immunity to the effects of poisons by exposing yourself to controlled doses of them.

Benefit: You gain a +4 bonus on Fortitude saves against poison.

Resistance to Energy [General]

You channel the power of nature to resist a particular energy type (fire, cold, electricity, acid, or sonic).

Prerequisites: Base Fort save bonus +8.

Benefit: Choose an energy form. You gain resistance 5 against that type of energy. For example, if you choose fire, you ignore the first 5 points of fire damage you take each round, regardless of whether that damage stems from a mundane or a magical source.

Special: You can take this feat multiple times. If you choose the same energy form two or more times, the effects stack. This resistance does not stack with that provided by any spell or magic item.

Scent [Wild]

Your olfactory senses are as sharp as the wolf's.

Prerequisites: Ability to use *wild shape* to become a wolf, Wis 11.

Benefit: You gain the scent extraordinary ability (airbreather's type, as described in Chapter 3 of the DUNGEON MASTER's Guide), which operates regardless of your form.

Shadow [General]

You have a better chance than most to trail someone unnoticed.

Benefit: You gain a +2 bonus on Hide and Spot checks.

Snatch [General]

You can grapple more easily with your claws or bite.

Prerequisite: Access to a form with either claws or bite as natural weapons.

Benefit: If you hit with a claw or bite attack, you automatically attempt to start a grapple as a free action without provoking an attack of opportunity. If you get a hold with a claw on a creature four or more size categories smaller than yourself, you squeeze each round for automatic claw damage. If you get a hold with your bite on a creature three or more size categories smaller than yourself, you automatically deal bite damage each round, or if you do not move and take no other action in combat, you deal double bite damage to the snatched creature.

As a free action, you can drop a creature you have snatched, or you can use a standard action to fling it aside. A flung creature travels 10 feet (and takes 1d6 points of damage) for each size category greater than Small that you are. If you fling a creature while you are flying, it suffers either flinging or falling damage, whichever is greater.

Speaking *Wild Shape* [Wild]

While in *wild shape*, you can communicate with animals or elementals of the same kind as your current form.

Prerequisites: Ability to use *wild shape*, Int 13.

Benefit: While in a *wild shape*, you operate as if you were under a continuous *speak with animals* effect with respect to animals of the same kind. For example, if you use *wild shape* to take the form of a wolf, you can communicate with wolves as long as you are in that form. You speak in growls, squawks, chitters, or whatever other sounds such an animal would typically use to communicate with others of its kind. If you are able to use *wild shape* to become an elemental, you can also communicate with elementals of the same kind as yourself, using their language. This feat does not enable mental communication.

Supernatural Blow [General]

Choose one favored enemy that is immune to critical hits. You know how to place blows against this opponent for best effect.

Prerequisites: Base attack bonus +7, favored enemy immune to critical hits.

Benefit: Whenever your attack roll against this favored enemy would otherwise be a critical hit, you inflict +1d6 points of extra damage per damage die that your weapon would do on a critical hit. In addition, your favored enemy damage bonus applies to this creature type normally.

Normal: Creatures that are immune to critical hits are also immune to the favored enemy damage bonus.

Wingover [General]

You change direction quickly once per round while airborne.

Prerequisite: Ability to fly.

Benefit: This feat allows you to turn at an angle of up to 180 degrees in addition to any other turns you are normally allowed, regardless of your maneuverability. You cannot gain altitude during the round you execute a wingover, but you can dive. For more information, see Tactical Aerial Movement in Chapter 3 of the DUNGEON MASTER's Guide.

CHAPTER 3: TOOLS OF THE TRADE

"Good tools make your work easier, whether your chosen occupation is war or peace. Choose your tools carefully."

—Soveliss

Every adventurer depends on equipment. Without arms, armor, and other equipment, both magical and mundane, a hero can't defeat enemies, mount a proper defense, or overcome the obstacles presented by the dungeon and the outside world. This chapter presents new exotic weapons and new magic items, most of which are designed for use in the outdoor world. The last section of the chapter describes a new type of magic item, the infusion.

EXOTIC WEAPONS

"He hit me. With a tree!"

—A dazed Krusk

The weapons presented below can be useful to characters in the outdoors. Exotic weapons such as these may be in common use in distant corners of the campaign world, and they present interesting options for characters who learn to use them.

Weapon Descriptions

Ankus: The ankus is a hooked device used to steer elephants. It deals only subdual damage, but because of its hook, you can also use it to make trip attacks. You can drop the ankus to avoid being tripped during your own trip attempt. The ankus has 10-foot reach.

Blowgun: The blowgun is a long tube through which you blow air to fire needles. A needle does 1 point of damage, and it can deliver an injury or contact type poison.

Blowgun, Greater: The greater blowgun fires blowgun darts, which are slightly smaller than thrown darts. These darts do 1d4 points of damage in addition to delivering poisons.

Caber: A caber is a heavy pole that you can throw at one or more targets grouped closely together. To throw a caber, you must target a 10-foot-square area and hit AC 15. Success means that everyone in the target area must make a Reflex save (DC = your attack roll) or move 5 feet backward. If a creature or object in the target area is incapable of movement, it takes 2d6 points of damage. The caber is normally used for breaking up military formations.

Crossbow, Winch: The winch crossbow fires a rope and pulley attached to a special crossbow bolt. The bolt is split down the head and center of the shaft, with the split head bending away from the shaft like a two-headed snake. A thin rope secured to each tip slows the bolt in flight (hence the reduced range increment). On a successful hit, the bolt snaps apart like a wishbone, taking the attached ropes past the target to wrap around and entangle it. If the target is a movable object of your size category or smaller, you can use the ropes to pull it toward you.

An entangled creature suffers a −2 penalty on attack rolls and a −4 penalty to Dexterity. It can move only at half speed and cannot charge or run. If you control the

TABLE 3–1: NEW EXOTIC WEAPONS

Exotic Weapons—Melee

Weapon	Cost	Damage	Critical	Range Increment	Weight	Type	Hardness	Hit Points
Large								
Ankus†	15 gp	2d4§	×2	—	15 lb.	Bludgeoning	5	10

Exotic Weapons—Ranged

Weapon	Cost	Damage	Critical	Range Increment	Weight	Type		
Medium-size								
Blowgun*	1 gp	1	×2	10 ft.	2 lb.	Piercing	5	3
Needles, blowgun (20)	1 gp	—	—	—	*	—	2	1
Crossbow, winch**	75 gp	1d8§	19–20/×2	50 ft.	10 lb.	Piercing	10	10
Bolts, winch crossbow (10)	5 gp	—	—	—	1/2 lb.	—	10	1
Nagaika**	25 gp	1d6	×3	—	4 lb.	Slashing	7	5
Nagaika, mighty**								
+1 Str bonus	225 gp	1d6	×3	—	5 lb.	Slashing	7	8
+2 Str bonus	325 gp	1d6	×3	—	6 lb.	Slashing	7	8
+3 Str bonus	425 gp	1d6	×3	—	7 lb.	Slashing	7	8
+4 Str bonus	525 gp	1d6	×3	—	8 lb.	Slashing	7	8
Large								
Blowgun, greater**	10 gp	1d4	×2	10 ft.	4 lb.	Piercing	5	4
Darts, blowgun (10)	1 gp	—	—	—	1 lb.	—	2	1
Caber**	10 gp	—	×2	10 ft.	100 lb.	Bludgeoning	5	120

*No weight worth noting.
**See the description of this weapon for special rules.
†Reach weapon.
§The weapon deals subdual damage rather than normal damage.

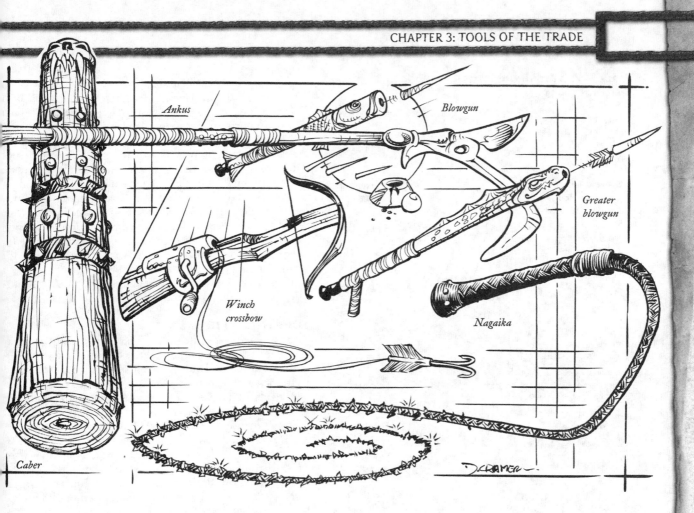

Ankus

Blowgun

Greater blowgun

Winch crossbow

Nagaika

Caber

D.CRAMER

trailing rope by succeeding at an opposed Strength check while holding it, the entangled creature can move only within the limits that the rope allows. Casting a spell while entangled requires a successful Concentration check (DC 15).

The entangled creature can escape the ropes with an Escape Artist check (DC 20), which is a full-round action. The rope has 5 hit points and can be burst (see Chapter 8 of the *Player's Handbook*) with a Strength check (DC 25, also a full-round action).

A winch crossbow's entangling effect is useful only against creatures between Tiny and Large size, inclusive. The subdual damage can affect any creature.

A winch crossbow requires two hands for effective use, regardless of the user's size. Loading a winch crossbow is a full-round action that provokes attacks of opportunity.

A Medium-size or larger creature can shoot, but not load, a winch crossbow with one hand at a –4 penalty. A Medium-size or larger creature can shoot a winch crossbow with each hand at a –6 penalty, plus the usual –4 penalty for the off-hand attack (–6 primary hand/–10 off hand). The Two-Weapon Fighting feat does not reduce these penalties because it represents skill with melee weapons, not ranged ones. The Ambidexterity feat lets you avoid the –4 off-hand penalty, bringing the penalties to –6 for both the primary hand and the off hand.

Nagaika: The nagaika is a leather lash studded with glass. Unlike the whip, it deals normal damage and can damage armored foes. Although you keep it in your hand, treat it as a projectile weapon with a maximum range of 15 feet and no range penalties.

Because the nagaika can wrap around an enemy's leg or other limb, you can make trip attacks with it. You can drop it to avoid being tripped during your own trip attempt. You also gain a +2 bonus on your opposed attack rolls when using the nagaika to disarm an opponent (including the roll to keep from being disarmed if your attempt fails).

Nagaika, Mighty: A character who takes Exotic Weapon Proficiency (nagaika) is also proficient with the mighty nagaika. This weapon is made of exceptionally strong leather, which allows the user to apply his or her Strength bonus on damage rolls (within the weapon's limit).

NEW MAGIC ITEMS

"The Wolf represents overconfidence. He is inclined to let his prey have a head start, only to bound farther and faster than the prey. But the Wolf ignores the long run. Someday, something will be faster than the Wolf and will not give him a head start."
—The Deck of Ages

This section describes several new magic items of various types. Many of these items are especially useful to characters who spend most of their time outdoors and to those who deal with animals.

Several of these devices are designed for use by animals. An animal can wear only one collar, saddle, bridle, or other such item at a time.

TABLE 3–2: NEW MAGIC ITEMS

Armor and Shield

Special Ability	Market Price
Aquatic	+2 bonus
Aquatic (with water breathing)	+3 bonus
Ease	+1 bonus
Wild	+3 bonus

Specific Armor

	Market Price
Gray ironwood suit	137,650 gp
Equerry's armor	10,670 gp

Magic Weapon

Special Ability	Type	Market Price
Exhausting	Melee, ranged	+1 bonus
Hunting	Melee, ranged	+1 bonus
Opposable	Melee, ranged	+1 bonus

Specific Weapon

	Market Price
Arrow of cure light wounds	107 gp
Arrow of cure moderate wounds	607 gp
Arrow of cure serious wounds	1,507 gp
Arrow of cure critical wounds	2,807 gp
Berserker blade (+1)	6,335 gp
Berserker blade (+2)	15,335 gp

Potion

	Market Price
Animal logic	150 gp
Natural clarity	150 gp
Unerring direction	150 gp

Wondrous Item

	Market Price
Boots of endurance	16,000 gp
Collar of cleverness (1 trick)	700 gp
Collar of cleverness (2 tricks)	1,400 gp
Collar of cleverness (3 tricks)	2,100 gp
Collar of resistance (+1)	490 gp
Collar of resistance (+2)	1,960 gp
Collar of resistance (+3)	4,410 gp
Collar of resistance (+4)	7,840 gp
Collar of resistance (+5)	12,250 gp
Goggles of following	2,000 gp
Helm of bonding	7,200 gp
Necklace of favored enemy detection	34,000 gp
Standing stone (0-level)	10,676 gp
Standing stone (1st-level)	10,850 gp
Standing stone (2nd-level)	12,600 gp
Standing stone (3rd-level)	15,750 gp
Standing stone (4th-level)	20,300 gp
Standing stone (5th-level)	26,250 gp
Standing stone (6th-level)	33,600 gp
Standing stone (7th-level)	42,350 gp
Standing stone (8th-level)	49,700 gp
Standing stone (9th-level)	57,750 gp
Torc of animal speech	12,000 gp
Wilding clasp	4,000 gp

Armor and Shield Special Abilities

Armor or a shield with a special ability must have at least a +1 enhancement bonus.

Aquatic: Armor and shields with this enchantment appear streamlined and possess a greenish glint. A suit of armor or shield with this enchantment enables its wearer to move freely through water without the need for Swim checks. Drowning rules still apply unless the item is also enchanted with *water breathing*.

Caster Level: 7th; *Prerequisites:* Craft Magic Arms and Armor, *freedom of movement*, *water breathing*; *Market Price:* +2 bonus, or +3 bonus with *water breathing*.

Ease: A suit of armor with this enchantment allows its wearer to rest comfortably overnight without removing it, regardless of how heavy it is. The wearer can don ease armor in only 5 rounds, or remove it in a single round.

Caster Level: 5th; *Prerequisites:* Craft Magic Arms and Armor, *soften earth and stone*; *Market Price:* +1 bonus.

Wild: The armor and enhancement bonuses of this item remain in effect even while the wearer is in *wild shape*. Such items meld into the wearer's *wild shape* and thus cannot be seen in that form.

Caster Level: 9th; *Prerequisites:* Craft Magic Arms and Armor, *meld into stone*; *Market Price:* +3 bonus.

Specific Armors

The following specific suits of armor are usually preconstructed with exactly the qualities described here.

Gray Ironwood Suit: When first found, this +2 *full plate* often appears to be made of steel. In actuality, it is composed of wood that has been permanently rendered into *ironwood*.

Caster Level: 11th; *Prerequisites:* Craft Magic Arms and Armor, *ironwood*; *Market Price:* 137,650 gp.

Equerry's Armor: This armor appears to be finely crafted +2 *full plate* specifically cut for someone who fights from atop a mount. Its wearer gains a +1 competence bonus on Ride checks. In addition, equerry's armor grants the wearer's mount a +2 enhancement bonus to Dexterity and increases its speed by +10 feet.

Caster Level: 6th; *Prerequisites:* Craft Magic Arms and Armor; *Market Price:* 10,670 gp.

Magic Weapon Special Abilities

A magic weapon with a special ability must have at least a +1 enhancement bonus.

Exhausting: A weapon with this ability deals +1d6 points of damage with each successful hit. However, all the damage it deals (the normal amount for a weapon of its kind plus all applicable bonuses) is subdual rather than normal damage. Bows, crossbows, and slings so enchanted bestow the exhausting effect upon their ammunition.

Caster Level: 8th; *Prerequisites:* Craft Magic Arms and Armor, *soften earth and stone*; *Market Price:* +1 bonus.

Hunting: When used by a ranger against a favored enemy, a hunting weapon doubles the wielder's favored enemy bonus on weapon damage rolls.

Caster Level: 6th; *Prerequisites:* Craft Magic Arms and Armor, *greater magic fang*; *Market Price:* +1 bonus.

Opposable: Even a creature that lacks the proper hands for weapon use can wield an opposable weapon. This enchantment creates one or more thumblike projections on the weapon. These artificial "thumbs" fold around the appropriate limb of the wielder to allow proper use. To wield an opposable weapon, a creature must be corporeal, have limbs, have proficiency with the weapon, and be able to stand without the limb(s) that wield the opposable weapon.

Caster Level: 6th; *Prerequisites:* Craft Magic Arms and Armor, *greater magic fang*; *Market Price:* +1 bonus.

Potion Descriptions

The following are nonstandard potions of interest to barbarians, druids, and rangers.

Animal Logic: A character drinking this potion gains an intuitive empathy with animals (in the form of a +10 circumstance bonus on Handle Animal checks) for 1 hour. An imbiber with ranks in Animal Empathy also gains a +10 circumstance bonus on Animal Empathy checks.

Caster Level: 2nd; *Prerequisites:* Brew Potion, spellcaster level 6th; *Market Price:* 150 gp.

Natural Clarity: A character drinking this potion gains a +10 circumstance bonus on Wilderness Lore checks for 1 hour.

Caster Level: 2nd; *Prerequisites:* Brew Potion, spellcaster level 6th; *Market Price:* 150 gp.

Unerring Direction: A character drinking this potion gains a +10 circumstance bonus on Intuit Direction checks for 1 hour.

Caster Level: 2nd; *Prerequisites:* Brew Potion, spellcaster level 6th; *Market Price:* 150 gp.

Wondrous Item Descriptions

The following wondrous items are designed primarily for use by barbarians, druids, and rangers.

Boots of Endurance: These boots grant the wearer a +4 circumstance bonus on checks for performing any physical action that extends over a period of time, such as running, swimming, or breath-holding. The wearer also gains a +4 circumstance bonus on Fortitude saves to avoid subdual damage caused by exposure to heat or cold, and a +4 circumstance bonus on Constitution checks made to prevent subdual damage from thirst or starvation.

Caster Level: 3rd; *Prerequisites:* Craft Wondrous Item, *endurance*; *Market Price:* 16,000 gp; *Weight:* 1 lb.

Collar of Cleverness: This animal collar expands to fit its wearer. While wearing this item, an animal can perform one or more additional tricks over and above those it knows. The creator of the collar must designate the specific trick or tricks it can grant. An animal can wear only one collar at a time.

Caster Level: 5th; *Prerequisites:* Craft Wondrous Item, animal trick (see Chapter 6); *Market Price:* 700 gp (1 trick), 1,400 gp (2 tricks), or 2,100 gp (3 tricks); *Weight:* 1 lb.

Collar of Resistance: This animal collar expands to fit its wearer. While wearing this item, an animal gains a +1 to +5 resistance bonus on all saving throws (Fortitude, Reflex, and Will). An animal can wear only one collar at a time.

Caster Level: 5th; *Prerequisites:* Craft Wondrous Item, *resistance*; *Market Price:* 490 gp (+1), 1,960 gp (+2), 4,410 gp (+3), 7,840 (+4), or 12,250 gp (+5); *Weight:* 1 lb.

Goggles of Following: The lenses of these goggles are tinted with shades of green and yellow. They grant the wearer a +10 competence bonus on Wilderness Lore checks made for tracking.

Caster Level: 3rd; *Prerequisites:* Craft Wondrous Item, Wilderness Lore 5 ranks; *Market Price:* 2,000 gp; *Weight:* —.

Helm of Bonding: This helm of animal hide looks to be of poor quality. Once per day, the wearer can bond telepathically with a single animal within his or her sight. For the next hour, the wearer can communicate mentally with that animal, both sending and receiving messages. The helm also bestows a *speak with animals*

Specific Weapons

The following specific weapons are usually preconstructed with exactly the qualities described here.

Arrow of Cure Light Wounds: When this otherwise normal +1 *arrow* strikes a target, it does no damage. Instead, the target is affected as if by a *cure light wounds* spell, which cures 1d8+1 points of damage. If such an arrow strikes an undead target, the creature is entitled to spell resistance and a Will save (DC 11) for half damage.

An *arrow of cure moderate wounds* cures 2d8+3 points of damage and has a save DC of 12. An *arrow of cure serious wounds* cures 3d8+5 points of damage and has a save DC of 13. An *arrow of cure critical wounds* cures 4d8+7 points of damage and has a save DC of 14.

Caster Level: 1st (light), 3rd (moderate), 5th (serious), 7th (critical); *Prerequisites:* Craft Magic Arms and Armor, *cure light wounds* (light), *cure moderate wounds* (moderate), *cure serious wounds* (serious), or *cure critical wounds* (critical); *Market Price:* 107 gp (light), 607 gp (moderate), 1,507 gp (serious), or 2,807 gp (critical); *Cost to Create:* 57 gp + 4 XP (light), 307 gp + 24 XP (moderate), 757 gp + 60 XP (serious), or 1,407 gp + 112 XP (critical).

Berserker Blade: The enhancement bonus of this +1 or +2 bastard sword increases by +1 when the wielder flies into a barbarian rage.

Caster Level: 7th; *Prerequisites:* Craft Magic Arms and Armor, *emotion* (rage); *Market Price:* 6,335 gp (+1 weapon) or 15,335 gp (+2 weapon); *Cost to Create:* 3,335 gp + 240 XP (+1 weapon) or 7,835 gp + 600 XP (+2 weapon).

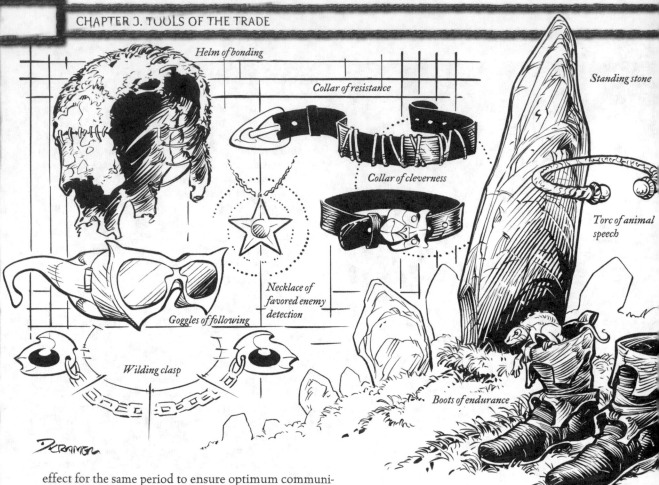

Helm of bonding
Collar of resistance
Standing stone
Collar of cleverness
Necklace of favored enemy detection
Torc of animal speech
Goggles of following
Wilding clasp
Boots of endurance

effect for the same period to ensure optimum communication. If the distance between the animal and the helm's wearer ever exceeds one mile, the connection is suspended until either the duration expires or the animal is once again within range. The user can select a different animal for each use.

Caster Level: 3rd; *Prerequisites:* Craft Wondrous Item, *speak with animals; Market Price:* 7,200 gp; *Weight:* 2 lb.

Necklace of Favored Enemy Detection: This star-shaped necklace is made of pure silver. When one of the wearer's favored enemies is within one mile, the necklace emits a low hum. By concentrating, the wearer can detect the direction of the nearest favored enemy within that range.

Caster Level: 11th; *Prerequisites:* Craft Wondrous Item, *detect favored enemy; Market Price:* 34,000 gp; *Weight:* —.

Standing Stone: This massive stone obelisk increases a druid's ability to cast a single spell when in contact with it. The creator chooses a druid spell for the stone to affect and a specific sacrifice (such as a cow or a pile of gems) that activates it. Thereafter, any druid can use the *meld into stone* spell to merge with the *standing stone* and discover those two pieces of information. Once she has done so, she can activate the *standing stone* for herself only by making the designated sacrifice.

From that point forward, whenever the druid is in contact with the activated stone, she casts that spell as if it were affected by the feats Empower Spell, Enlarge Spell, and Extend Spell. Because each *standing stone* affects only one spell, these items are typically arranged in circles with no more than 30 feet between any adjacent pair, so that a druid may move to a new stone to cast a new spell each round. The caster level and market price (not in-

cluding transportation) are determined by the level of the spell the stone affects, as follows.

Spell Level	Caster Level	Market Price	Cost to Create
0	3rd	10,676 gp	5,338 gp + 427 XP
1st	3rd	10,850 gp	5,425 gp + 434 XP
2nd	3rd	12,600 gp	6,300 gp + 504 XP
3rd	5th	15,750 gp	7,875 gp + 630 XP
4th	7th	20,300 gp	10,150 gp + 812 XP
5th	9th	26,250 gp	13,125 gp + 1,050 XP
6th	11th	33,600 gp	16,800 gp + 1,344 XP
7th	13th	42,350 gp	21,175 gp + 1,694 XP
8th	14th	49,700 gp	24,850 gp + 1,988 XP
9th	15th	57,750 gp	28,875 gp + 2,310 XP

Caster Level: 5th (or high enough to cast the chosen spell); *Prerequisites:* Craft Wondrous Item, *meld into stone,* ability to cast the chosen spell; *Weight:* 8,000 lb.

Torc of Animal Speech: This beaten steel necklace is unadorned by pendant or ornament. Its wearer can use a *speak with animals* effect at will.

Caster Level: 6th; *Prerequisites:* Craft Wondrous Item, *speak with animals; Market Price:* 12,000 gp; *Weight:* 1 lb.

Wilding Clasp: Appearing as a 3-inch-long gold chain, this item works only when attached to an amulet, vest, or similar item. The clasp prevents both itself and the attached item from melding into the wearer's new form when transforming magic (such as *polymorph self* or *wild shape*) is used. The item is still worn in the same manner it previously was and remains available for use in the new form. For example, a druid with a *wilding clasp* attached to her *periapt of Wisdom* could use *wild shape* to become a wolf, but the periapt and the *wilding clasp* would remain in their normal forms, fully functional. Some forms may be harmful to certain items; for instance, it would be unwise to take the form of a fire elemental while retaining a functional *necklace of fireballs*.

Caster Level: 5th; *Prerequisites:* Craft Wondrous Item, *polymorph self* or *wild shape* ability; *Market Price:* 4,000 gp; *Weight:* —.

INFUSIONS

"This forest is our home. We derive strength from its roots. You do not, unless we say so."

—Vadania

Since sentient beings first walked upon the land, they have been quick to take advantage of the bounty of life before them. When human and elven foragers discovered that eating the leaves of a certain vine could stave off infection, the science of herbalism was born. Experimentation over the years, across the continents and oceans, proved that nature held secret cures for many of the diseases and weaknesses that the world knew. This section presents another use for herbs in the creation of infusions—magic items that can be imbued with the power of spells.

What Is an Infusion?

An infusion is a divine spell stored within a specially treated herb. It works like a scroll, except that it is use-activated—to activate the spell, the user must consume the herb. This makes infusions ideal for the druid; she can hide several of them for later consumption, thus gaining access to spell effects while she is in *wild shape* and has no voice or hands to cast spells or use standard items.

Physical Description

Infusions vary widely in appearance, from red berries to dirt-covered roots. In general, they are very small and essentially weightless items—a bag of ten weighs only a single pound. An infusion is quite delicate, with an AC of 9, 1 hit point, a hardness of 0, and a break DC of 6.

Activation

In addition to consumption of the herb, several other steps and conditions come into play when activating an infusion.

Analyze the Chemistry: To determine what spell an infusion contains, a character must analyze its chemistry. This requires a *read magic* spell or a successful Spellcraft check (DC 15 + spell level). Analyzing an infusion does not activate it unless it is a specially designed cursed infusion.

Of course, it is possible to activate an infusion without first analyzing its chemistry. In that case, the user simply doesn't know what spell he or she is about to use.

Activate the Infusion: To attempt to activate an infusion, the user simply eats it. This is a standard action requiring no material components or focus. (The creator of the infusion provided those.) Some spells (such as *ironwood*) are effective only when cast on an item. In that case, the user must provide the item at the time of activation or the spell is wasted. An infusion cannot be administered to an unconscious creature.

Like drinking a potion, eating an infusion provokes attacks of opportunity. A successful attack against the user forces a Concentration check (DC = 10 + damage dealt). Failure means the character cannot eat the infusion in that round. If desired, an attacker may direct the attack of opportunity against the infusion rather than the character, destroying the item on a successful hit (see Attack an Object in Chapter 8 of the *Player's Handbook*).

To successfully activate an infusion, the user must meet the following requirements:

- Have the spell it contains on his or her class list (see Chapter 11 of the *Player's Handbook* for spells available to various classes).
- Have the requisite ability score to cast the spell (for example, Wisdom 15 for a druid casting a 5th-level spell).
- Have a caster level at least equal to that of the infusion.

If the user meets all the above requirements, the spell stored in the infusion takes effect immediately after consumption. Otherwise, the infusion acts as an ingestive poison. The user must make a Fortitude save (DC 10 + one-half of the infusion's caster level) or become nauseated. A second saving throw at the same DC and with the same consequence for failure must be made 1 minute later.

Determine the Effect: A spell successfully activated from an infusion works like a spell prepared and cast in the normal way. The infusion's caster level is always the minimum required for that spell, unless the caster is of a different class or specifically desires otherwise. For example, a 12th-level druid might want to create a *flame strike* infusion at caster level 12 rather than the minimum for the spell (caster level 7) to get the extra level-dependent benefits.

Since infusions are consumed during activation, they cannot be reused.

Random Generation

You can randomly generate infusions just as you can divine scrolls. See Chapter 8 of the *Dungeon Master's Guide* for details.

Creating Infusions

The process for creating infusions is similar to that for creating scrolls. The creator needs a supply of prepared herbs, the cost of which is subsumed in the cost for creating the infusion—25 gp per spell level times the caster level. The creator must pay the full cost for creating the infusion regardless of how many times he or she has previously created the same one.

The creator must have prepared the spell to be infused and must provide any material components or focuses required. If casting the spell would reduce the caster's XP total, the creator pays that cost upon beginning the infusion in addition to the XP cost for making the infusion itself. Likewise, any material components are consumed

when the process begins, but focuses are not. (A focus used in creating an infusion can be reused.) The act of infusing triggers the prepared spell, making it unavailable for casting until the character has rested and regained spells. (That is, the spell slot is expended from the creator's currently prepared spells, just as if it had been cast.)

Creating an infusion requires one day per 1,000 gp value of the completed infusion.

Item Creation Feat Required: Create Infusion.

TABLE 3–3: INFUSION BASE PRICES AND COSTS

Spell Level	Base Price	Base Cost to Create
0	25 gp	12 gp 5 sp + 1 XP
1	50 gp	25 gp + 2 XP
2	300 gp	150 gp + 12 XP
3	750 gp	375 gp + 30 XP
4	1,400 gp	700 gp + 46 XP
5	2,250 gp	1,125 gp + 90 XP
6	3,300 gp	1,650 gp + 132 XP
7	4,550 gp	2,275 gp + 182 XP
8	6,000 gp	3,000 gp + 240 XP
9	7,650 gp	3,825 gp + 306 XP

These costs assume that the creator makes the infusion at the minimum caster level.

Variant: Doing It Yourself

A character who's at home in the outdoors and has a good working knowledge of plants may be able to collect and prepare the components for an infusion personally rather than paying the local herbalist for them. With a little time and energy, a character with ranks in Profession (herbalist) and Wilderness Lore can remove the merchant from the equation and save some money in the process.

Collecting

Different infusions require different herbs. Not surprisingly, the higher the spell level, the more rare and prized is the herb required for an infusion of it. Thus, not only is the herb for a *heal* infusion different from the one for a *cure light wounds* infusion, it is also harder to find. Herbs for the highest-level spells may grow only in the remotest locales, so collection may require long journeys.

A character can use Wilderness Lore to forage for an herb while moving at one-half his or her normal overland movement rate through a forested or other natural area. Make a Wilderness Lore check (DC = 10 + twice the level of the spell to be infused) at the end of each day spent foraging. Success indicates that the character has found a sufficient quantity of the herb for a single infusion of the desired spell; failure means none was found. Casting *detect animals or plants* grants the character a +2 circumstance bonus on that day's check.

While foraging in this fashion, a character can also forage for sustenance, as detailed in the Wilderness Lore skill description in Chapter 4 of the *Player's Handbook*.

Gardening

Though growing herbs for infusions seems like a good idea, seldom does an adventuring character actually do so. Maintaining an herb garden requires hours of work each day in a single locale, and most adventurers cannot abide this degree of attachment to one place. Still, any

character wishing to undertake the challenge of gardening may attempt it according to the following rules.

Once the character has acquired a sample of the desired herb (see Collecting, above), he or she can attempt to cultivate it. A single character can care for a number of herbs equal to twice the number of ranks he or she has acquired in Wilderness Lore. With proper care, an herb garden produces a harvest twice a year.

To produce an herb crop, the character must make a Wilderness Lore or Profession (farmer) check for each week of cultivation, plus an additional Wilderness Lore check at harvest time. The DC for the weekly cultivation check is one-half the DC required to find the herb (see Collecting, above). If this check fails by 5 or more, the herb withers and dies. Each time it fails by less than 5, a cumulative −1 penalty is imposed on the final Wilderness Lore check for harvesting the crop. If that last check is successful, the herbs harvested are sufficient for a number of infusions equal to one-half the check result. Failure indicates that no usable herbs are produced.

Hiring a gardener to perform this task may be a reasonable option. A skilled gardener earns 1 gp per day, or about 180 gp per season. (This does not include the cost of acquiring the herb for planting, nor the cost of the land for the garden.) The average gardener can cultivate two herbs per season, each of which produces enough herbs for 1d4 infusions.

Preparing

Before an herb can be used in an infusion, it must be properly prepared. Some herbs must be treated or dried; others must be baked, steamed, or doused with a solution of oil or seawater. Again, the higher the level of the spell to be infused, the more difficult and complex the preparation becomes. Preparing an herb for infusion requires a Profession (herbalist) check.

To determine how long the preparation takes, first find the base cost to create the infusion on Table 3–3 and convert the price to silver pieces (1 gp = 10 sp). Then make a Profession (herbalist) check (DC = 10 + twice the level of the spell to be infused) representing one week's worth of work. If the check succeeds, multiply the check result by the DC. A total equal to or greater than the base cost for creation means that the herb is ready to be infused with the desired spell. A total below that price represents the progress made that week. Make another check the subsequent week and, if it is successful, add that check result times the DC to the previous week's result. As soon as the sum of these weekly totals equals or exceeds the price of

the item in silver pieces, the preparation is complete.

Failure at any point indicates that the character makes no progress that week. Failure by 5 or more means the character ruins the raw materials and must begin again with a fresh supply of the herb.

Optional Rule: Benefits of Hard Work

Taking the time and trouble to collect or grow each herb, prepare it, and infuse it with a spell is hard work. By so doing, however, characters attune themselves to nature and her bounty. Making an infusion "from scratch" raises its caster level by +1. This increase alters neither the cost of creating the infusion nor the difficulty of using it.

Optional Rule: Tailored Infusions

The fantasy world of the DUNGEONS & DRAGONS game teems with distinctive and individual animals, beasts, and plants. Rather than assuming that a certain infusion uses some nameless herb, reference the spell's level and school on Table 3–4 to find the name of the herb needed.

TABLE 3–4: TAILORED INFUSIONS

Spell Level	Abjuration	Conjuration	Divination	Enchantment	Evocation	Illusion	Necromancy	Transmutation	Universal
0	mayflower	oregano	marigold	asparagus root	thyme	rose	castor	chives	mistletoe
1	rosemary	colewort	ginseng	juniper berry	mace	ash bark	hazelwort	garlic	
2	marjoram	red cockscomb	benne	adrue	benzoin	parsnip	dandelion	waybread	
3	felonwort	plantain	chamomile	muira-puama	lucerne	chaulmoogra oil	senna	comfrey root	
4	white horehound	lily of the valley	quince	asafetida	nux vomica	sweet balm	agaric	beth root	
5	jewel weed	hyssop	angelica	pomegranate	fenugreek	thoughtwort	stickwort	mandragora	
6	knight's spur	spikenard	fennel	scopolis	foxglove	berberis	hellebore	hartstongue	
7	mudar bark	felwort	cardamom	wolfsbane	black horehound	butterbur	fenugreek	throatwort	
8	unicorn root	blackbane	cyclopstongue	belladonna	dragonhart	madwort	corpsetoe	leapleaf	
9	turtlewort	shamblerstalk	seerglove	feybread	firecomb	madweed	assassin seed	ironmoss	

CHAPTER 4: ANIMALS

"The Brine Lord's coral castle is surrounded by hungry sharks. He calls the toothy creatures to his home, then lets them roam free. He doesn't bother controlling them; something always comes by to make the sharks want to stay."

—Soveliss

Animals are among nature's most potent resources. They offer sustenance with their milk, their eggs, and their very flesh. Their skins and hides provide clothing and shelter from the elements. Some can also serve as transportation for characters and goods, or even guard against predators.

This chapter begins with an expanded discussion of how to choose, acquire, and care for an animal companion, as well as what a character can expect from that relationship. Following this are statistics for several new dire animals. Finally, a new subtype of animal is presented—the legendary animal—along with statistics for several creatures of that subtype.

ANIMAL COMPANIONS

Druids and rangers have deeper and more complex relationships with animals than other characters do, but even so, the basics are unchanged. These special guardians of nature are just as likely as any other character to consume the bounty of nature in the form of hunted animals—that's part of the cycle of life. Hide armor is popular among druids, and rangers frequently use horses or other creatures as mounts or beasts of burden. The difference is that both the druid and the ranger have a fundamental respect for the natural world they live in. Not only are they committed to studying the outdoors through the Knowledge (nature) and Wilderness Lore skills, but they also maintain special relationships with animal companions.

Animal companions are an important part of a druid's (and to a lesser extent, a ranger's) power. The druid lacks some of the cleric's spellcasting versatility and casts fewer spells per day, but her powerful animal companions go a long way toward compensating. An animal companion can serve as a protector, tracker, scout, mount, and warrior—sometimes all at once. It can even be a friend capable of offering advice, thanks to the magic of *awaken*. Moreover, the Hit Dice of an adventuring druid's animal companion can equal her own, whereas followers and cohorts almost always have fewer Hit Dice than their leaders.

The typical druid chooses a wolf as her first animal companion. The wolf attacks as well as a fighter of comparable Hit Dice, plus it can track. Five levels later, the druid could have a brown bear, which averages a whopping 51 hit points and has three attacks with the potential to do more than 20 points of damage per round. Later, the dire tiger offers 120 hit points on average, plus even more damage potential through its claw, bite, pounce, grab, and rake attacks. Thus, regardless of their limitations, animal companions are incredibly valuable.

Shopping for an Animal

The 1st-level druid starts out with an animal companion, but throughout the rest of her adventuring career, she must do a bit of work to acquire new ones—as must the ranger. The first step is to choose the desired kind of animal from the options described in the *Monster Manual* and in Chapter 1 of this book.

Since having animal companions is a core ability of the druid and the ranger, the DM shouldn't make it particularly difficult or challenging to find one. The simplest option is to allow the character a couple of days between adventures to find the desired companion. As long as he or she searches in a terrain that is home to that species, it takes only a day or two to find an appropriate creature. (Of course, it's impossible to find a lion in polar regions or a shark on land.)

To play this out a bit more, have the druid or ranger make a Wilderness Lore check (DC 10 for most animals) to discover the creature's regular territory, then use the Track feat to locate one specimen. The *detect animals or plants* spell allows the character to focus the search on a single species within range. *Power sight*, a new spell described in Chapter 6, can reveal the exact Hit Dice of a target animal and thus whether or not the character can befriend it. Assume that with the use of Wilderness Lore and a *detect animals or plants* spell, the character has a 30% chance to locate an animal for each day spent searching in an appropriate terrain and climate.

If the DM wants to center a campaign around individual heroes and their quests, the party could have a good time seeking out the lair of the evil sorcerer who has imprisoned animals for diabolical purposes, or rescuing a bear from a frost giant's kitchen before it lands on the supper table. A few such quests could be interesting and give the animal companion a special place in the party, but it may not be appropriate to reserve game time for this sort of activity if the character is changing animal companions frequently.

Better than Average Animals

It's simplest to assume that the druid and the ranger always find animal companions that are average for their species, with the ability scores and average hit points given in the *Monster Manual*. But some creatures deviate from this norm, with hit points above or below the average, or even unusual ability scores. Wolves with 18 hit points instead of 13 exist, and so do lions with Strength 25 instead of 21. While it may be simplest to assume that all animal companions are average, it's in a character's best interest to seek out creatures that exceed the norm.

The obvious way to do this is to generate an animal's hit points and ability scores randomly whenever the character encounters one. Rolling for hit points is easy, and generating ability scores isn't tough (see Ability Scores for Monsters in Chapter 2 of the DUNGEON

Previous Sources

The core rulebooks of the DUNGEONS & DRAGONS game offer plenty of material about animal companions. The description of the druid in the *Player's Handbook* lays out the basic concepts. The *animal friendship* spell, in Chapter 11 of the same book, gives still more information. Finally, the sidebar on Animal Companions in Chapter 2 of the DUNGEON MASTER's Guide continues the discussion and introduces the concept of training and teaching tricks.

MASTER's Guide). The disadvantage of this method is that it involves a lot of dice-rolling and could result in day after day of searching for the picky character.

The best solution is not to reveal an animal's ability scores or hit points. After all, while it may be easy to identify a sick animal, it's tough to differentiate between two animals whose Strength scores differ by 2 points. And no animal is likely to tolerate a barrage of tests designed to determine whether it's a worthy companion before the character has magically befriended it. Intending to perform such tests after casting *animal friendship* is a violation of the spell's parameters, since it functions only for a caster who has a true heart and actually wishes to be the animal's friend. Only after the character has adventured with the animal for weeks or months (assume 2d4 weeks as an average) should the DM consider revealing its ability scores and hit points. At that point, the character can abandon the animal and begin anew, if desired. However, doing this too often may call the character's "true heart" into question.

Two ability scores actually have limitations. First, an animal's Intelligence score never exceeds 2 without the assistance of magic. Most mammals, lizards, and birds have Intelligence 2, while snakes, fish, and lower-order animals have Intelligence 1. Second, only one normal animal (the wolverine) has a Charisma score greater than 7, and no dire animal has a Charisma greater than 11.

The Bond

The bond created by an *animal friendship* spell is not a magical one. It cannot be dispelled, though *dominate animal* or some other magical compulsion could cause the animal to act against the character's wishes. The animal acknowledges the character as its friend—something like a special denmate or a member of the pack. The animal may realize that the character isn't really one of its own, but true conscious thought along those lines is beyond most animals' ability.

As the Animal Companions sidebar in Chapter 2 of the *DUNGEON MASTER's Guide* states, a companion is still only an animal. It cannot understand human speech. Other than following its friend and performing the tricks it has been taught, it cannot respond to directions. An empathic link exists between the wizard and her familiar and between the paladin and her mount, but not between a druid (or a ranger) and an animal companion. Thus, an animal companion makes a poor scout, since it has no way to communicate what it sees—and even if it did, its low Intelligence prevents it from knowing what to look for or how to analyze what it finds.

The animal expects its friend to either provide it with sustenance or give it adequate time to find food and water on its own. In addition, though the animal naturally defends its friend, and may even attack his or her enemies, it doesn't enjoy combat. While the druid and the ranger can accept that some pain is necessary in the service of good or the defense of the land, these concepts are lost on the lion, hawk, or lizard that is being struck, mauled, or energy drained. The animal expects its friend to try to keep it safe, so painful fight after painful fight may cause it to grow weary of the punishment.

Animal Mood and Attitude

The player whose character has befriended an animal usually controls it. As long as that character continues to fulfill the obligations and duties of friendship, this is a fine way to run things. Should anything complicate or challenge that relationship, however, the DM may want to step in and control the animal's reactions.

When a character befriends an animal through *animal friendship,* its attitude toward its new friend automatically becomes helpful (see Chapter 5 of the *DUNGEON MASTER's Guide.*) Should the character ever abuse the animal physically or expose it to adverse situations that strain its loyalty, the DM can adjust its attitude appropriately—to friendly, indifferent, or worse as the situation requires. A friendly animal may or may not aid its friend, and an indifferent one certainly won't. An animal that has become unfriendly or hostile looks for the first chance to depart or lash out at the "friend" who has clearly abused its trust. However, through roleplaying and judicious use of the Animal Empathy skill, a character may be able to repair such a breach of trust. Use Table 5–4: Influencing NPC Attitude in the *DUNGEON MASTER's Guide* to determine the DC for the check.

The animal has no special tie to its friend's fellow adventurers, so its initial attitude toward them is indifferent. It doesn't protect them unless ordered, but neither does it attack them unless provoked. Roleplaying and the use of Animal Empathy can adjust the animal's attitude about other party members in the same manner as described above.

Limitations and Problems

The presence of animal companions in an adventuring party can present a variety of problems. Wild animals are generally not accepted inside a city or within the lord's keep. To most peasants, a wild animal is something to be feared, driven off, or put down, just like a troll or a griffon would be. Only the most famous druid or ranger heroes can expect an urban population to accept wild creatures walking along the streets—even in the company of humanoids.

Most characters solve this problem by simply asking their companions to stay in the wilderness outside town. An animal companion can accept such a parting of the ways as long as it remains short (less than a week), or the character's visits are frequent. Of course, leaving a wild animal outside town can present another problem—the creature may think that the domesticated cows, chickens, or horses on the nearby farms are meant for its consumption.

Another tough situation is the dungeon. Most animals (other than bats, lizards, rats, snakes, toads, and the dire versions thereof) are unaccustomed to dwelling underground. Bears, even though they live in caves, are not truly native to subterranean habitats. Surface-dwelling

The Best Animal Companion?

What's the best animal to befriend? You should try to maintain your maximum allowed Hit Dice of companions, and whenever possible, invest all those Hit Dice in a single animal. Unless you want an animal companion just to serve as a distraction, it needs the best hit points and attack bonus possible. Most magical beasts and underground denizens can overpower an animal of equal Hit Dice, so you have to work hard to keep animal companions competitive.

That said, some animals tend to make better companions than others. A horse makes some sense, perhaps, though it's just as easy to purchase one. In general, you can't go wrong choosing the most combat-effective animal you can get. Depending on the Hit Dice, that means a wolf, lion, bear, or tiger—or a dire version thereof.

animals are reluctant to proceed into confined spaces and tight, sunless corridors. Even if they can be convinced to enter the dungeon, most animals have great difficulty dealing with pits, steep inclines, narrow crevices, and similar dungeon challenges. Without magical levitation or the ability to fly, a creature such as a dire tiger could easily get stuck somewhere in the Underdark. Because of this, some characters choose to leave their animal companions outside the dungeon. Alternatively, the calm trick (see Chapter 2) can enhance a creature's ability to deal with dungeon environments.

Food and Care

A character with an animal companion must see to its care and feeding during adventures. The obvious option, of course, is to carry food for it. The biggest problem with doing this is typically the weight, not the cost. For an herbivore, a day's worth of feed costs a mere 5 cp and weighs 10 pounds; for a carnivore, it costs 5 sp and weighs 10 pounds. Each day, a Medium-size herbivore or carnivore drinks at least a gallon of water, which weighs about 8 pounds (plus the weight of the container), and a Large animal drinks at least 3 gallons a day. Given the typical horse's carrying capacity, it can be a real challenge to carry more than two weeks of food for an animal companion. On extended trips, a druid can rely upon *create water* and *goodberry*. One *goodberry* can provide sustenance for one Medium-size herbivore or carnivore; a Large animal requires two per day, and a Huge creature requires four. As a final option, a character may be able to convince a hungry carnivore to eat the flesh of a slain monster—particularly a beast, dragon, giant, humanoid, magical beast, or monstrous humanoid.

Another option is to allow the animal to graze or hunt for itself. It must eat at least once every third day, just like a human, or begin to suffer the effects of starvation (see Chapter 3 of the DUNGEON MASTER'S Guide). Grazing animals need only grassland or a hayfield; no skill check is required. To forage for water or to hunt, the animal must make a Wilderness Lore check (DC 10). Success indicates that it has acquired a day's worth of food and water; failure means no suitable sustenance was found. If the animal is foraging in its native terrain and climate, it suffers no penalties on the check; otherwise, a circumstance penalty of at least –4 and as much as –8 applies. If the animal moves at one-half its overland movement rate or slower, it can hunt while traveling; otherwise, it requires 4 hours per day to hunt.

Finally, animals aren't prepared for climates other than their own. Those adapted for the cold, such as bears, perform poorly in warm deserts, and cold-blooded animals such as snakes and lizards suffer in cold regions. When outside its native environment, an animal must make Fortitude saving throws at regular intervals to avoid taking subdual damage. The rules for this are the same as those given for characters in the Heat Dangers and Cold Dangers sections in Chapter 3 of the DUNGEON MASTER'S Guide, except that the animal's Wilderness Lore skill provides no bonuses on these saves. A character, however, may provide bonuses to an animal companion with a successful Wilderness Lore check, as noted in the Wilderness Lore skill description in the Player's Handbook. Eventually, though, the character must make a choice: Take the animal out of the foreign environment, cast a protection spell such as *endure elements*, or watch the creature perish.

Breaking the Limits

Often, the best way to improve the abilities of animal companions and overcome some of their limitations is the use of spells and magic items.

Enhancing Magic: *Magic fang* and *nature's favor* enhance an animal companion's combat ability. *Might of the oak*, *persistence of the waves*, and *speed of the wind* each enhance one of an animal's ability scores at the expense of another. *Animal growth* improves an animal's combat effectiveness through increased Hit Dice, Strength, Constitution, damage, and hit points. Finally, *nature's avatar* increases an animal's hit points and grants it the benefits of *haste*, thus transforming it into a fearsome destructive machine. The lower-level spells, especially *nature's favor*, are excellent for use in wands. See Chapter 6 for spell descriptions.

Barding: Horses, ponies, riding lizards, and riding dogs typically accept armor in the form of barding, but wild creatures simply refuse the burden. With the armor trick (see Chapter 2), a character can adapt any animal to the use of armor. Barding is available in all armor types (including masterwork and magical versions), but it always costs more than comparable human armor. See Chapter 7 of the Player's Handbook for additional rules on barding.

Communication: Adopting an animal form through *wild shape* or *polymorph self* doesn't impart the ability to communicate with that species (at least, not without the Speaking *Wild Shape* feat described in Chapter 2). The *speak with animals* spell is the one of the best ways to converse with animal companions, but a *helm of bonding* or a *torc of animal speech* (see Chapter 3 for magic item descriptions) also allows communication. Direct conversation lets the creature understand instructions beyond the tricks it has learned, but even so, the animal's intelligence places an obvious limit on the interaction.

Loyalty: Most animals have poor Will saving throws. As friendly and loyal as an animal companion is to its druid or ranger friend, an enemy can all too easily use magic to control or dominate it. A druid with foresight can either carry spells (such as *dispel magic* or *calm animal*) to neutralize this threat or equip her companions with *collars of resistance*.

More Animals: The obvious way to acquire additional animal companions is to gain class levels in druid or ranger, but magic items provide a second option. One *ring of animal friendship* adds 12 Hit Dice to the character's

---

Raising a Companion

The realistic way to get a better than average animal is to raise it from infancy. An animal that never goes hungry and gets ample exercise is likely to grow up stronger, tougher, and slightly more intelligent than the average creature of its kind. To reflect this, the DM may allow an animal companion that a character has raised and trained from birth to have 2 bonus hit points per Hit Die, an extra 3 points for its ability scores (distributed as the player sees fit), and the ability to learn one additional trick per point of Intelligence.

Rearing a wild animal takes one year and requires one Handle Animal check (DC 15 + HD of animal). No skill check is required if the creature has already become an animal companion to a druid or ranger, but most adventurers choose to befriend animals only after they are old enough to be helpful. Paying someone to raise an animal may be a more feasible option for adventuring characters. A professional trainer charges 250 gold pieces per Hit Die of the animal to rear it.

This method of acquiring animal companions requires more planning than just searching for one does, but it's also useful for nonadventuring druids who aren't likely to gain levels (and thus require new animal companions) very frequently.

limit, a second raises that to 24, and a *hand of glory* allows the use of a third such ring for a total of 36 additional Hit Dice of animal companions. At a price of only 9,500 gp per ring and 7,200 gp for the *hand of glory*, these items are cheap for their benefits.

Regardless of the total Hit Dice of animal companions an adventuring character can have, none of them can exceed his or her own Hit Dice.* That is, an 8th-level druid wearing with a *ring of animal friendship* can befriend two dire lions (8HD creatures), but not a dire tiger (16HD creature), or any creature with more than 8 Hit Dice. On the other hand, two dire lions can pack quite a punch.

*This information supersedes that presented in the *animal friendship* spell in the *Player's Handbook*.

Abandoning a Companion

Characters want to replace their animal companions from time to time, and there is no penalty for doing so. Reasons for making a change abound—for example, a druid may not wish to expose comparatively weak animals to dangers they cannot handle, or she may need to travel to a region where her existing companions could not survive.

The real issue is the conditions under which a character abandons an animal companion. Leaving it in a foreign land, or worse, in the depths of some dungeon, is an evil act. Even neutral and evil druids should be loath to betray their companions in this way.

Improving a Companion

Some characters, abhorring the prospect of abandoning a trusted friend every level or two, seek a way out of this situation. Long ago, druids developed a magical ritual to deal with this problem. During this ritual, which takes a full day to perform at a holy site or natural glade, the druid's touch imbues one animal companion with additional strength. The druid loses 200 XP, as if she had cast a spell with that XP cost. Only animals with a listing for "advancement" in their statistics can improve through this ritual.

At the end of the ritual, the animal's Hit Dice increase by +1. As a result, it gains additional hit points and a bonus on attack rolls, if the new Hit Dice total warrants that. The additional Hit Die may also increase the animal's size (see the rules for advancement in the introduction of the *Monster Manual*). Since it is an animal, the companion gains neither feats nor skills as it advances.

Awakened Animals

Awaken is a 5th-level spell available to druids. Because it grants humanlike sentience and intelligence to an animal, the creature's type changes to magical beast. This spell greatly changes the relationship between druid and animal companion. Armed with intelligence and the ability to speak at least one language, the animal no longer needs training to understand the druid's wishes. Thus, the druid gains a source of advice and ready conversation in addition to a guard and a servant. Of course, as a fully sentient creature, an *awakened* animal develops its own desires and ambitions.

While normally a creature with such a high intelligence isn't subject to *animal friendship*, an animal *awakened* by a druid remains her companion as long as she treats it with respect, as discussed above. The animal continues to count against the druid's Hit Dice limit for animal companions. For a time, the *awakened* animal can even exceed the druid's level. (For example, an *awakened* dire bear suddenly has 14 HD, but it remains with a 12th-level druid). Until the druid once again exceeds the animal in Hit Dice, however, she cannot gain new animal companions.

As a general rule, an *awakened* animal continues to assist the druid, at least as long as she continues to include it among her companions. When she elects to leave that animal behind (by befriending a new one), it soon departs. The animal remains friendly with the druid and may assist her from time to time, but it no longer accompanies her on adventures.

DIRE ANIMALS

	Dire Toad Small Animal	Dire Hawk Medium-Size Animal	Dire Snake Large Animal
Hit Dice:	4d8+8 (26 hp)	5d8+10 (32 hp)	7d8+21 (52 hp)
Initiative:	+2 (Dex)	+6 (Dex)	+5 (Dex)
Speed:	20 ft.	10 ft., fly 80 ft. (average)	20 ft., climb 20 ft., swim 20 ft.
AC:	15 (+1 size, +2 Dex, +2 natural)	19 (+6 Dex, +3 natural)	18 (−1 size, +5 Dex, +4 natural)
Attacks:	Tongue +6 ranged	2 claws +9 melee and bite +4 melee	Bite + 10 melee
Damage:	Tongue poison	Claw 1d4+1; bite 1d6	Bite 1d6 +9 and poison
Face/Reach:	5 ft. by 5 ft./5 ft.	5 ft. by 5 ft./5 ft.	5 ft. by 10 ft. (coiled)/10 ft.
Special Attacks:	Poison	—	Improved grab, constrict 1d6+9, poison
Special Qualities:	—	—	Scent
Saves:	Fort +6, Ref +6, Will +3	Fort +6, Ref +10, Will +3	Fort +8, Ref +10, Will +3
Abilities:	Str 6, Dex 14, Con 14, Int 2, Wis 14, Cha 7	Str 12, Dex 22, Con 14, Int 2, Wis 14, Cha 10	Str 22, Dex 20, Con 16, Int 1, Wis 12, Cha 10
Skills:	Hide +16, Jump +9, Listen + 7, Spot +11	Listen +8, Move Silently +8, Spot +8*	Balance +14, Climb +14, Hide +6, Listen +9, Spot +9
Feats:	—	Weapon Finesse (claws, bite)	—

Climate/Terrain:	Temperate and warm land, aquatic, and underground	Any forest, hill, plains, and mountains	Temperate and warm land, aquatic, and underground
Organization:	Solitary or swarm (10–100)	Solitary or pair	Solitary
Challenge Rating:	2	2	4
Treasure:	None	None	None
Alignment:	Always neutral	Always neutral	Always neutral
Advancement:	5–6 HD (Small); 7–10 HD (Medium-size)	5–8 HD (Medium-size); 9–12 HD (Large)	8–12 HD (Large); 13–16 HD (Huge)

	Dire Horse Large Animal	Dire Elk Huge Animal	Dire Elephant Gargantuan Animal
Hit Dice:	8d8+48 (84 hp)	12d8+60 (114 hp)	20d8+200 (290 hp)
Initiative:	+1 (Dex)	+0	+0
Speed:	60 ft.	50 ft.	30 ft., climb 10 ft.
AC:	16 (–1 size, +1 Dex, +6 natural)	15 (–2 size, +7 natural)	10 (–4 size, +4 natural)
Attacks:	2 hooves +11 melee and bite +6 melee	Slam +14 melee and 2 hooves +9 melee; or gore +14 melee	Slam +26 melee and 2 stamps +21 melee; or gore +26 melee
Damage:	Hoof 1d6+6; bite 1d4+3	Slam 2d6+7, hoof 2d4+3; gore 2d8+10	Slam 2d8+15, stamp 2d8+7, gore 4d6+22
Face/Reach:	5 ft. by 10 ft./5 ft.	10 ft. by 20 ft./10 ft.	20 ft. by 40 ft./10 ft.
Special Attacks:	—	Trample 2d8+10	Trample 4d6+22
Special Qualities:	Scent	Scent	Scent
Saves:	Fort +12, Ref +7, Will +4	Fort +13, Ref +8, Will +4	Fort +22, Ref +12, Will +8
Abilities:	Str 22, Dex 13, Con 22, Int 2, Wis 14, Cha 10	Str 24, Dex 11, Con 20, Int 2, Wis 11, Cha 6	Str 40, Dex 10, Con 30, Int 2, Wis 14, Cha 8
Skills:	Hide –3, Listen +8, Spot +8	Hide –4, Listen +6, Spot +6	Climb +23, Hide –12, Listen +8, Spot +8
Feats:	—	—	—
Climate/Terrain:	Any land	Temperate and cold forest, hill, and mountains	Warm forest and plains
Organization:	Solitary or herd (6–30)	Solitary or herd (6–30)	Solitary or herd (6–30)
Challenge Rating:	4	7	10
Treasure:	None	None	None
Alignment:	Always neutral	Always neutral	Always neutral
Advancement:	9–16 HD (Large); 17–24 HD (Huge)	13–16 HD (Huge); 17–36 HD (Gargantuan)	21–30 HD (Gargantuan); 31–45 HD (Colossal)

Dire animals are larger, tougher, and meaner versions of normal animals. They tend to have a feral, prehistoric look.

Dire Toad

These small amphibians are generally nonaggressive insect hunters. In large groups, however, they can make good use of their poison attacks.

Combat

Poison (Ex): Bite, Fort save (DC 14); initial and secondary damage 1d6 temporary Con.

Improved Grab (Ex): To use this ability, the dire toad must hit with a tongue attack. If it gets a hold, it can attempt to swallow the foe.

Swallow Whole (Ex): A dire toad can try to swallow a grabbed opponent of Tiny or smaller size by making a successful grapple check. Once inside the dire toad, the opponent takes 1d6 points of crushing damage +1d4 points of acid damage per round from the creature's stomach. A swallowed creature can climb out of the stomach with a successful grapple check. This returns it to the dire toad's mouth, where another successful grapple check is needed to get free. A swallowed creature can also cut its way out by dealing 10 or more points of damage to the stomach (AC 13) with claws or a Tiny slashing weapon. Once that swallowed creature exits, muscular action closes the hole; another swallowed opponent must cut its own way out.

The dire toad's interior holds up to two Tiny, four Diminutive, or eight Fine opponents.

Skills: A dire toad receives a +4 racial bonus on Hide, Listen, and Spot checks, and a +8 racial bonus on Jump checks.

Dire Hawk

A bird of prey capable of taking down pigs, sheep, and even the occasional small horse, the dire hawk prefers high, remote nesting spots.

A typical dire hawk is 5 feet long and has a wingspan of 11 feet.

Skills: A dire hawk receives a +8 racial bonus on Spot checks in daylight.

Dire Snake

The dire snake combines all the strength and power of the constrictor with the venomous bite of a viper. It can constrict an opponent of up to Large size.

Combat

Poison (Ex): Bite, Fort save (DC 16), initial and secondary damage 1d6 temporary Con.

Improved Grab (Ex): To use this ability, the dire snake must hit with its bite attack. If it gets a hold, it can constrict.

Constrict (Ex): A dire snake deals 1d6+9 points of damage with a successful grapple check against a Large or smaller creature.

Skills: The dire snake receives a +4 racial bonus on Hide, Listen, and Spot checks, and a +8 racial bonus on Balance checks. A dire snake with higher Dexterity than Strength can use its Dexterity modifier on Climb checks.

Dire Horse

Aggressive, wild equines that roam the wilderness, dire horses resist domestication as much as any wild animal does. A dire horse can fight while carrying a rider, but the rider cannot also attack unless he or she succeeds at a Ride check (DC 10).

Carrying Capacity: A light load for a dire horse is up to 519 pounds, a medium load is 520–1,038 pounds, and a heavy load is 1,039–1,557 pounds. A dire horse can drag 7,785 pounds.

Dire Elk

A bull dire elk is an imposing and aggressive beast during the mating season. His enormous antlers can span up to 12 feet, and he can weigh up to 3 tons. If this creature believes himself challenged, he tries to drive off the interloper by bellowing loudly and pawing the ground. If that doesn't work, the dire elk charges with his head lowered to deliver a vicious gore with his oversized antlers, then follows up with stamping and trampling attacks. Females are not antlered (no gore attack) and are less aggressive than males, but cow dire elks are still formidable when their calves are threatened. In the spring, the bull sheds his antlers, after which his gore attack is not available until he regrows them the following autumn.

Combat

Trample (Ex): A dire elk can trample Medium-size or smaller creatures for automatic gore damage. Opponents who do not make attacks of opportunity against the dire elk can attempt a Reflex save (DC 23) to halve the damage.

Skills: A dire elk receives a +4 racial bonus on Hide checks.

Dire Elephant

These titanic herbivores are somewhat unpredictable and likely to attack. Giants sometimes use them as mounts or beasts of burden.

Combat

Trample (Ex): A dire elephant can trample Large or smaller creatures for automatic gore damage. Opponents who do not make attacks of opportunity against it can attempt a Reflex save (DC 35) to halve the damage.

LEGENDARY ANIMALS

	Legendary Eagle Small Animal	Legendary Ape Medium-Size Animal	Legendary Wolf Medium-Size Animal
Hit Dice:	12d8+36 (90 hp)	13d8+39 (97 hp)	14d8+70 (133 hp)
Initiative:	+10 (Dex)	+3 (Dex)	+9 (Dex)
Speed:	10 ft., fly 100 ft. (average)	40 ft., climb 20 ft.	60 ft.
AC:	25 (+1 size, +10 Dex, +4 natural)	19 (+3 Dex, +6 natural)	24 (+9 Dex, +5 natural)
Attacks:	2 claws +20 melee and bite +15 melee	2 claws +19 melee and bite + 14 melee	Bite +19 melee
Damage:	Claw 1d6+2; bite 1d8+1	Claw 1d8+10; bite 2d6+5	Bite 2d6 +10
Face/Reach:	5 ft. by 5 ft./5 ft.	5 ft. by 5 ft./5 ft.	5 ft. by 5 ft./5 ft.
Special Attacks:	—	Rend 2d8+15	Trip
Special Qualities:	—	Scent	Scent
Saves:	Fort +11, Ref +18, Will +7	Fort +11, Ref +11, Will +7	Fort +14, Ref +18, Will +6
Abilities:	Str 14, Dex 30, Con 16, Int 2, Wis 16, Cha 12	Str 30, Dex 16, Con 16, Int 2, Wis 16, Cha 10	Str 24, Dex 28, Con 20, Int 2, Wis 14, Cha 10
Skills:	Hide +14, Listen +10, Spot +10*	Climb +19, Move Silently +11, Spot +9	Hide +13, Listen +10, Move Silently +12, Spot +10, Wilderness Lore +4*
Feats:	Weapon Finesse (claws, bite)	—	Weapon Finesse (bite)
Climate/Terrain:	Any forest, hill, plains, and mountains	Warm forest and mountains, and underground	Any forest, hill, mountain, plain, and underground
Organization:	Solitary or pair	Solitary or company (2–5)	Solitary or herd (5–8)
Challenge Rating:	6	7	7
Treasure:	None	None	None
Alignment:	Always neutral	Always neutral	Always neutral
Advancement:	12–24 HD (Small)	14–26 HD (Medium-size)	15–30 HD (Medium-size)

	Legendary Snake Large Animal	Legendary Horse Large Animal	Legendary Bear Large Animal
Hit Dice:	16d8+112 (184 hp)	18d8+144 (225 hp)	20d8+20 (230 hp)
Initiative:	+7 (Dex)	+2 (Dex)	+2 (Dex)
Speed:	30 ft., climb 30 ft., swim 30 ft.	80 ft.	50 ft.
AC:	22 (–1 size, +7 Dex, +6 natural)	19 (–1 size, +2 Dex, +8 natural)	21 (–1 size, +2 Dex, +10 natural)
Attacks:	Bite +19 melee	2 hooves +21 melee and bite +16 melee	2 claws +27 melee and bite +22 melee
Damage:	Bite 1d8+12 and poison	Hoof 2d6+9, bite 1d6+4	Claw 2d6+13, bite 4d6+6
Face/Reach:	5 ft. by 10 ft. (coiled)/10 ft.	5 ft. by 10 ft./5 ft.	5 ft. by 10 ft./5 ft.
Special Attacks:	Improved grab, constrict 1d8 +12, poison	—	Improved grab
Special Qualities:	Scent	Scent	Scent
Saves:	Fort +17, Ref +17, Will +7	Fort +19, Ref +13, Will +8	Fort +19, Ref +14, Will +9
Abilities:	Str 26, Dex 24, Con 24, Int 1, Wis 14, Cha 7	Str 28, Dex 14, Con 26, Int 2, Wis 14, Cha 10	Str 36, Dex 14, Con 24, Int 2, Wis 16, Cha 12
Skills:	Balance +24, Climb +18, Hide +14, Listen +12, Spot +12	Hide –2, Listen +8, Spot +8	Hide –2, Listen +8, Spot +8, Swim +18
Feats:	—	—	—
Climate/Terrain:	Temperate and warm land, aquatic, and underground	Any land	Any forest, hill, mountains, plains, or underground
Organization:	Solitary	Solitary or herd (6–30)	Solitary or pair
Challenge Rating:	8	8	9
Treasure:	None	None	None
Alignment:	Always neutral	Always neutral	Always neutral
Advancement:	17–32 HD (Large)	19–36 HD (Large)	21–40 HD (Large)

	Legendary Tiger Large Animal	Legendary Shark Huge Animal
Hit Dice:	26d8+182 (299 hp)	30d8+210 (345 hp)
Initiative:	+4 (Dex)	+4 (Dex)

Speed:	50 ft.	Swim 100 ft.
AC:	23 (−1 size, +4 Dex, +10 natural)	22 (−2 size, +4 Dex, +10 natural)
Attacks:	2 claws +29 melee and bite +24 melee	Bite +29 melee
Damage:	Claw 2d6+11; bite 2d8+5	Bite 2d8+13
Face/Reach:	5 ft. by 10 ft./5 ft.	10 ft. by 20 ft./10 ft.
Special Attacks:	Improved grab, pounce, rake 2d6+5	Improved grab, swallow whole
Special Qualities:	Scent	Keen scent
Saves:	Fort +22, Ref +19, Will +10	Fort +24, Ref +21, Will +12
Abilities:	Str 32, Dex 18, Con 24, Int 2, Wis 14, Cha 10	Str 28, Dex 18, Con 24, Int 1, Wis 14, Cha 6
Skills:	Hide +7*, Jump +15, Listen +5, Move Silently +13, Spot +7, Swim +14	Listen +9, Spot +9
Feats:	—	—
Climate/Terrain:	Any forest, hill, mountains, plains, and underground	Any aquatic
Organization:	Solitary or pair	Solitary or school (2–5)
Challenge Rating:	10	10
Treasure:	None	None
Alignment:	Always neutral	Always neutral
Advancement:	27–48 HD (Large)	31–60 HD (Huge)

Legendary animals are animals of incredible strength, speed, and power. According to some theories, they have been imbued with power beyond all other animals to serve as nature's defenders. Whatever their origin, legendary animals are extraordinarily rare.

Legendary animals represent another step in the animal power curve. Although the same size as their normal counterparts, they are significantly more powerful than even dire versions of their kind. Thus, they make appropriate animal companions for high-level druids. Making this option available ensures that a druid's animal companions remain valuable to her as she continues to advance.

As the druid gains levels, her spellcasting ability and overall power improve measurably, but her trusted servants begin to pale in comparison. Given the limitation that the total Hit Dice of an adventuring druid's animal companions cannot exceed her own level (except at 1st level, when she can have 2 HD worth of animal companions), she eventually outdistances her animal friends in terms of power. This is easy to see by considering the challenge ratings of the available creatures. For example, a 1st-level adventuring druid can have a 2-HD wolf companion (a CR 1 creature), which improves her combat ability (and thus her overall survivability) dramatically. At 6th level, she can maintain a 6-HD animal companion, such as a brown bear, which still adds significantly to her prowess, though it is only a CR 4 creature. But when she reaches 16th level and acquires a 16-HD dire tiger as an animal companion, she has gained only a CR 8 creature. In terms of encounter levels, the addition of a CR 8 creature to a 16th-level character results in a negligible improvement. The dire tiger is by no means an unworthy companion, but the druid just isn't getting the "bang for her buck" that she did earlier. Sadly, she also loses versatility, since the toughest animal companions are also Large, or even

Huge. Fitting these oversized creatures into cramped dungeon corridors is a challenge.

Legendary animals rarely appear except in the company of druids or other high-level characters. In fact, they are never even created until they are needed. They are created from normal animals of their kind through the power of nature (or a deity) whenever a character of appropriate level needs such a companion. Thus, when a high-level druid goes out to search for a new animal companion, nature mystically makes one available.

Legendary animals are treated as dire animals for the purpose of determining how spells affect them. For instance, a legendary animal is allowed a saving throw to resist the *calm animals* spell, just as a dire animal would be.

Legendary Eagle

With its feathers of white and yellow, the legendary eagle has a reputation for being an omen of good weather and good times to come. Like all birds of prey, the legendary eagle is a carnivore that hunts other birds and small reptiles, snakes, and mammals.

Skills: *A legendary eagle receives a +12 racial bonus on Spot checks in daylight.

Legendary Ape

This ape appears no different from the common ape in color and markings, but even the casual observer can tell that it is stronger, faster, and tougher than others of its kind.

Combat

Legendary apes are aggressive and territorial.

Rend (Ex): A legendary ape that hits with both claw attacks latches onto the opponent's body and tears the flesh. This automatically deals an additional 2d8+15 points of damage.

Legendary Wolf

A fierce-looking wolf with black, white, or gray fur, this animal is generally not aggressive toward humanoids, though hunger may make it attack.

Combat

Legendary wolves encountered singly may fight, or they may retreat to call together the pack. Whenever possible, legendary wolves hunt in groups.

Trip (Ex): A legendary wolf that hits with a bite attack can attempt to trip the opponent as a free action (see Trip in Chapter 8 of the *Player's Handbook*) without making a touch attack or provoking an attack of opportunity. If the attempt fails, the opponent cannot react to trip the legendary wolf.

Skills: A legendary wolf receives a +2 racial bonus on Listen, Move Silently, and Spot checks, and a +4 racial bonus on Hide checks. *It also receives a +8 racial bonus on Wilderness Lore checks when tracking by scent.

Legendary Snake

A strong constrictor with a potent venomous bite, the legendary snake is frequently found in lakes, rivers, and streams. It attacks only when threatened.

Combat

Poison (Ex): Bite, Fort save (DC 25), initial and secondary damage 1d8 temporary Con.

Improved Grab (Ex): To use this ability, the dire snake must hit with its bite attack. If it gets a hold, it can constrict.

Constrict (Ex): A legendary snake deals 1d8+12 points of damage with a successful grapple check against Large or smaller creatures.

Skills: A legendary snake receives a +8 racial bonus on Hide, Listen, and Spot checks, and a +16 racial bonus on Balance checks. A legendary snake with higher Dexterity than Strength can use its Dexterity modifier on Climb checks.

Legendary Horse

Legendary horses can never be domesticated, only befriended. Ancient stories tell of heroes riding these creatures, but even the tales have become very rare. A legendary horse can fight while carrying a rider, but the rider cannot also attack unless he or she succeeds at a Ride check (DC 10).

Carrying Capacity: A light load for a legendary horse is up to 1,200 pounds, a medium load is 1,201–2,400 pounds, and a heavy load is 2,401–3,600 pounds. A legendary horse can drag 18,000 pounds.

Legendary Bear

The legendary bear doesn't usually attack humans despite its great strength. Its diet consists primarily of plants and fish.

Combat

Improved Grab (Ex): To use this ability, the legendary bear must hit with a claw attack.

Legendary Tiger

The legendary tiger is the fiercest and most dangerous land predator in the animal kingdom. It measures 8–10 feet long and weighs up to 600 pounds.

Combat

Pounce (Ex): If a legendary tiger leaps upon a foe during the first round of combat, it can make a full attack even if it has already taken a move action.

Improved Grab (Ex): To use this ability, the legendary tiger must first hit with a bite attack. If it succeeds, it has grabbed its prey and can then rake.

Rake (Ex): A legendary tiger can make two attacks (+29 melee) against a held creature with its hind legs for 2d6+5 points of damage each. If the legendary tiger pounces on an opponent, it can also rake.

Skills: A legendary tiger receives a +8 racial bonus on both Hide and Move Silently checks. *In areas of tall grasses or heavy undergrowth, the Hide bonus improves to +16.

Legendary Shark

The legendary shark hunts anything it finds in the sea.

Combat

Improved Grab (Ex): To use this ability, the legendary shark must hit with a bite attack. If it gets a hold, it can try to swallow the foe.

Swallow Whole (Ex): A legendary shark can try to swallow a grabbed opponent of Large or smaller size by making a successful grapple check. Once inside the legendary shark, the opponent takes 2d8+13 points of crushing damage plus 1d8+4 points of acid damage per round from the creature's digestive juices. A swallowed creature can climb out of the stomach with a successful grapple check. This returns it to the legendary shark's mouth, where another successful grapple check is needed to get free. A swallowed creature can also cut its way out by dealing 50 or more points of damage to the stomach (AC 18) with claws or a Tiny slashing weapon. Once that swallowed creature exits, muscular action closes the hole; another swallowed opponent must cut its own way out.

The shark's gullet holds up to two Large, three Medium-size, four Small, eight Tiny, sixteen Diminutive, or thirty-two Fine or smaller opponents.

Keen Scent (Ex): A legendary shark notices creatures by scent in a 180-foot radius and detects blood in the water at ranges of up to a mile.

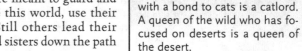

Chapter 5: Prestige Classes

"Yes, yes, I am the famous slayer of the demon-wyrm Korthos. Be awed and move on."

—The dragon hunter Jalyn

Introduced in the *Dungeon Master's Guide*, prestige classes are character classes with prerequisites. Unless noted otherwise, you must follow all standard rules for multiclassing when adding prestige classes to your PCs.

Animal Lord

For the animal lord, a humanoid form is simply an accident of birth. In spirit, she belongs with the wild pack of wolves, the running herd of horses, or the dancing school of fish. Her nearly hairless, two-legged form is just a hindrance to being one with her true kind, but it is a hindrance she can overcome.

Each animal lord forms a bond with one group of animals. Apelords, bearlords, birdlords, catlords, equinelords, marinelords, snakelords, and wolflords all exist. Animals in her selected group accept the animal lord as a sister and a leader. They offer her their support, and she in turn watches over them.

Individual animal lords may approach their calling in very different ways. Some are simple defenders of their kind, content to live as part of the natural cycle of predator and prey. Others, believing that nature's creatures are meant to guard and ultimately improve this world, use their gifts to do good. Still others lead their animal brothers and sisters down the path of selfishness or vengeance.

Because they are so close to nature, elves and half-elves are the most likely races to lay aside

Special Prestige Classes

Three of the prestige classes presented here—the animal lord, the foe hunter, and the king/queen of the wild—have a special rule. They each require a specialization that defines the character's focus. For example, a character who becomes a foe hunter must select a hated enemy. This choice defines her class—a hater of goblins becomes a goblin hunter, for example. Similarly, an animal lord with a bond to cats is a catlord. A queen of the wild who has focused on deserts is a queen of the desert.

Table 5–1: The Animal Lord

Class Level	Base Attack Bonus	Fort Save	Ref Save	Will Save	Special	Spells per Day 1st	2nd	3rd	4th
1st	+0	+2	+2	+0	Animal bond, animal sense	0	–	–	–
2nd	+1	+3	+3	+0	Animal speech, first totem	1	–	–	–
3rd	+2	+3	+3	+1	*Lesser wild shape*	1	0	–	–
4th	+3	+4	+4	+1	*Animal farspeech, summon animal* (1/day)	1	1	–	–
5th	+3	+4	+4	+1	Second totem, *share lesser form*	1	1	0	–
6th	+4	+5	+5	+2	*Animal perception, summon animal* (2/day)	1	1	1	–
7th	+5	+5	+5	+2	*Lesser wild shape* (dire)	2	1	1	0
8th	+6	+6	+6	+2	Third totem, *summon animal* (dire, 2/day)	2	1	1	1
9th	+6	+6	+6	+3	*Share greater form*	2	2	1	1
10th	+7	+7	+7	+3	*Lesser wild shape* (legendary)	2	2	2	1

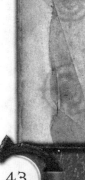

the burdens of the humanoid form. Halflings and gnomes rarely become animal lords because of their strong community ties, and half-orcs are even less likely to do so because of their typically rapacious attitudes. Though rangers, druids, and barbarians are the most likely characters to adopt this class, some arcane spellcasters (especially bards) choose to become animal lords late in their adventuring careers.

A character can choose this prestige class more than once but must select a different group of associated animals and start at 1st level each time. Levels of different animal lord classes do not stack when determining level-based class features.

Eight animal lords are presented here (the DM is free to create others). The various kinds of animals from the *Monster Manual* they are associated with are as follows.

Apelord: ape, baboon, monkey.

Bearlord: black bear, brown bear, polar bear.

Birdlord: eagle, hawk, owl, raven.

Catlord: cat, cheetah, leopard, lion, tiger.

Equinelord: donkey, heavy horse, heavy warhorse, light horse, light warhorse, mule, pony, warpony.

Marinelord: crocodile, giant crocodile, octopus, giant octopus, porpoise, shark (all), squid, giant squid, whale (all).

Snakelord: constrictor, giant constrictor, viper (all).

Wolflord: dog, riding dog, wolf.

Hit Die: d8.

Requirements

To become an animal lord, a character must fulfill the following criteria.

Alignment: Neutral good, lawful neutral, neutral, chaotic neutral, or neutral evil.

Skills: Animal Empathy 6 ranks, Wilderness Lore 8 ranks, plus 2 ranks in the appropriate skill from the following list: Apelord—Climb; Bearlord—Intimidate; Birdlord—Intuit Direction; Catlord—Move Silently; Equinelord—Jump; Marinelord,—Swim; Snakelord—Escape Artist; Wolflord—Hide.

Feats: Animal Control and the appropriate feat from the following list: Apelord, Skill Focus (Climb); Bearlord, Power Attack; Birdlord, Improved Flight; Catlord, Weapon Finesse (any); Equinelord, Run; Marinelord, Skill Focus (Swim); Snakelord, Resist Poison; Wolflord, Expertise.

Class Skills

The animal lord's class skills (and the key ability for each skill) are Animal Empathy (Cha, exclusive skill), Climb (Str), Handle Animal (Cha), Heal (Wis), Hide (Dex), Intuit Direction (Wis), Knowledge (nature) (Int), Jump (Str), Listen (Wis), Spellcraft (Int), Spot (Wis), Swim (Str), and Wilderness Lore (Wis). See Chapter 4 of the *Player's Handbook* for skill descriptions.

Skill Points at Each Level: 2 + Int modifier.

Class Features

The following are class features of the animal lord prestige class.

Weapon and Armor Proficiency: Animal lords gain no weapon or armor proficiencies.

Spells: An animal lord can cast a small number of divine spells. Her spells are based on Wisdom, so casting any given spell requires a Wisdom score of at least 10 + the spell's level. The DC for saving throws against these spells is 10 + spell level + the animal lord's Wisdom modifier. When the table indicates that the animal lord is entitled to 0 spells of a given level (such as 0 1st-level spells at 1st level), she gets only those bonus spells that her Wisdom score allows. An animal lord prepares and casts spells just like a druid does, but she must choose them from the spell list below.

Animal Bond: Beginning at 1st level, the animal lord develops a bond with animals of her selected group (see above). For instance, the bearlord bonds with brown bears, black bears, and polar bears, and the apelord with monkeys, baboons, and apes. The marinelord's bond extends to porpoises, whales, and other aquatic mammals as well as fish. Because of this bond, all animals of the appropriate kinds automatically have a friendly attitude toward the animal lord.

Animal bond also allows the animal lord to have one or more animal companions chosen from among her selected group. This aspect of animal bond is a spell-like ability that functions like the druid's *animal friendship* spell, except that the animal lord can acquire companions only from among her selected group, and her maximum Hit Dice of animal companions (whether or not she adventures) equals twice her animal lord level. The character can train these animal companions just as the druid does (see Chapter 4 for details).

Animal Sense (Su): At 1st level, an animal lord can sense any animals of her selected group within a radius of miles equal to her animal lord level squared. For example, a 6th-level bearlord can sense brown bears, black bears, and polar bears within thirty-six miles. This ability does not allow the character to communicate with the animals she senses.

Animal Speech (Ex): At 2nd level, an animal lord can converse at will with any animals of her selected group as though a *speak with animals* spell were in effect. The creatures' responses, of course, are limited by their intelligence and perceptions.

First Totem: At 2nd level, the animal lord gains a benefit related to her selected group from the list below.

Lesser Wild Shape (Sp): At 3rd level, an animal lord can use *wild shape* to take the form of any kind of natural animal in her selected group. This ability otherwise functions like the druid's *wild shape*, except that the animal lord can use it as often as desired. At 7th level, an animal lord can use this ability to adopt the dire form of an animal in her selected group, and at 10th level, she can use it to adopt the legendary form of an animal in her selected group.

Animal Farspeech (Sp): At 4th level, an animal lord can use her animal speech ability to converse telepathically with any animal of her selected group that she can sense (see animal sense, above).

Summon Animal (Sp): Also at 4th level, an animal lord can summon 1d3 animals of her selected group once per day. This ability functions like the appropriate *summon nature's ally* spell, except that the duration is 1 round per animal lord level. At 6th level, the animal lord can use this ability twice per day, and at 8th level, she can use it to summon 1d3 dire animals of her selected group.

Share Lesser Form (Sp): Beginning at 5th level, an animal lord can share whichever animal form she is cur-

rently using with a number of willing individuals equal to her animal lord level. This effect is identical to that of the *polymorph other* spell, except that its duration is 1 hour per animal lord level.

Second Totem: At 5th level, an animal lord gains a benefit related to her selected group from the list below.

Animal Perception (Sp): At 6th level, an animal lord can share the sensory input of any animal of her selected group that is within range of her animal sense.

Third Totem: At 8th level, an animal lord gains a benefit related to her selected group from the list below.

Share Greater Form (Sp): At 9th level, an animal lord can share her dire form with her allies. This ability is otherwise identical to *share lesser form*, above.

Animal Lord Spell List

Animal lords choose their spells from the following list.

1st level—*alarm, animal trick*, calm animals, camouflage*, cure light wounds, detect animals or plants, pass without trace, purify food and drink, speak with animals.*

2nd level—*adrenaline surge*, animal reduction*, cure moderate wounds, animal trance, endure elements, hold animal, invisibility to animals, nature's favor*.*

3rd level—*cure serious wounds, embrace the wild*, lesser restoration, neutralize poison, protection from elements, remove disease.*

4th level—*awaken* (animals in selected group only), *animal growth* (animals in selected group only), *commune with nature, cure critical wounds, freedom of movement.*

*New spell described in Chapter 6 of this book.

Totems

Each animal lord gains special abilities according to her selected animal type as she rises in level.

Apelord

First Totem: The apelord gains Brachiation as a bonus feat.

Second Totem: The apelord gains a +2 inherent bonus to Intelligence.

Third Totem: The apelord gains the spell-like ability to scare by howling, hooting, and beating her chest. The Will save DC against this ability is 10 + the apelord's class level + her Charisma modifier. In all other ways, this effect is identical to the *scare* spell.

Bearlord

First Totem: The bearlord gains a +2 inherent bonus to Strength.

Second Totem: The bearlord gains Great Fortitude as a bonus feat.

Third Totem: The bearlord gains damage reduction 2/–. If she already has damage reduction, this does not stack with it.

Birdlord

First Totem: The birdlord gains a +2 inherent bonus to Dexterity.

Second Totem: The birdlord gains a +8 conditional bonus on Spot checks made in daylight.

Third Totem: The birdlord gains Improved Critical (claw) as a bonus feat.

Catlord

First Totem: The catlord gains Skill Focus (Move Silently) as a bonus feat.

Second Totem: Once per hour, the catlord can use the sprint extraordinary ability to move at ten times her normal speed as a charge action.

Third Totem: The catlord gains a +2 inherent bonus to Dexterity.

Equinelord

First Totem: The equinelord gains a bonus to her speed of +10 feet.

Second Totem: The equinelord gains a +2 inherent bonus to Constitution.

Third Totem: The equinelord gains Trample as a bonus feat.

Marinelord

First Totem: The marinelord gains the extraordinary ability to breathe water in her normal form. (She cannot, however, breathe air while in a form that can breathe only water.)

Second Totem: The marinelord gains Improved Swimming (see Chapter 2) as a bonus feat.

Third Totem: The marinelord gains a +2 inherent bonus to Wisdom.

Snakelord

First Totem: The snakelord gains Resist Poison (see Chapter 2) as a bonus feat.

Second Totem: The snakelord gains the extraordinary ability to produce poison once per day (Fortitude save DC 10 + class level; initial and secondary damage 2d6 temporary Constitution). She can produce only one dose of poison per day. The snakelord is skilled in the use of poison and never risks accidentally poisoning herself when applying poison to a blade.

Third Totem: The snakelord gains a +2 inherent bonus to Charisma.

Wolflord

First Totem: The wolflord gains Scent (see Chapter 2) as a bonus feat.

Second Totem: The wolflord gains a +4 circumstance bonus on Wilderness Lore checks made for tracking. This bonus stacks with any modifier provided by Scent.

Third Totem: The wolflord gains a +2 inherent bonus to Constitution.

BANE OF INFIDELS

The bane of infidels is the leader of a xenophobic tribe. He wants nothing to do with the outside world because the way his people do things is the way they have always done them, and the way they always will. Alone among his compatriots, the bane of infidels sees the possibilities of the outside world, but he considers progress dangerous. Allowing his people to advance would surely endanger them and imperil his leadership. Since visitors bring danger of change, they must die—and what better way than as sacrifices in the name of his tribe's religion?

The act of sacrifice empowers and rewards the bane of infidels and his tribe. Usually visitors and conquered foes serve as sacrifices, though in a pinch a criminal will do (or even an innocent, though this a risky move).

Though he is often ruthless, the bane of infidels is nonetheless respected by the members of his tribe, to whom he provides healing, guardianship, and unwavering direction in return for absolute loyalty. Druids are the most likely characters to embrace this lifestyle, though clerics, high-level rangers, and adepts can also adopt this prestige class. The tribe of a bane of infidels often includes fighters, rangers, barbarians, bards, and sorcerers, but other classes may not be as welcome.

Hit Die: d8.

Requirements

To become a bane of infidels, a character must fulfill the following criteria.

Alignment: Any nongood.

Skills: Intimidate 4 ranks; Knowledge (religion) 6 ranks or Knowledge (nature) 6 ranks.

Feats: Iron Will, Leadership.

Spells: Able to cast 3rd-level divine spells.

Class Skills

The bane of infidels's class skills (and the key ability for each skill) are Animal Empathy (Cha), Concentration (Con), Craft (any) (Int), Diplomacy (Cha), Handle Animal (Cha), Heal (Wis), Intimidate (Cha), Intuit Direction (Wis), Knowledge (nature) (Int), Knowledge (religion) (Int), Profession (any) (Wis), Scry (Int, exclusive skill), Sense Motive (Wis), Spellcraft (Int), Swim (Str), and Wilderness Lore (Wis). See Chapter 4 of the *Player's Handbook* for skill descriptions.

Skill Points at Each Level: 4 + Int modifier.

Class Features

The following are class features of the bane of infidens prestige class.

Weapon and Armor Proficiency: A bane of infidels gains no weapon or armor proficiencies.

Spells per Day/Spells Known: At each bane of infidels level, the character gains new spells per day (and spells known, if applicable) as if he had also gained a level in a spellcasting class to which he belonged before adding the prestige class. He does not, however, gain any other benefit a character of that class would have gained (additional *wild shape* options, metamagic or item creation feats, or the like). If the character had more than one spellcasting class before becoming a bane of infidels, the player must decide to which class to add each level for determining spells per day and spells known.

Energumen (Sp): Beginning at 1st level, the character may bestow a low-powered form of barbarian rage in any follower (as defined in Chapter 2 of the DUNGEON MASTER's Guide) who is an adherent of the same religion. The follower gains a +2 bonus to both Strength and Constitution, as well as a +1 morale bonus on Will saves. In all other respects, this effect is like barbarian rage. *Energumen* is usable once per day per bane of infidels level.

Pyre (Sp): At 1st level, the bane of infidels may cause a 5-foot-square area to burst into flame. Anyone in that

area must succeed at a Reflex save (DC 10 + bane of infidels level + Wisdom bonus of bane of infidels) or suffer 1d4 points of damage per bane of infidels level. This ability is usable once per day.

Hearth Protection (Sp): At 2nd level, the bane of infidels may perform an 8-hour ritual to designate an area with a radius of up to 5 feet per bane of infidels level as a hearth. This area then functions as a permanent *zone of truth*, though the bane of infidels is immune to that effect. The character may have only one hearth at a time.

Sacrifice (Su): Beginning at 2nd level, the bane of infidels may sacrifice any humanoid by killing it with a coup de grace in his hearth. This ritual increases his effective caster level for all spells by +2 for 1 hour. If the bane of infidels sacrifices a follower, he must make a Diplomacy check (DC 20). Failure indicates that all his remaining followers desert; success means he retains their loyalty. This effect does not stack with the bonuses gained from major sacrifice or mass sacrifice (see below). Sacrifice is usable once per day.

Secrets of Stone (Sp): At 3rd level, the bane of infidels gains the ability to discern the affected spell and necessary sacrifice of any *standing stone* (see Chapter 3) within 100 feet of him as a free action.

Detect Loyalty (Sp): At 4th level, the bane of infidels may examine a follower for faithfulness. If that individual has grossly violated the code of conduct that the bane of infidels has established or otherwise acted in a manner opposed to the latter's purposes and directions in the last 24 hours, the bane of infidels discovers it (no save, but spell resistance applies) and gains a +5 circumstance bonus on his Diplomacy check when sacrificing that follower. Using *detect loyalty* does not provoke an attack of opportunity.

Major Sacrifice (Su): This ability, gained at 5th level, is like sacrifice, except that the bane of infidels can increase his effective caster level for all spells by +4 for 1 hour by sacrificing a sentient creature with 5 or more Hit Dice. This effect does not stack with that of sacrifice or mass sacrifice.

Wicker Man (Sp): At 6th level, the bane of infidels learns to create a sacrificial totem trap. This ability produces the same effect as the *wall of thorns* spell, except as follows. The thorny briars form a humanoid shape 10 feet square, with a height equal to 10 feet per bane of infidels level. Anyone in that area when the *wicker man* appears gets a Reflex save (DC 10 + bane of infidels level + Wisdom bonus of bane of infidels) to avoid being caught in its body at a point halfway up its height. The *pyre* and *bonfire* abilities of the bane of infidels count as magical fire for purposes of igniting the wicker man and do their normal damage to everyone trapped inside each round until the *wicker man* burns away (per the *wall of thorns* spell) or they escape. This ability is usable once per day.

Bonfire (Sp): This ability, gained at 7th level, functions like *pyre*, except that it affects a 10-foot-square area.

Antipathy Field (Sp): At 8th level, the bane of infidels may protect his hearth with an *antipathy field* once per day. This functions like an *antipathy* spell, except that the target is the entire area of the hearth and the duration is 24 hours.

Mass Energumen (Sp): This ability (gained at 9th level) functions like *energumen* (above), except that it affects up to ten followers at once.

Mass Sacrifice (Su): At 10th level, the bane of infidels can increase his effective caster level by +2 (up to a maximum of +10) for each humanoid sacrificed within 10 rounds. This ability is otherwise like sacrifice. Its effect does not stack with that of sacrifice or major sacrifice.

TABLE 5–2: THE BANE OF INFIDELS

Class Level	Base Attack Bonus	Fort Save	Ref Save	Will Save	Special	Spells per Day/Spells Known
1st	+0	+2	+0	+2	*Energumen, pyre*	+1 level of existing class
2nd	+1	+3	+0	+3	*Hearth protection*, sacrifice	+1 level of existing class
3rd	+2	+3	+1	+3	*Secrets of stone*	+1 level of existing class
4th	+3	+4	+1	+4	*Detect loyalty*	+1 level of existing class
5th	+3	+4	+1	+4	Major sacrifice	+1 level of existing class
6th	+4	+5	+2	+5	*Wicker man*	+1 level of existing class
7th	+5	+5	+2	+5	*Bonfire*	+1 level of existing class
8th	+6	+6	+2	+6	*Antipathy field*	+1 level of existing class
9th	+6	+6	+3	+6	*Mass energumen*	+1 level of existing class
10th	+7	+7	+3	+7	Mass sacrifice	+1 level of existing class

BLIGHTER

When a druid turns away from the land, the land turns away from her. Some ex-druids make peace with this change; others seek to restore the bond. A few, however, actually embrace their disconnection from nature and become forces of destruction. These few, called blighters, leave their mark wherever they tread.

A blighter gains her spellcasting ability by stripping the earth of life. A swath of deforested land always marks her path through the wilderness.

The vast majority of blighters are no-madic loners constantly in search of green lands to destroy. Some are grim; others laugh at the destruction they wreak. Almost all, however, are friendless and mad. What puts them over the edge is the knowledge that nature gets the last laugh: To gain their spells, they must seek out the richest forests of the land, even if it's only to destroy them. Thus, even though they've turned away from nature, they must constantly return to it.

Only human ex-druids seem attracted in any number to the blighter's path. Legends say that a few elven druids have also turned to destruction over the millennia—a terrifying prospect given how much land they could destroy in their long lifetimes.

Hit Die: d8.

Requirements

To qualify as a blighter, a character must fulfill the following criteria.

Alignment: Any non-good.

Special: The character must be an ex-druid previously capable of casting 3rd-level druid spells.

Class Skills

The blighter's class skills (and the key ability for each skill) are Animal Empathy (Cha), Concentration (Con), Craft (any) (Int), Diplomacy (Cha), Handle Animal (Cha), Heal (Wis), Intuit Direction (Wis), Knowledge (nature) (Int), Profession (herbalist) (Wis), Scry (Int), Spellcraft (Int), Swim (Str), and Wilderness Lore (Wis). See Chapter 4 of the *Player's Handbook* for skill descriptions.

Skill Points at Each Level: 4 + Int modifier.

Class Features

The following are class features of the blighter prestige class.

Weapon and Armor Proficiency: Blighters gain no weapon or armor proficiencies.

Spells per Day: At each blighter level, the character gains spells per day according to Table 5–3. She does not, however, gain any other benefit that a druid of that level would have gained. She must choose her spells from the blighter spell list, below. The blighter's caster level is equal to her blighter level plus her druid level.

The blighter gains access to her daily spells through *deforestation* (see below). If she goes more than 24 hours without deforesting a wooded area, she cannot cast spells until she does so.

The default divine focus for any spell cast by a blighter is a desiccated sprig of holly or

TABLE 5–3: THE BLIGHTER

Class Level	Base Attack Bonus	Fort Save	Ref Save	Will Save	Special	Spells per Day						
						0	1st	2nd	3rd	4th	5th	6th
1st	+0	+2	+0	+2	*Deforestation*	2	1	0	–	–	–	–
2nd	+1	+3	+0	+3	Burning hands, sustenance	2	2	1	0	–	–	–
3rd	+2	+3	+1	+3	*Undead wild shape 1/day*	3	2	2	0	–	–	–
4th	+3	+4	+1	+4	*Speak with dead animal, undead wild shape 2/day*	3	3	2	1	0	–	–
5th	+3	+4	+1	+4	Contagious touch 1/day, *undead wild shape (Large)*	4	3	3	2	0	–	–
6th	+4	+5	+2	+5	Animate dead animal, *undead wild shape 3/day*	4	4	3	3	1	0	–
7th	+5	+5	+2	+5	Contagious touch 2/day, *undead wild shape (incorporeal)*	5	4	4	3	2	0	–
8th	+6	+6	+2	+6	*Unbond, undead wild shape 4/day*	5	5	4	4	2	1	0
9th	+6	+6	+3	+6	Contagious touch 3/day, *undead wild shape (Huge)*	6	5	5	4	3	2	1
10th	+7	+7	+3	+7	Plague, *undead wild shape 5/day*	6	6	5	5	3	2	2

mistletoe. Any material component for a blighter's spell must have been dead for at least a day before use.

Deforestation (**Sp**): Beginning at 1st level, the blighter can kill all nonsentient plant life within a radius of 50 feet per blighter level as a full-round action once per day. If a potentially affected plant is under the control of another (such as a druid's *liveoak* or a dryad's home tree), the controller can make a Fortitude save (DC 10 + blighter level + blighter's Wisdom bonus) to keep it alive. Affected plants immediately cease photosynthesis, root tapping, and all other methods of sustenance. Like picked flowers, they appear vibrant for several hours, but within a day, they turn brown and wither. Except for plants saved by a controller, nothing can grow in a deforested area until it has a *hallow* spell cast upon it and it is reseeded.

Deforestation enables the blighter to cast her daily allotment of spells. This ability works in any terrain, but deforesting a sandy desert, ice floe, or other environment with only sparse vegetation does not empower the character to cast spells.

Burning Hands (**Su**): This ability, gained at 2nd level, functions like the *burning hands* spell, except that the blighter can use it as often as desired, turning it on or off as a move-equivalent action, and it does 1d4 points of fire damage per round.

Sustenance (**Ex**): At 2nd level, the blighter no longer needs food or water to survive.

Undead Wild Shape (**Sp**): At 3rd level, the blighter regains a version of the *wild shape* ability. *Undead wild shape* functions like *wild shape*, except that the forms available are those of undead creatures (specifically skeletons) formerly of the animal type. A skeletal animal has the statistics of a skeleton of the appropriate animal's size category (see the skeleton entry in the *Monster Manual*).

The blighter gains one extra use per day of this ability for every two additional blighter levels she acquires. In addition, she gains the ability to take the shape of a Large skeletal animal at 5th level, an incorporeal skeletal animal (see Incorporeality in Chapter 3 of the *Dungeon Master's Guide*) at 7th level, and a Huge skeletal animal at 9th level.

Speak with Dead Animal (**Sp**): At 4th level, the blighter can converse with dead animals. This ability functions like a *speak with dead* spell cast by a cleric of a level equal to the total of the character's druid and blighter levels, except that it affects only corpses of animal creatures. It is usable once per day.

Contagious Touch (**Su**): At 5th level, the blighter can produce an effect like that of a *contagious touch* spell once per day. She gains 1 extra use per day of this ability for every two additional blighter levels she acquires.

Animate Dead Animal (**Sp**): This ability, gained at 6th level, functions like an *animate dead* spell, except that it affects only corpses of animal creatures and requires no material component. It is usable once per day.

Unbond (**Sp**): At 8th level, the blighter can temporarily separate a bonded animal or magical beast (such as an animal companion, familiar, or mount) from its master once per day. The target creature must be within 40 feet of both its master and the blighter. If the master fails a Will save (DC 10 + blighter level + blighter's Wisdom modifier), the bond terminates as if the servitor had died,

though this does not cause experience loss in the case of a familiar. Normally hostile creatures attack their masters but are otherwise unaffected. The bond returns after 5 rounds per blighter level, restoring all benefits. Alternatively, the master can regain the servitor through the normal methods of acquisition.

Plague (**Su**): At 10th level, the blighter can spread disease over a large area. This ability functions like the contagious touch ability, except that no attack roll is required and it affects all targets the blighter designates within a 20-foot radius. Plague is usable once per day and costs one daily use of the contagious touch ability.

Blighter Spell List
Blighters choose their spells from the following list.

0 level—*darkseed**, *detect magic*, *detect poison*, *flare*, *ghost sound*, *inflict minor wounds*, *read magic*.

1st level—*bane*, *burning hands*, *curse water*, *decomposition**, *detect undead*, *doom*, *endure elements*, *inflict light wounds*, *invisibility to animals*, *ray of enfeeblement*.

2nd level—*chill metal*, *chill touch*, *darkness*, *death knell*, *fire trap*, *flaming sphere*, *heat metal*, *inflict moderate wounds*, *miasma**, *produce flame*, *resist elements*, *warp wood*.

3rd level—*contagion*, *deeper darkness*, *desecrate*, *diminish plants*, *dispel magic*, *inflict serious wounds*, *poison*, *protection from elements*, *stinking cloud*, *vampiric touch*.

4th level—*antiplant shell*, *animate dead*, *blight**, *death ward*, *flame strike*, *inflict critical wounds*, *kiss of death**, *languor**, *repel vermin*, *rusting grasp*, *transmute mud to rock*, *transmute rock to mud*, *unhallow*, *wall of fire*.

5th level—*acid fog*, *antilife shell*, *circle of death*, *contagious touch**, *create undead*, *firestorm*, *forbiddance*, *greater dispelling*, *protection from all elements**, *repel wood*.

6th level—*antipathy*, *control undead*, *earthquake*, *epidemic**, *finger of death*, *foresight*, *horrid wilting*, *invulnerability to elements**.

*New spell described in Chapter 6 of this book.

BLOODHOUND
A bandit king is raiding caravans on the road. An ogre is pillaging the farms to the north. A sorcerer has kidnapped the mayor's son and hidden him somewhere in the marsh. And the soldiers of the king cannot seem to stem the tide. The terrified citizens have only one choice, and it isn't cheap. They call in a bloodhound.

The bloodhound tracks down wrongdoers and brings them to whatever justice awaits them. Low-level bloodhounds depend on their keen senses and careful training to hunt their targets. As they gain experience, their obsessive determination gives them supernatural abilities that make them nearly unstoppable.

Most bloodhounds work for money (usually a lot of it), but some accept jobs for justice, revenge, or enjoyment. When a bloodhound accepts a job, he designates his target as a mark. Thereafter, he does not abandon the case until it is finished, which occurs when the mark is apprehended or when either the mark or the bloodhound dies.

Though some bloodhounds leave calling cards or even brands on their marks, most don't kill their targets if they can help it. They prefer instead to subdue their marks and bring them in. For those of good alignment, this

Table 5—4: The Bloodhound

Class Level	Base Attack Bonus	Fort Save	Ref Save	Will Save	Special
1st	+1	+0	+2	+0	Determination, mark, no subdual penalty
2nd	+2	+0	+3	+0	Dead or alive, fast tracking, ready and waiting
3rd	+3	+1	+3	+1	Pacekeeping, restlessness
4th	+4	+1	+4	+1	Improved subdual, move like the wind
5th	+5	+1	+4	+1	Shatter, traceless track
6th	+6	+2	+5	+2	Ignore scrying, *locate creature*
7th	+7	+2	+5	+2	Fracture, see invisibility
8th	+8	+2	+6	+2	Subdual resistance
9th	+9	+3	+6	+3	Ignore magical barriers
10th	+10	+3	+7	+3	*Find the path*

practice satisfies some deeply held belief in the cause of justice. For neutral and evil bloodhounds, it ensures a steady stream of income from catching the same marks over and over when they break out of jail.

Rangers and barbarians make the best bloodhounds, but rogues, bards, druids, and fighters can also excel in this role. Occasionally a paladin shoulders the mantle, but never for money. Most bloodhounds are human, though elves and half-elves sometimes find this lifestyle satisfying. Some of the best bloodhounds are humanoids such as gnolls, hobgoblins, and bugbears.

Hit Die: d10.

Requirements

To become a bloodhound, a character must fulfill the following criteria.

Base Attack Bonus: +4.

Skills: Gather Information 4 ranks, Move Silently 4 ranks, Wilderness Lore 4 ranks.

Feats: Run, Track.

Class Skills

The bloodhound's class skills (and the key ability for each skill) are Appraise (Int), Bluff (Cha), Climb (Str), Diplomacy (Cha), Disguise (Cha), Forgery (Dex), Gather Information (Cha), Heal (Wis), Hide (Dex), Intimidate (Cha), Intuit Direction (Wis), Jump (Str), Listen (Wis), Move Silently (Dex), Open Lock (Dex), Ride (Dex), Search (Int), Sense Motive (Wis), Spot (Wis), Swim (Str), Use Rope (Dex), and Wilderness Lore (Wis). See Chapter 4 of the *Player's Handbook* for skill descriptions.

Skill Points at Each Level: 6 + Int modifier.

Class Features

The following are class features of the bloodhound prestige class.

Weapon and Armor Proficiency: Bloodhounds are proficient with light armor, shields, and both simple and martial weapons.

Determination (Ex): At 1st level, the character gains an insight bonus equal to his bloodhound level on Gather Information, Spot, and Wilderness Lore checks made to determine the whereabouts of a mark (see below).

Mark (Ex): At 1st level, the character can target, or mark, an individual humanoid foe. To do so, the bloodhound must focus on a foe who is present and visible, or on the depiction or description of one who is not, for 10 minutes. Any interruption ruins the attempt and forces the bloodhound to start the process again. Once this study is complete, that target is called a mark, and the bloodhound receives a variety of advantages against him or her (see below). A bloodhound may have up to one mark per two bloodhound levels (rounded up) at once, but only if all of them are within 30 feet of one another for the duration of the marking process. For example, a 6th-level bloodhound could mark three bugbears in such a group, but not a bugbear on one side of the kingdom and a troll on the other. If a bloodhound chooses a new mark before apprehending an existing one, the latter is unmarked, and the bloodhound loses XP equal to the amount he would have gotten for defeating that creature. The bloodhound can mark an individual once a week.

No Subdual Penalty (Ex): Also at 1st level, the bloodhound can use a melee weapon that deals normal damage to deal subdual damage instead without suffering the usual −4 penalty on his attack roll.

Dead or Alive (Ex): At 2nd level, the bloodhound learns to strike for subdual at just the right moment to avoid killing a mark. Immediately after striking a blow that would reduce a mark from positive to negative hit points, the bloodhound may convert the normal damage dealt by that blow to subdual damage before it takes effect. The bloodhound cannot use this ability while raging or after 1 round has passed.

Fast Tracking: At 2nd level, the bloodhound no longer suffers a –5 penalty on Wilderness Lore checks for tracking while moving at normal speed.

Ready and Waiting (Ex): Also at 2nd level, the bloodhound may, as a free action, designate a particular move-equivalent, standard, or full-round action that a mark who is flat-footed might perform. If the mark actually performs this action within 10 minutes thereafter, the bloodhound can make an attack of opportunity against him or her with a drawn weapon, either melee or ranged. This counts against the bloodhound's attacks of opportunity for that round.

Pacekeeping (Ex): At 3rd level, a bloodhound tracking a mark can raise his own speed by up to +5 feet per bloodhound level, to a maximum value equal to the mark's speed.

Restlessness (Ex): When the bloodhound reaches 3rd level, he gains damage reduction 5/– against subdual damage from a forced march while in pursuit of a mark.

Improved Subdual (Ex): At 4th level, the bloodhound uses his Intelligence bonus on the damage roll for any attack that deals only subdual damage.

Move Like the Wind (Su): At 4th level, the bloodhound ignores armor check penalties on his Move Silently and Hide checks. In addition, he no longer suffers the –5 penalty on those checks when moving at speeds between half and full.

Traceless Track (Su): At 5th level, the bloodhound can track a creature moving under the influence of *pass without trace* or a similar effect, though he suffers a –10 circumstance penalty on his Wilderness Lore checks.

Shatter (Su): At 5th level, the bloodhound can destroy an object that stands between himself and his mark when the latter is within 100 feet. This ability functions like a *shatter* spell cast by a sorcerer of the character's bloodhound level.

Ignore Scrying (Ex): At 6th level, the bloodhound gains spell resistance equal to 10 + his bloodhound level against divination spells. This stacks with any other spell resistance he has that includes spells of that school.

Locate Creature **(Sp):** Once per day, the bloodhound can produce an effect identical to that of a *locate creature* spell cast by a sorcerer of the bloodhound's character level.

Fracture (Su): At 7th level, the character can use his shatter ability to destroy weight-equivalent portions of larger objects, such as doors and walls, regardless of their construction.

See Invisibility (Su): This ability, gained at 7th level, functions like a *see invisibility* spell, except that it is constantly in effect and it reveals only marks.

Subdual Resistance: At 8th level, the bloodhound gains damage reduction 20/+3 against subdual damage.

Ignore Magical Barriers (Ex): At 9th level, the bloodhound gains spell resistance equal to 15 + his bloodhound level against magical barriers (*wall of force*, *entangle*, *prismatic wall*, and so forth).

Find the Path **(Sp):** At 10th level, the bloodhound can produce an effect like a *find the path* spell cast by a druid of the bloodhound's character level. It is usable three times per day.

Organization: The Bloodhounds

"Eyes . . . I saw his eyes before he pounced. That was all. He had no body until he was upon me. If he had meant to kill me, I would have been as helpless as a babe."
—Tordek, on meeting a Bloodhound

The organization known as the Bloodhounds is dedicated to finding people and bringing them to justice (or whatever fate awaits them). Some Bloodhounds limit themselves to tracking down criminals; others are willing to hunt anyone for a client who can pay the price. The group's leaders don't concern themselves with such issues, only with maintaining the organization's reputation as the place to go to find someone.

Membership in the Bloodhounds is by invitation only. Members report on capable trackers they encounter in their travels, and from these reports the organization's leaders select candidates for membership. A member of the organization tracks each candidate surreptitiously for a while. If the Bloodhound reports that the candidate had the necessary fervor and talents, the leaders offer him or her a chance to try out for membership. A candidate who actually noticed the Bloodhound following is almost guaranteed an offer.

To be accepted for membership, the candidate must track a Bloodhound considerably more experienced than himself. The Bloodhound makes the job difficult by leaving false trails, telling locals deceitful stories, and even hiring brigands to ambush the candidate along the way. The Bloodhound must not assist the candidate in this task; otherwise the test is void. A candidate who succeeds in finding the target passes the test and may join the organization.

Bloodhounds can take any assignments they choose. Some jobs come directly from clients who contact individual Bloodhounds. Others come through the grapevine, since members pass word to each other. Individual bloodhounds are fiercely competitive, and should one succeed where another has failed, the winner gloats over the victory. In fact, Bloodhounds often tell each other about the assignments they've taken, in effect challenging their compatriots to beat them to the quarry. Members may work together, but most work alone or with nonmembers so that word spreads of their personal fame. Thus, whenever several Bloodhounds form a posse to catch a particularly elusive foe, word spreads far and wide.

Despite this rivalry, when a mark is too important to go free, a Bloodhound can spread the word of a "free" bounty among the membership. This means that any member who brings in the mark can claim the prize. Members who spread free bounties lose no face in the organization for doing so.

Bloodhounds resent the concept of giving their earnings to anyone. Thus, the organization does not demand a piece of its members' earnings. No Bloodhounds guildhalls or strongholds exist because no self-respecting Bloodhound would limit himself to one base of operations.

Since so many of the Bloodhounds' marks are human, ranger Bloodhounds who have taken humans as favored enemies have an advantage in assignments. Thus, a large percentage of the membership is nonhuman, and differing alignments are rarely an impediment to teaming up. In fact, rumor has it that a good elven Bloodhound and an evil gnoll Bloodhound regularly work together, since between them they can function in any society. The gulf between their alignments is simply not as wide as the bridge of their common goals.

DEEPWOOD SNIPER

An arrow flies from a high mountain aerie, unerringly striking a paladin's mount. Expecting only a flesh wound, the paladin is stunned to watch his companion of many adventures crumple to the earth. This unfortunate knight has trespassed into the domain of the deepwood sniper, and he may not make it out alive.

A deepwood sniper is patient, careful, quiet, and deadly accurate. She is a stealthy, long-range terminator whose arrows sail accurately from much longer ranges than those of other archers. In addition, she has magical abilities to help her shafts fly true.

Because of their alertness, dexterity, patience, and affinity for the bow, elves of almost any character class make excellent deepwood snipers. For a long time, elves would train only those of their own race in these techniques, but more recently some half-elves, halflings, and humans have joined the ranks of the deepwood sniper.

Hit Die: d8.

Requirements

To qualify as a deepwood sniper, a character must fulfill the following criteria.

Base Attack Bonus: +5.

Skills: Hide 4 ranks, Move Silently 4 ranks, Spot 4 ranks.

Feats: Far Shot, Point Blank Shot, Weapon Focus (any bow or crossbow).

Class Skills

The deepwood sniper's class skills (and the key ability for each skill) are Balance (Dex), Climb (Str), Craft (bowmaking) (Int), Escape Artist (Dex), Intuit Direction (Wis), Hide (Dex), Jump (Str), Knowledge (nature) (Int), Listen (Wis), Move Silently (Dex), Profession (Wis), Search (Int), Sense Motive (Wis), Spot (Wis), Swim (Str), and Wilderness Lore (Wis). See Chapter 4 of the *Player's Handbook* for skill descriptions.

Skill Points at Each Level: 4 + Int modifier.

Class Features

The following are class features of the deepwood sniper prestige class.

Weapon and Armor Proficiency: Deepwood snipers gain no weapon or armor proficiencies. All weapon-related abilities of this prestige class apply only to projectile ranged weapons with which the character is proficient.

TABLE 5–5: THE DEEPWOOD SNIPER

Class Level	Base Attack Bonus	Fort Save	Ref Save	Will Save	Special
1st	+1	+0	+2	+0	Keen arrows, range increment bonus +10 ft./level
2nd	+2	+0	+3	+0	Concealment reduction 10%, *magic weapon*, projectile improved critical +1
3rd	+3	+1	+3	+1	Safe poison use
4th	+4	+1	+4	+1	Take aim +2
5th	+5	+1	+4	+1	Consistent aim 1/day
6th	+6	+2	+5	+2	Concealment reduction 20%, *keen edge*
7th	+7	+2	+5	+2	Consistent aim 2/day, projectile improved critical +2
8th	+8	+2	+6	+2	Take aim +4
9th	+9	+3	+6	+3	Consistent aim 3/day
10th	+10	+3	+7	+3	Concealment reduction 30%, *true strike*

Keen Arrows (Ex): At 1st level, all projectiles the deepwood sniper fires behave as if they were keen weapons in addition to any other properties they might possess. Thus, a normal arrow fired by a deepwood sniper has a threat range of 19–20 instead of 20. This effect does not stack with any other keen effect.

Range Increment Bonus (Ex): With each level the deepwood sniper gains, the range increments of her projectile weapons increase by +10 feet (added after all multipliers). Thus, a 10th-level deepwood sniper who has the Far Shot feat would have a 280-foot range increment with a heavy crossbow (120 feet × 1.5 + 100 feet).

Concealment Reduction (Ex): When the deepwood sniper reaches 2nd level, her miss chance against opponents with concealment drops by 10%. Thus, she has a miss chance of 10% rather than 20% against an opponent with one-half concealment. Her miss chance drops by an additional 10% per four deepwood sniper levels she gains thereafter, but this ability never reduces her miss chance against any opponent below 0%.

Magic Weapon **(Sp):** At 2nd level, the character can produce an effect identical to that of a *magic weapon* spell cast by a cleric of her deepwood sniper level. This ability is usable once per day on projectile weapons only.

Projectile Improved Critical (Ex): When the deepwood sniper reaches 2nd level, the critical damage multipliers of all her projectile weapons increase by +1. Thus, an arrow that normally deals damage ×3 on a critical hit instead does damage ×4 in her hands. When she reaches 7th level, these critical multipliers increase by an additional +1.

Safe Poison Use (Ex): At 3rd level, a deepwood sniper can use poison without any chance of poisoning herself (see Perils of Using Poison in Chapter 3 of the DUNGEON MASTER's *Guide*).

Take Aim (Ex): A 4th-level deepwood sniper can gain a +2 bonus on her attack rolls against a stationary target by aiming carefully. Taking aim is a full-round action, and if the target moves more than 5 feet during that period, the bonus is lost. No additional benefit exists for spending more than 1 round aiming. This bonus increases to +4 at 8th level.

Consistent Aim (Su): Once per day, a 5th-level deepwood sniper can reroll one attack roll that she has just made with a projectile weapon. She must keep that result, even if it is worse than the original roll. She can use this ability twice per day at 7th level and three times per day at 10th level, though each use must relate to a different attack roll.

True Strike **(Sp):** At 10th level, the deepwood sniper can produce an effect identical to that of a *true strike* spell cast by a cleric of her deepwood sniper level. This ability is usable once per day on projectile weapons only.

EXOTIC WEAPON MASTER

Swords and axes do not a warrior make. Such might be the unvoiced motto of the exotic weapon master—a student of her world's most unusual and bizarre weapons. For the exotic weapon master, the intricacies of the shuriken, the siangham, the dire flail, and the hand crossbow pose no difficulty at all. These unusual weapons are her trade, and in her hands, they become instruments of destruction.

Characters of any race or background can become exotic weapon masters; the only real requirement is commitment and perseverance. Nevertheless, most are human, because members of that race have the most exposure to new cultures and thus the most opportunities to take up exotic weapons.

Hit Die: d10.

Requirements

To become an exotic weapon master, a character must fulfill the following criteria.

Base Attack Bonus: +6.
Feats: Exotic Weapon Proficiency (any three).
Special: Ability to rage.

Class Skills

The exotic weapon master's class skills (and the key ability for each skill) are Craft (any) (Int) and Profession (any) (Int). See Chapter 4 of the *Player's Handbook* for skill descriptions.

Skill Points at Each Level: 2 + Int modifier.

Class Features

The following are class features of the exotic weapon master prestige class.

Weapon and Armor Proficiency: Exotic weapon masters gain no weapon or armor proficiencies.

Partial Exotic Proficiency: At 1st level, the exotic weapon master can use any exotic weapon with which she is not already proficient at a –2 penalty instead of a –4 penalty on the attack roll. This penalty is reduced to –1 at 2nd level.

Full Exotic Proficiency: At 3rd level, the exotic weapon master becomes proficient with all exotic weapons.

Improvised Throwing Weapons: At 3rd level, the exotic weapon master can use artisan's tools to fashion a usable throwing weapon from any object (rock, branch, melee weapon, or the like) that she can lift. This process takes at least 1 hour, or more if conditions are poor. The range increment for such an improvised weapon is 10 feet. It deals 1d6 points of damage (×2 on a critical hit), and its threat range is 20. The exotic weapon master is au-

TABLE 5–6: THE EXOTIC WEAPON MASTER

Class Level	Base Attack Bonus	Fort Save	Ref Save	Will Save	Special
1st	+1	+2	+0	+0	Partial exotic proficiency +2
2nd	+2	+3	+0	+0	Partial exotic weapon proficiency +3
3rd	+3	+3	+1	+1	Full exotic proficiency, improvised throwing weapons
4th	+4	+4	+1	+1	Exotic focus, improvised melee weapons
5th	+5	+4	+1	+1	Exotic specialization, greater improvised weapons

tomatically proficient with her improvised throwing weapon; anyone else who wishes to use it must spend an Exotic Weapon Proficiency feat to avoid the –4 nonproficiency penalty. Most objects do bludgeoning damage; sharp items do piercing damage instead.

Exotic Focus: At 4th level, the exotic weapon master gains a +1 bonus on her attack rolls when using any exotic weapon. This bonus does not stack with that provided by the Weapon Focus feat.

Improvised Melee Weapons: Also at 4th level, the exotic weapon master can use artisan's tools to fashion a usable melee weapon from any object (rock, branch, projectile weapon, or the like) that she can lift. This process takes at least 1 hour, or more if conditions are poor. Such an improvised melee weapon deals 1d6 points of damage (×2 on a critical hit), and its threat range is 20. The exotic weapon master is automatically proficient with her improvised melee weapon; anyone else who wishes to use it must spend an Exotic Weapon Proficiency feat to avoid the –4 nonproficiency penalty. Most objects do bludgeoning damage; sharp items do piercing damage instead. Long items (such as ladders) have reach according to their length, and items with many protrusions (such as chairs) give the exotic weapon master a +2 bonus on disarm attempts.

Exotic Specialization: At 5th level, the exotic weapon master gains a +2 bonus on damage rolls when using any exotic weapon. (For ranged weapons, this damage bonus applies only if the target is within 30 feet.) This modifier does not stack with that provided by the Weapon Specialization feat.

Greater Improvised Weapons: At 5th level, the exotic weapon master can make an improvised throwing or melee weapon that deals 2d6 points of damage. This ability otherwise functions like the improvised throwing weapons or improvised melee weapons ability, depending on the kind of weapon desired.

EYE OF GRUUMSH

Most people think they've seen the worst that orcs can breed when an orc barbarian comes raging over a hilltop—at least until they see a one-eyed orc barbarian come raging over a hilltop. This creature may well be an eye of Gruumsh, an orc so devoted to his evil deity that he has disfigured himself in Gruumsh's name.

In an epic battle at the dawn of time, the elven deity Corellon Larethian stabbed out Gruumsh's left eye. Filled with rage and hatred, the orc deity called for followers loyal enough to serve in his image. Those who heed this call are known as the eyes of Gruumsh. They sacrifice their right eyes instead of their left ones so that their impaired vision balances that of their deity. Thus, symbolically at least, they can see what he cannot. These living martyrs to Gruumsh are some of the toughest orcs and half-orcs in the world.

The eye of Gruumsh is a true prestige class in the sense that all orcs respect those who achieve it. If a candidate proves capable with the brutal orc double axe and has no moral code to stand in the way of his service, only the test remains—to put out his own right eye in a special ceremony. This is a bloody and painful ritual, the details of which are best left undescribed. If the candidate makes a sound during the process, he fails the test. No consequences for failure exist, except that he can never become an eye of Gruumsh—and he's lost one eye.

Barbarians gain the most value from this prestige class, since it encourages raging as a fighting style. Fighters, clerics, rangers, and even rogues also heed this calling. Orcs and half-orcs are the obvious candidates for the class, and some orc tribes whisper of barbarians from other races who have adopted this mantle. Of course, these may just be legends meant to inspire young orcs to jealous rage.

Hit Die: d12.

Requirements

To qualify as an eye of Gruumsh, a character must fulfill the following criteria.

Race: Orc or half-orc. (A character of another race who grows up among orcs may also adopt this prestige class if the DM permits.)

Alignment: Chaotic evil, chaotic neutral, or neutral evil.

Base Attack Bonus: +6.

Feats: Exotic Weapon Proficiency (orc double axe), Weapon Focus (orc double axe).

Special: The character must be a worshiper of Gruumsh and must put out his own right eye in a special ritual. None of the eye of Gruumsh's special abilities function if he regains sight in both eyes.

Class Skills

The eye of Gruumsh's class skills (and the key ability for each skill) are Intimidate (Cha), Jump (Str), Ride (Dex), and Swim (Str). See Chapter 4 of the *Player's Handbook* for skill descriptions.

Skill Points at Each Level: 2 + Int modifier.

Class Features

The following are class features of the eye of Gruumsh prestige class.

Weapon and Armor Proficiency: Eyes of Gruumsh are proficient with light and medium armor, shields, and all simple and martial weapons.

Blind-Fight: At 1st level, the eye of Gruumsh gains Blind-Fight as a bonus feat.

Follow Orders Blindly: At 1st level, the eye of Gruumsh may grant a +2 morale bonus on Will saves to any nongood orcs or half-orcs with HD lower than his character level within 30 feet of him. Any recipient who willingly goes against the eye of Gruumsh's directions loses this bonus immediately. Using this ability is a standard action, and the effect lasts for 1 hour per eye of Gruumsh level.

Rage: Also at 1st level, the eye of Gruumsh gains the ability to rage as a barbarian of a level equal to the total of his barbarian and eye of Gruumsh levels. Thus, a Bbn14/eye of Gruumsh2 can use rage 5 times per day.

Ritual Scarring: Through frequent disfiguration of his own skin, the eye of Gruumsh gains a +1 natural armor bonus at 3rd level. This bonus increases by +1 for every three eye of Gruumsh levels gained thereafter.

Swing Blindly (Ex): At 2nd level, the eye of Gruumsh gains an additional +2 bonus to his Strength score while raging. While this ability is in effect, the character provokes attacks of opportunity as though he were casting a spell whenever he takes any kind of attack action.

Blinding Spittle (Ex): The eye of Gruumsh can launch blinding spittle at any opponent within 20 feet. Using a ranged touch attack (at a –4 penalty), he spits his stomach acid into the target's eyes. An opponent who fails a Reflex save (DC 10 + eye of Gruumsh level + eye of

TABLE 5–7: THE EYE OF GRUUMSH

Class Level	Base Attack Bonus	Fort Save	Ref Save	Will Save	Special
1st	+1	+2	+0	+0	Blind-Fight, follow orders blindly, rage
2nd	+2	+3	+0	+0	Swing blindly
3rd	+3	+3	+1	+1	Ritual scarring +1
4th	+4	+4	+1	+1	Blinding spittle 1/hour
5th	+5	+4	+1	+1	Blindsight, 5-foot radius
6th	+6	+5	+2	+2	Ritual scarring +2
7th	+7	+5	+2	+2	Blinding spittle 2/hour
8th	+8	+6	+2	+2	Blindsight, 10-foot radius
9th	+9	+6	+3	+3	Ritual scarring +3
10th	+10	+7	+3	+3	Sight of Gruumsh

Gruumsh's Constitution bonus) is blinded until he or she can rinse away the spittle. This attack has no effect on creatures that don't have eyes or don't depend on vision. Blinding spittle is usable once per hour at 4th level and twice per hour at 7th level.

Blindsight (Ex): At 5th level, the eye of Gruumsh gains blindsight in a 5-foot radius. This ability is otherwise identical to the hearing-based version described in the introduction of the *Monster Manual*. Its range increases to 10 feet at 8th level.

Sight of Gruumsh: At 10th level, the eye of Gruumsh sees the moment of his own death through his missing eye. This foreknowledge gives him a +2 morale bonus on all saving throws from then on. (Whether or not the vision is accurate is irrelevant—the character believes it to be true.)

Organization: The Eyes Of Gruumsh

"The cycle of my father's people is a simple one. You kill, you get better at killing, and you kill again. Break the cycle, and you die."
—Krusk

Though orcs revere eyes of Gruumsh for their unique clarity of vision, the average eye of Gruumsh isn't particularly well qualified to think for an entire tribe—even though he often assumes leadership of a tribe early in his career. Thus, he relies on a cleric of Gruumsh for wise counsel. To discourage any unhealthy confusion among their followers about who is in charge, both the eye of Gruumsh and the cleric encourage war against other races at every opportunity.

Since eyes of Gruumsh seek to avenge Corellon Larethian's insult to their deity, most are so obsessed with the destruction of elves that they attack any elven community on sight. Inspired by their leaders' rage, other orcs often throw themselves heedlessly at elven hordes.

Multiple eyes of Gruumsh usually don't work well together because they commonly have competing ideas about which course of action serves their deity best. Every few decades or so, however, several eyes of Gruumsh get the same idea in their heads—a crusade! (After all, a holy crusade involving hundreds of tribes under the command of dozens of eyes of Gruumsh is just the thing to inspire the younger generation to the deity's service.) When this occurs, the eyes of Gruumsh meet and declare truces between competing tribes by closing their functional left eyes all at once—thus blinding them to their own bickering. Then they go out and try to eradicate some other species.

FOE HUNTER

The foe hunter has but one purpose in life: to kill creatures of the type she hates. She is willing to pay any price or risk any danger to prevail against this hated foe. Her blade is anathema to such creatures, and her body is more often than not proof against their attacks. Though her hatred of this enemy is boundless and unending, it is not unthinking or rash. She lives to put an end to her hated foe, but she does not throw away her own life needlessly.

The foe hunter's path is open to any creature, good or evil. Some hunt humans or even celestials; others hunt the foulest spawn of the underworld. NPC foe hunters can be fierce allies against formidable enemies or implacable opponents dedicated to killing those the heroes love.

A character can choose this prestige class more than once but must select a different hated enemy and start again at 1st level each time. Levels of different foe hunter classes do not stack when determining level-based class features.

Hit Die: d10.

Requirements

To become a foe hunter, a character must fulfill the following criteria.

Base Attack Bonus: +7.
Feats: Track, Weapon Focus (any).
Language: The language (if any) of the intended hated enemy.
Special: The character must have a favored enemy.

Class Skills

The foe hunter's class skills (and the key ability for each skill) are Climb (Str), Intimidate (Cha), Jump (Str), Listen (Wis), Ride (Dex), Spot (Wis), Swim (Str), and Wilderness Lore (Wis). See Chapter 4 of the *Player's Handbook* for skill descriptions.

Skill Points at Each Level: 4 + Int modifier.

Class Features

The following are class features of the foe hunter prestige class.

TABLE 5–8: THE FOE HUNTER

Class Level	Base Attack Bonus	Fort Save	Ref Save	Will Save	Special
1st	+0	+2	+2	+0	Hated enemy, rancor +1d6
2nd	+1	+3	+3	+0	Hated enemy damage reduction 3/–
3rd	+2	+3	+3	+1	Rancor +2d6
4th	+3	+4	+4	+1	Hated enemy damage reduction 5/–, hated enemy spell resistance
5th	+3	+4	+4	+1	Rancor +3d6
6th	+4	+5	+5	+2	Hated enemy damage reduction 7/–
7th	+5	+5	+5	+2	Rancor +4d6
8th	+6	+6	+6	+2	Hated enemy damage reduction 9/–
9th	+6	+6	+6	+3	Rancor +5d6
10th	+7	+7	+7	+3	Death attack, hated enemy damage reduction 11/–

Hated Enemy Spell Resistance (Ex): Beginning at 4th level, the foe hunter can avoid the effects of spells and spell-like abilities that would directly affect her, as long as they originate from her hated enemy. Against such effects, the foe hunter has spell resistance equal to 15 + her foe hunter class level. This stacks with any other applicable spell resistance the character may have.

Death Attack (Ex): At 10th level, the foe hunter can make a death attack against a hated enemy that is denied its Dexterity bonus to AC (whether or not it actually has one). This ability functions like the assassin's death attack (see Assassin in Chapter 2 of the DUNGEON MASTER's Guide), except that the foe hunter need only make a melee attack that successfully does damage, not a sneak attack.

FORSAKER

Magic is evil. Magic tempts. Magic perverts. Magic corrupts. Anyone who cannot embrace these truths has no business considering the path of the forsaker.

The forsaker rebels against the magic of the fantastic world around him. It's not that he doesn't believe in it; he knows full well that magic is real. He has felt its all too tangible power burn over his skin or wrest control of his mind from him. While others may ignore the dangers of magic and succumb to its siren call of power, the forsaker knows better. To him, sorcery is nothing but a crutch that coddles and weakens its users. By depending upon his own resources alone, the forsaker becomes stronger, tougher, smarter, and more nimble than any of his companions. To that end, he treads a lonely path, deliberately depriving himself of magic's benefits and destroying any magic items he finds.

Forsakers can take up any standard or philosophy, though they tend more toward chaos than law. Evil forsakers hunt down and kill the most powerful users of magic that they can find, as if to demonstrate the ultimate weakness of the wizard and the sorcerer. Good forsakers commit themselves to expunging evil sorcery from their world, but they too see themselves as examples of how mundane strength can conquer foul enchantments.

Though forsakers do their best to resist all spells—even beneficial ones—cast upon them, some eventually learn to tolerate their companions' magic. A few claim that they are leading by example; others rationalize that only by consorting with lesser villains can they defeat greater ones. Whatever justification they use, the alliance between forsaker and spellcaster, no matter how temporary or how necessary, is seldom a peaceful one.

Few characters other than dwarven fighters and human or half-orc barbarians can appreciate the lifestyle of the forsaker. Elves, half-elves, and gnomes are surrounded by the benefits of magic from birth, so they are unlikely to choose this path. Dwarves, on the other hand, are naturally suspicious of sorcery, and many rural humans are just as distrustful. Certainly, no spellcaster should consider this career choice, since it means the virtual end of advantages gained from a former class. Even paladins and rangers must think hard before leaving behind their spells and spell-like abilities. Fighters and rogues occasionally take up this prestige class, but most forsakers are barbarians. Some say that only such a prim-

Weapon and Armor Proficiency: Foe hunters gain no weapon or armor proficiencies.

Hated Enemy: At 1st level, the foe hunter chooses one creature type that she has already selected as a favored enemy to be the target of her hatred. This choice determines what kind of foe hunter she becomes—orc hunter, giant hunter, or the like. The choice of hated enemy is irreversible.

Rancor (Su): The foe hunter can deliver a powerful blow to her hated enemy. Once per round, on her action, she can designate one of her attacks against a hated enemy as a rancor attack before the attack roll is made. A successful rancor attack by a 1st-level foe hunter deals +1d6 points of extra damage. This amount increases by +1d6 points for every two additional foe hunter levels the attacker acquires. Should the foe hunter score a critical hit with a rancor attack, this extra damage is not multiplied. The extra damage from a rancor attack applies even if that hated enemy is immune to critical hits.

With a sap or an unarmed strike, the foe hunter can deal subdual damage instead of normal damage with a rancor attack. She cannot, however, do subdual damage with a weapon that deals normal damage in a rancor attack, even when taking the usual –4 penalty.

Hated Enemy Damage Reduction (Ex): At 2nd level, the foe hunter can shrug off 3 points of damage from each successful attack by her hated enemy. This damage reduction increases by 2 points for every two additional foe hunter levels she has. Damage reduction can reduce damage to 0, but not below that. Hated enemy damage reduction does not stack with any other damage reduction the character has.

itive, focused mind could ever manage to forsake magic for good.

Hit Die: d12.

Requirements

To qualify as a forsaker, a character must fulfill the following criteria.

Feats: Great Fortitude, Iron Will, Lightning Reflexes.

Special: The character must once have been the victim of a magical attack that seriously wounded him or threatened his life. He must also sell or give away all his magic items (including magic weapons, armor, and potions) and renounce the use of any spellcasting and spell-like abilities he previously used.

Class Skills

The forsaker's class skills (and the key ability for each skill) are Climb (Str), Craft (any) (Int), Handle Animal (Wis), Heal (Wis), Intimidate (Cha), Intuit Direction (Wis), Jump (Str), Listen (Wis), Ride (Dex), Sense Motive (Wis), Swim (Str), Tumble (Dex), and Wilderness Lore (Wis). See Chapter 4 of the *Player's Handbook* for skill descriptions.

Skill Points at Each Level: 2 + Int modifier.

Class Features

The following are class features of the forsaker prestige class.

Weapon and Armor Proficiency: Forsakers gain no weapon or armor proficiencies.

Ability Bonus (Ex): Beginning at 1st level, the character gains a +1 inherent bonus to any desired ability score for each forsaker level.

Fast Healing (Ex): Forsakers regain hit points at an exceptionally fast rate. At 1st level, the character regains 1 hit point per round, to a maximum of 10 hit points per day. The number of hit points regained per round increases by +1 for every four forsaker levels, and the maximum restorable per day increases by 10 for every two forsaker levels. Except as noted above, this ability works like the fast healing ability described in the introduction of the *Monster Manual*.

Forsake Magic: In addition to avoiding all use of spellcasting, spell-like abilities, and magic items, the forsaker must also refuse any benefits from others' magic—including magical healing. Thus, he must attempt a saving throw against any spell that allows one. For most beneficial spells, such as *displacement* or *neutralize poison*, a successful save negates the spell's effects; for a *cure* spell, it halves the benefit. Any forsaker who unwittingly uses a magic item or casts a spell (while under the influence of a *charm person* or *dominate person* spell, for example) loses all the special abilities of the prestige class for one week.

Spell Resistance (Ex): At 1st level, the forsaker gains spell resistance 11. This value increases by +1 with each forsaker level gained and stacks with any other applicable spell resistance he has.

TABLE 5–9: THE FORSAKER

Class Level	Base Attack Bonus	Fort Save	Ref Save	Will Save	Special
1st	+1	+2	+0	+2	Ability bonus +1, fast healing 1 (10), forsake magic, SR 11
2nd	+2	+3	+0	+3	Ability bonus +1, damage reduction 3/+1, magic destruction, SR 12
3rd	+3	+3	+1	+3	Ability bonus +1, fast healing 1 (20), natural weapons, SR 13, tough defense
4th	+4	+4	+1	+4	Ability bonus +1, damage reduction 5/+2, SR 14
5th	+5	+4	+1	+4	Ability bonus +1, fast healing 2 (30), SR 15
6th	+6	+5	+2	+5	Ability bonus +1, damage reduction 7/+3, slippery mind, SR 16
7th	+7	+5	+2	+5	Ability bonus +1, fast healing 2 (40), SR 17
8th	+8	+6	+2	+6	Ability bonus +1, damage reduction 9/+4, SR 18
9th	+9	+6	+3	+6	Ability bonus +1, fast healing 3 (50), SR 19
10th	+10	+7	+3	+7	Ability bonus +1, damage reduction 11/+5, SR 20

Damage Reduction (Ex): At 2nd level, the forsaker gains damage reduction 3/+1. This damage resistance rises by 2/+1 for every two forsaker levels he gains thereafter. This ability remains in effect only as long as the forsaker destroys the required value of magic items every 24 hours (see Magic Destruction, below). This does not stack with any other damage reduction he already has.

Magic Destruction: The forsaker gains access to his damage reduction ability (see above) through the destruction of magic items. If he goes more than 24 hours without destroying magic items whose market prices total at least 100 gp per point of damage reduction, he loses that ability until he does so.

Tough Defense (Ex): At 3rd level, a forsaker gains a natural armor bonus equal to his Constitution bonus (if any).

Natural Weapons (Ex): Beginning at 3rd level, the forsaker can fight as though he and his weapon were one. Any weapon he uses functions as if it were a natural weapon for overcoming damage reduction (see Damage Reduction in the introduction of the *Monster Manual*). That is, if the forsaker has damage reduction 3/+1, any weapon he uses functions as if it were a +1 weapon for overcoming a foe's damage reduction.

Slippery Mind (Ex): At 6th level, the forsaker can wriggle free from magical effects that would otherwise control or compel him. If he fails his saving throw against an enchantment effect, he can attempt his saving throw again 1 round later. He gets only one extra chance to succeed at his saving throw.

Ex-Forsakers

Forsakers can multiclass normally, as long as they continue to abide by the strictures of the prestige class. Any forsaker who willingly violates those strictures by using magic items or casting spells loses all special abilities of the prestige class and can progress no further as a forsaker. If he thereafter remains pure (uses no magic) for a period of a year and a day, his abilities are reinstated at their previous levels and he may once again progress in the prestige class.

FRENZIED BERSERKER

The random madness of the thunderstorm and the unpredictability of the slaadi come together in the soul of the frenzied berserker. Unlike most other characters, she does not fight to achieve some heroic goal or defeat a loathsome villain. Those are mere excuses—it is the thrill of combat that draws her. For the frenzied barbarian, the insanity of battle is much like an addictive drug—she must constantly seek out more conflict to feed her craving for battle.

Along the wild borderlands and in the evil kingdoms of the world, frenzied berserkers often lead warbands that include a variety of character types—and even other frenzied berserkers. Some such groups turn to banditry and brigandage; others serve as specialized mercenaries. Whatever their origin, such warbands naturally gravitate toward situations of instability and conflict, because wars and civil strife are their bread and butter. Indeed, the

coming of a frenzied berserker is the most obvious herald of troubled times.

The frenzied berserker's path is unsuited for most adventurers—a fact for which the peace-lovers of the world can be thankful. Because of their traditional love for battle, orc and half-orc barbarians are the ones who most frequently adopt this prestige class, though human and dwarven barbarians also find it appealing. It might seem that elves would be good candidates because of their chaotic nature, but the elven aesthetic and love of grace are at odds with the frenzied berserker's devaluation of the self. Spellcasting characters and monks almost never become frenzied berserkers.

Hit Die: d12.

Requirements

To become a frenzied berserker, a character must fulfill the following criteria.

Alignment: Any nonlawful.
Base Attack Bonus: +6.
Feats: Cleave, Destructive Rage, Intimidating Rage, Power Attack.

Class Skills

The frenzied berserker's class skills (and the key ability for each skill) are Climb (Str), Intimidate (Cha), Jump (Str), Ride (Dex), and Swim (Str). See Chapter 4 of the *Player's Handbook* for skill descriptions.

Skill Points at Each Level: 2 + Int modifier.

Class Features

The following are class features of the frenzied berserker prestige class.

Weapon and Armor Proficiency: Frenzied berserkers gain no weapon or armor proficiencies.

Frenzy (Ex): Beginning at 1st level, the frenzied berserker can enter a frenzy during combat. While frenzied, she gains a +6 bonus to Strength and a single extra attack each round at her highest bonus. (This latter effect is not cumulative with *haste*.) However, she also suffers a –4 penalty to AC and takes 2 points of subdual damage per round. A frenzy lasts for a number of rounds equal to 3 + the frenzied berserker's Constitution modifier. To end the frenzy before its duration expires, the character may attempt a Will save (DC 20) once per round as a free action. Success ends the frenzy immediately; failure means it continues. The effects of frenzy stack with those from rage.

At 1st level, the character can enter a frenzy once per day. Thereafter, she gains one additional use per day of this ability for every two frenzied berserker levels she acquires. The character can enter a frenzy as a free action. Even though this takes no time, she can do it only during her action, not in response to another's action. In addition, if she suffers damage from an attack, spell, trap, or any other source, she automatically enters a frenzy at the start of her next action, as long as she still has at least one daily usage of the ability left. To avoid entering a frenzy in response to damage, the character must make a successful Will save (DC 10 + points of damage suffered since her last action) at the start of her next action.

TABLE 5–10: THE FRENZIED BERSERKER

Class Level	Base Attack Bonus	Fort Save	Ref Save	Will Save	Special
1st	+1	+2	+0	+0	Frenzy 1/day, Remain Conscious
2nd	+2	+3	+0	+0	Supreme cleave
3rd	+3	+3	+1	+1	Frenzy 2/day
4th	+4	+4	+1	+1	Deathless frenzy
5th	+5	+4	+1	+1	Frenzy 3/day, improved power attack
6th	+6	+5	+2	+2	Inspire frenzy 1/day
7th	+7	+5	+2	+2	Frenzy 4/day
8th	+8	+6	+2	+2	Greater frenzy, inspire frenzy 2/day
9th	+9	+6	+3	+3	Frenzy 5/day
10th	+10	+7	+3	+3	Inspire frenzy 3/day, no longer winded after frenzy, supreme power attack

While frenzied, the character cannot use skills or abilities that require patience or concentration (such as Move Silently), nor can she cast spells, drink potions, activate magic items, or read scrolls. She can use any feat she has except Expertise, item creation feats, metamagic feats, and Skill Focus in a skill that requires patience or concentration. She can, however, use her special ability to inspire frenzy (see below) normally.

During a frenzy, the frenzied berserker must attack those she perceives as foes to the best of her ability. Should she run out of enemies before her frenzy expires, her rampage continues. She must then attack the nearest creature (determine randomly if several potential foes are equidistant) and fight that opponent without regard to friendship, innocence, or health (the target's or her own).

When a frenzy ends, the frenzied berserker is fatigued (–2 penalty to Strength and Dexterity, unable to charge or run) for the duration of the encounter, or until she enters another frenzy, whichever comes first. At 10th level, she is no longer fatigued after a frenzy, though she still suffers the subdual damage for each round it lasts.

Starting at 8th level, the character's frenzy bonus to Strength becomes +10 instead of +6.

Remain Conscious: The frenzied berserker gains Remain Conscious as a bonus feat.

Supreme Cleave: At 2nd level, the frenzied berserker can take a 5-foot step between attacks when using the Cleave or Great Cleave feat. She is still limited to one such adjustment per round, so she cannot use this ability during a round in which she has already taken a 5-foot step.

Deathless Frenzy (Ex): At 4th level, the frenzied berserker can scorn death and unconsciousness while in a frenzy. Should her hit points to fall to 0 or below because of hit point loss, she continues to fight normally until her frenzy ends. At that point, the effects of her wounds apply normally. This ability does not prevent death from spell effects such as *slay living* or *disintegrate*.

Improved Power Attack: Beginning at 5th level, the frenzied berserker gains a +3 bonus on her melee damage rolls for every –2 penalty she takes on her melee attack rolls when using the Power Attack feat.

Inspire Frenzy (Su): Beginning at 6th level, the frenzied berserker can inspire frenzy in her allies while she herself is frenzied. When she uses this ability, all allies within 10 feet of her gain the benefits and the disadvantages of frenzy as if they had that ability themselves.

Those who do not wish to be affected can make a Will save (DC 10 + frenzied berserker level + frenzied berserker's Charisma modifier) to resist the effect. The frenzy of affected allies lasts for a number of rounds equal to 3 + the frenzied berserker's Constitution modifier, regardless of whether they remain within 10 feet of her.

The frenzied berserker gains one additional use of this ability per day for every two additional frenzied berserker levels she acquires, though the ability is still usable only once per encounter.

Supreme Power Attack: At 10th level, the frenzied berserker gains a +2 bonus on her melee damage rolls for every –1 penalty she takes on her melee attack rolls when using the Power Attack feat. This effect does not stack with that of Improved Power Attack.

GEOMANCER

The cleric reaches out to a higher power. The wizard trusts only in eldritch tomes. The druid looks to nature for her spells. To the geomancer, however, all magic is the same.

Geomancy is the art of channeling magical energy from many sources through the land itself. A geomancer may research like a wizard, pray like a cleric, or sing like a bard, but he casts spells as only a geomancer can. In the area he calls home (be it high on a mountain, deep in a forest, or even beneath an ocean) he weaves ley lines—powerful connections to the land itself. The spells he casts through these connections with the earth are reflections of his own strength of will. As the geomancer progresses, however, the effort of gathering magic through the earth takes a physical toll on him, making him more and more like the land and its creatures.

Only characters with more than one spellcasting class can become geomancers. The most popular combinations are druid/sorcerer and druid/wizard. Clerics with arcane spellcasting ability can also qualify; those with access to the Plant or Animal domain are the most likely to consider this path. A bard or a ranger who picks up a second, more focused spellcasting class can also adopt this lifestyle.

Hit Die: d6.

Requirements

To qualify as a geomancer, a character must fulfill the following criteria.

Skills: Knowledge (arcana) 6 ranks, Knowledge (nature) 6 ranks.

Spells: Ability to cast 2nd-level arcane spells and 2nd-level divine spells.

Class Skills

The geomancer's class skills (and the key ability for each skill) are Alchemy (Int), Animal Empathy (Cha), Concentration (Con), Craft (any) (Int), Diplomacy (Cha), Handle Animal (Cha), Heal (Wis), Intuit Direction (Wis), Knowledge (arcana), Knowledge (nature), Scry (Int), Spellcraft (Int), Swim (Str), and Wilderness Lore (Wis). See Chapter 4 of the *Player's Handbook* for skill descriptions.

Skill Points at Each Level: 4 + Int modifier.

Class Features

The following are class features of the geomancer prestige class.

Weapon and Armor Proficiency: Geomancers gain no weapon or armor proficiencies.

Spells per Day/Spells Known: At each geomancer level, the character gains new spells per day (and spells known, if applicable) as if he had also gained a level in a spellcasting class to which he belonged before adding the prestige class. He does not, however, gain any other benefit a character of that class would have gained (additional *wild shape* options, metamagic or item creation feats, or the like). Since the character had more than one spellcasting class before becoming a geomancer, the player must decide to which class to add each geomancer level for determining spells per day and spells known.

Spell Versatility: At 1st level, the geomancer learns to blend divine and arcane magic. He still acquires and prepares his spells in the normal manner for his individual spellcasting classes. When he casts them, however, he can mix or match spellcasting parameters from any of his classes to gain the maximum possible advantage for any spell with a spell level equal to or less than his spell versatility score. Thus, as a 4th-level geomancer, he can cast any of his 3rd-level or lower sorcerer/wizard spells with no chance of arcane spell failure from armor. (The druidic prohibition against metal armor still applies to druid/geomancers, however, since this stricture stems from a spiritual oath rather than a practical limitation.) The geomancer may use his Wisdom bonus to set the save DC for arcane spells, or his Charisma or Intelligence bonus (whichever he would normally use for arcane

spells) to set the save DC for divine spells. If a spell requires either an arcane material component or a divine focus, he may use either. A cleric/geomancer who also has levels of wizard, sorcerer, or bard can spontaneously convert any prepared arcane or divine spell (except a domain spell) of an appropriate level into a *cure* or *inflict* spell of equal or lower level, though he must be capable of casting the latter as a cleric.

Drift: The character slowly becomes closer to nature. At each geomancer level, choose a drift from the appropriate stage (see Drift, below).

Ley Lines: At 2nd level, the geomancer learns to create magical connections with a specific type of terrain. Choose one of the following terrain types: aquatic, desert, forest, hills, marsh, mountains, or plains. In that terrain, the geomancer's effective caster level for all spells increases by +1. At 6th level and again at 10th level,

TABLE 5–11: THE GEOMANCER

Class Level	Base Attack Bonus	Fort Save	Ref Save	Will Save	Special	Spells per Day/Spells Known
1st	+0	+2	+0	+2	Drift 1, spell versatility 0	+1 level of existing class
2nd	+1	+3	+0	+3	Drift 1, ley lines +1, spell versatility 1	+1 level of existing class
3rd	+2	+3	+1	+3	Drift 2, spell versatility 2	+1 level of existing class
4th	+3	+4	+1	+4	Drift 2, spell versatility 3	+1 level of existing class
5th	+3	+4	+1	+4	Drift 3, spell versatility 4	+1 level of existing class
6th	+4	+5	+2	+5	Drift 3, ley lines +2, spell versatility 5	+1 level of existing class
7th	+5	+5	+2	+5	Drift 4, spell versatility 6	+1 level of existing class
8th	+6	+6	+2	+6	Drift 4, spell versatility 7	+1 level of existing class
9th	+6	+6	+3	+6	Drift 5, spell versatility 8	+1 level of existing class
10th	+7	+7	+3	+7	Drift 5, ley lines +3, spell versatility 9	+1 level of existing class

the character may either choose a new terrain in which to receive the benefit (at +1), or increase his effective caster level in a previously chosen terrain by an additional +1.

Drift

Drift is a gradual devolution into some other natural form. Those who experience this phenomenon gain attributes of animals and plants as time goes by. Geomancers experience drift at every level. As a variant rule, high-level druids who spend all their lives away from civilization may also experience drift at the Dungeon Master's discretion—perhaps once every ten years.

Drift is divided into stages. You must choose one drift from stage 1 the first time you experience the phenomenon. Your second drift must also be from stage 1. Thereafter, you may choose from a higher stage only after you have acquired at least two drifts from the previous stage. For example, a stage 4 drift may be chosen only after you have at least two stage 1 drifts, two stage 2 drifts, and two stage 3 drifts. You may, however, choose drifts from stages below your maximum whenever you wish. For example, you if you have two stage 1 drifts, you may choose a third stage 1 rather than a stage 2, if desired.

Stage 1 drifts have no game effect. Each drift of stage 2 and beyond grants a permanent extraordinary ability. Natural attacks allow for Strength bonuses on damage rolls, except in the case of poison and acid.

Stage 1

1. Leopard spots appear on your body.
2. You grow a cat's tail.
3. You sprout feathers (but not wings).
4. Your eyebrows become green and bushy.
5. Your hair becomes a tangle of short vines.
6. Light, downy fur covers your skin.
7. Your skin turns green and scaly.
8. Your touch causes flowers to wilt.
9. Your voice sounds like a dog's, though it is still intelligible.
10. Zebra stripes appear on your body.

Stage 2

1. A small camel's hump grows on your back. (You can go without water for up to five days.)
2. You grow a coat of white fur like a polar bear's. (You gain a +8 bonus on Hide checks in snowy areas.)
3. The pads of your feet become sticky, like those of a lizard. (You gain a +4 bonus on Climb checks.)
4. You become as swift as an elk. (Your land speed increases by +5 feet.)
5. You become as comely as a dryad. (You gain a +4 bonus on Diplomacy checks.)
6. You become as graceful as a cat. (You gain a +4 bonus on Balance checks.)
7. You sprout leaves and become photosynthetic. (You can subsist on 1 hour/day of sunlight in lieu of food, though you still require the same amount of water as before.)
8. Your blood flows as slowly as tree sap. The speed at which progressive damage, such as that from *wounding* or *decomposition* (see Chapter 6), affects you is halved.

9. Your eyes become as sharp as a rat's. (You gain low-light vision.)
10. Your skin adapts like that of an octopus. (You can change color to blend with your surroundings, gaining a +4 bonus on Hide checks.)

Stage 3

1. Deer antlers grow from your forehead. (You gain a gore attack for 1d6 points of damage.)
2. Thorns grow on your body. (Your unarmed attacks do piercing damage, and those striking you with natural weapons suffer 1d3 points of piercing damage per successful hit.)
3. You can constrict like a snake. (You deal 1d3 points of damage with a successful grapple check against a creature of your size category or smaller.)
4. You can spin a web like a spider. (You can use your web to snare prey as described in the monstrous spider entry in the *Monster Manual*, but you cannot attack with it.)
5. You sprout fish gills. (You can breathe both water and air.)
6. Your eyes become as sharp as an eagle's. (You gain a +4 bonus on Spot checks in daylight.)
7. Your eyes become as sharp as an owl's. (You gain a +4 bonus on Spot checks in dusk and darkness.)
8. Your fingers grow hawklike talons. (You gain Weapon Finesse [claw] and can make two claw attacks per round for 1d3 points of damage each.)
9. Your mouth extends like a crocodile's. (You gain a bite attack for 1d6 points of damage.)
10. Your toes grow lionlike claws. (You can make two rake attacks for 1d4 points of damage each if you gain a hold on your target.)

Stage 4

1. You grow an acid stinger like that of a giant ant. (You can sting for 1d4 points of piercing damage + 1d4 points of acid damage.)
2. You can trip like a wolf. (If you hit with a natural attack, you can attempt to trip your target as a free action; see the wolf entry in the *Monster Manual*.)
3. You can rage like a wolverine. (If you take damage, you rage as a 1st-level barbarian—see Barbarian in the *Player's Handbook*—or gain +1 effective level of any class you have that grants rage as a class feature, but only for determining the benefits of rage.)
4. You gain a boar's ferocity. (You continue to fight without penalty even while disabled or dying.)
5. You can grab like a bear. (You gain the improved grab ability as described in the introduction of the *Monster Manual*.)
6. You can pounce like a leopard. (If you leap on a foe in the first round of combat, you can make a full attack action even if you have already taken a move action.)
7. Your hands become as strong as a gorilla's. (You gain a +2 bonus on Strength checks to break objects.)
8. Your jaw becomes as powerful as a weasel's (You can attach to an opponent with a successful bite and inflict 1d3 points of damage per round until unattached. However, you lose your Dexterity bonus to AC while attached.)
9. You can fire an ink cloud as does a squid. (In water, you can emit a cloud of jet-black ink 10 feet on a side once

per minute as a free action; this provides total conceal-ment and those within the cloud suffer the effects of total darkness.)

10. Your nose becomes as sensitive as a hound's. (You gain the Scent feat; see Chapter 2.)

Stage 5

1. You grow a unicorn horn. (You gain a +4 bonus on Fortitude saves against poison and a gore attack for 1d8 points of damage.)
2. Feathered or batlike wings grow from your back. (You gain a fly speed of 60 feet.)
3. You can curl into a spiny ball like a hedgehog. (When curled, you gain a +4 natural armor bonus to AC, but you may not move or attack. Curling or uncurling is a standard action.)
4. You are as graceful as a pixie. (You gain a +2 bonus on Reflex saves.)
5. You gain the tremorsense of an earthworm. (You can sense anything in contact with the ground within 30 feet of you.)
6. Your canine teeth exude poison. (If you hit with a bite attack, your target must make a Fortitude save (DC 10 + 1/2 your character level + your Constitution modifi-er) against poison. Initial damage is 1d2 points of tem-porary Dexterity damage; secondary damage is 1d4 points of temporary Dexterity damage.)
7. Your senses become as sharp as a bat's. (You gain the Blindsight feat; see Chapter 2.)
8. Your feet extend to elephantine width. (You gain the trample ability as described in the introduction of the *Monster Manual*. Your trample attack does 2d4

points of bludgeoning damage, and the Reflex save DC is 10 + 1/2 your character level + your Strength modifier.)
9. You can move like a cheetah. (Once per hour, you can take a charge action to move ten times your normal speed.)
10. Your skin becomes tree bark. (You gain a +1 natural armor bonus to AC.)

HEXER

"Do not meet the gaze of the shaman with the evil eye," warn townsfolk who have crossed paths with a hexer. Unfortunately, the typical intrepid adventurer rarely hears such advice in time. The hexer profits by this igno-rance, surprising his victims with the power of his gaze. Many hexers inflict curses that follow their victims like a plague. The more powerful practitioners can engender fear, cause magical slumber, or enthrall their victims as slaves with a mere glance.

Hexers are unknown among civilized peoples; they are found only among tribes of goblins, ogres, and orcs. Prior to pursuing the path of the hexer, most of them were adepts who served as witch doctors for their tribes. Hexers often assume leadership of their tribes as well—who would dare to gainsay them, after all?

Most hexers are villainous, evil cretins lacking any code of morality, and the vast majority of them hate humans, elves, dwarves, and other civilized races. Neu-tral hexers are no less dangerous, especially when some-thing threatens the welfare of their tribes.

Hit Die: d6.

TABLE 5-12: THE HEXER

Class Level	Base Attack Bonus	Fort Save	Ref Save	Will Save	Special	Spells per Day/Spells Known
1st	+1	+0	+0	+2	Hex 1/day	+1 level of existing class
2nd	+2	+0	+0	+3	Bonus spell, hex 2/day	+1 level of existing class
3rd	+3	+1	+1	+3	Sicken hex	+1 level of existing class
4th	+4	+1	+1	+4	Bonus spell, hex 3/day	+1 level of existing class
5th	+5	+1	+1	+4	Fear hex	+1 level of existing class
6th	+6	+2	+2	+5	Bonus spell, hex 4/day	+1 level of existing class
7th	+7	+2	+2	+5	Sleep hex	+1 level of existing class
8th	+8	+2	+2	+6	Bonus spell, hex 5/day	+1 level of existing class
9th	+9	+3	+3	+6	Charm hex	+1 level of existing class
10th	+10	+3	+3	+7	Bonus spell, hex 6/day	+1 level of existing class

Requirements

To become a hexer, a character must fulfill the following criteria.

Race/Type: Monstrous humanoid, giant, goblinoid, or other primitive humanoid, such as orc or gnoll.

Alignment: Any nongood.

Skills: Knowledge (arcana) 10 ranks, Spellcraft 8 ranks, Wilderness Lore 10 ranks.

Spellcasting: Able to cast *lightning bolt* as a divine spell.

Class Skills

The hexer's class skills (and the key ability for each skill) are Alchemy (Int), Concentration (Con), Craft (any) (Int), Handle Animal (Cha), Heal (Wis), Knowledge (any) (Int), Profession (any) (Wis), Scry (Int, exclusive skill) Spellcraft (Int), and Wilderness Lore (Wis). See Chapter 4 of the *Player's Handbook* for skill descriptions.

Skill Points at Each Level: 2 + Int modifier.

Class Features

The following are class features of the hexer prestige class.

Weapon and Armor Proficiency: Hexers gain no weapon or armor proficiencies.

Spells per Day/Spells Known: At each hexer level, the character gains new spells per day (and spells known, if applicable) as if he had also gained a level in a spellcasting class to which he belonged before adding the prestige class. He does not, however, gain any other benefit a character of that class would have gained (additional *wild shape* options, metamagic or item creation feats, or the like). If the character had more than one spellcasting class before becoming a hexer, the player must decide to which class to add each hexer level for determining spells per day and spells known.

Hex **(Sp):** At 1st level, the hexer gains a gaze attack. He can use this ability once per day at 1st level and twice per day at 2nd level. Thereafter, he gains one additional use per day of this ability for every two hexer levels he acquires.

Activating this power is a standard action, and it lasts for a number of rounds equal to the character's hexer level. Each round, the hexer's gaze attack automatically works against one creature within 30 feet that is looking at (attacking or interacting with) him. Targets who avert their eyes have a 50% chance of avoiding the gaze,

but the hexer gains one-half concealment (20% miss chance) relative to those who successfully avoid the gaze. Targets can also close their eyes or turn away entirely; doing so prevents the *hex* from affecting them but grants the gazer total concealment (50% miss chance) relative to them.

An affected target must make a Will save (DC 10 + hexer level + hexer's Wisdom modifier) or suffer a –4 enhancement penalty on attack rolls, saving throws, ability checks, and skill checks. These effects are permanent until removed with a *break enchantment, limited wish, miracle, remove curse,* or *wish* spell. This is an enchantment effect and cannot be dispelled.

A *hex* does not affect undead creatures or extend beyond the plane that the hexer occupies. The hexer is subject to the effects of his own reflected gaze and is allowed a saving throw against them.

Bonus Spell: At 2nd level, the hexer adds a new spell of his choice to his spell list. This spell must come from the wizard/sorcerer spell list and must be of a spell level that the hexer can cast. He can prepare this new spell at the same spell level as it appeared on the wizard/sorcerer list. He gains one additional bonus spell for every two hexer levels he has.

Sicken Hex **(Sp):** At 3rd level, the hexer can use his gaze attack to inflict a debilitating illness. This ability functions like the *hex* ability (above), except that the target must make a Fortitude save instead of a Will save to resist, and the effect is as described below. A *sicken hex* requires one daily use of the character's *hex* ability.

A target who fails the save is overcome with pain and fever, which causes him or her to move at one half normal speed, lose any Dexterity bonus to Armor Class, and suffer a –2 circumstance penalty on attack rolls. These effects are permanent until removed with a *break enchantment, limited wish, miracle, remove curse,* or *wish* spell. A *sicken hex* is a necromancy effect that cannot be dispelled.

Fear Hex **(Sp):** At 5th level, the hexer can use his gaze attack to engender fear. This ability functions like the *hex* ability (above), except that target is affected as if by a *fear* spell. A *fear hex* is a mind-influencing, compulsion, enchantment effect, and it requires one daily use of the character's *hex* ability.

Sleep Hex **(Sp):** At 7th level, the hexer can use his gaze to generate a *sleep* effect. This ability functions like the *hex* ability (above), except that duration is 10 minutes × the character's hexer level and the target is affected as if by a *sleep* spell. A *sleep hex* is a mind-influencing, compulsion, enchantment effect, and it requires one daily use of the character's *hex* ability.

Charm Hex (Sp): At 9th level, the hexer can use his gaze attack to generate a *charm monster* effect. This ability functions like the *hex* ability (above), except that duration is 1 day per hexer level and the target is affected as if by a *charm monster* spell. (Should the hexer fall victim to his own reflected gaze attack, he is affected as if by a *hold monster* spell.) A *charm hex* is a mind-influencing, charm, enchantment effect, and it requires one daily use of the character's *hex* ability.

KING/QUEEN OF THE WILD

Few are brave enough to climb the highest mountains and tread the deepest deserts. But where nature's fury is at its height, there you'll find the kings and queens of the wild, undaunted by the challenges before them—that is, if you're strong enough to look for them there.

When choosing this prestige class, you must specify one of the following eight terrain types: desert, forest, hills, marsh, mountain, plains, sea, skies, or underground. Other terrain types are not harsh enough to engender this kind of survivalism.

Anyone with a tie to nature and sufficient hardiness can become a king or queen of the wild. Rangers, barbarians, and druids tend to be the most comfortable with this lifestyle. However, many adventurers have clashed with snow wizards and desert sorcerers who

have augmented their powers by adopting this prestige class.

A character can choose this prestige class more than once but must select a different terrain type and start again at 1st level each time. Levels of different king/queen of the wild classes do not stack for determining level-based class features.

Hit Die: d12.

Requirements

To become a king or queen of the wild, a character must fulfill the following criteria.

Base Fortitude Save Bonus: +4.

Skills: Hide 4 ranks, Intuit Direction 4 ranks, Wilderness Lore 8 ranks, terrain-dependent prerequisite skill (see below) 4 ranks.

Feats: Endurance, Track.

Special: The character must choose a terrain type (see below) and live in or near such an area.

Class Skills

The king/queen of the wild's class skills (and the key ability for each skill) are Balance (Dex), Climb (Str), Craft (any) (Int), Handle Animal (Cha), Hide (Dex), Intuit Direction (Wis), Jump (Str), Listen (Wis), Move Silently (Dex), Ride (Dex), Spot (Wis), Swim (Str), Use Rope (Dex), and Wilderness Lore (Wis). See Chapter 4 of the *Player's Handbook* for skill descriptions.

Skill Points at Each Level: 4 + Int modifier.

Class Features

The following are class features of the king/queen of the wild prestige class.

Weapon and Armor Proficiency: Kings and queens of the wild gain proficiency with simple weapons and light armor.

Terrain Skill Bonuses: At 1st level, a king or queen of the wild gains a +2 insight bonus on both Wilderness Lore checks and checks made with his or her terrain-dependent prerequisite skill while in the chosen terrain.

Endure Elements (Ex): The king or queen of the wild can ignore some damage from the element associated with the chosen terrain type (see Terrain-Dependent Features, below) as though under a permanent *endure elements* effect. At 2nd level, the character ignores the first 5 points of damage from that element. (The terrain elements correspond to the five energy types: acid, cold, electricity, fire, and sonic.) This amount increases by an additional +5 at 5th, 8th, and 10th level.

Terrain Movement (Ex): At 2nd level, if the chosen terrain is land-based, the king or queen of the wild can move overland through it as if it were plains. A king of the sea or a queen of the marsh swims along the surface of water at one-half his or her land speed.

Attack Native Creatures (Ex): The king or queen of the wild gains a competence bonus on attack rolls against any creature that has the character's chosen terrain listed in the Climate/Terrain section of its statistics. (In the

Table 5–13: The King/Queen of the Wild

Class Level	Base Attack Bonus	Fort Save	Ref Save	Will Save	Special
1st	+1	+2	+0	+2	Terrain skill bonuses
2nd	+2	+3	+0	+3	Endure elements 5, terrain movement
3rd	+3	+3	+1	+3	Attack native creatures +1, terrain camouflage
4th	+4	+4	+1	+4	Bonus feat
5th	+5	+4	+1	+4	Attack native creatures +2, endure elements 10
6th	+6	+5	+2	+5	Detect animals or plants
7th	+7	+5	+2	+5	Adaptation, attack native creatures +3
8th	+8	+6	+2	+6	Bonus feat, endure elements 15
9th	+9	+6	+3	+6	Attack native creatures +4
10th	+10	+7	+3	+7	Endure elements 20, freedom of movement

case of a king or queen of the skies, this means any naturally flying creature who lives outdoors.) A creature with a listing of "Any land" does not trigger these bonuses. This bonus is +1 at 3rd level, and it increases by +1 for every two king/queen of the wild levels the character gains thereafter.

Terrain Camouflage (Ex): At 3rd level, kings and queens of the wild may use the raw materials of their chosen terrains to conceal their presence from others. This full-round action grants a character a +10 competence bonus on Hide checks in the chosen terrain.

Bonus Feat: At 4th and 8th level, a king or queen of the wild may choose a bonus feat from the list for his or her terrain type (see below). This is in addition to the feats that a character of any class normally gets every three levels. The character must still meet any prerequisites for these bonus feats.

Detect Animals and Plants (Sp): At 6th level, the character can use *detect animals or plants* within the chosen terrain as a druid of his or her king/queen of the wild level. This ability is usable three times a day.

Adaptation (Su): At 7th level, the character can function as if wearing a *necklace of adaptation* for a total of up to 30 minutes per day.

Freedom of Movement (Su): At 10th level, the king/queen of the wild can function as if under the influence of a *freedom of movement* spell for up to 30 minutes. This ability is usable once per day.

Terrain-Dependent Features

Each of the nine prestige classes derived from king/queen of the wild has different features depending on the terrain type chosen.

King/Queen of the Desert
Terrain Type: Desert.
Prerequisite Skill: Spot.
Terrain Element: Fire.
Bonus Feats: Great Fortitude, Mounted Combat, Run, Skill Focus (Spot), Toughness.

King/Queen of the Forest
Terrain Type: Forest.
Prerequisite Skill: Climb.
Terrain Element: Fire.
Bonus Feats: Alertness, Brachiation, Point Blank Shot, Run, Skill Focus (Climb).

King/Queen of the Hills
Terrain Type: Hills.
Prerequisite Skill: Climb.
Terrain Element: Cold.
Bonus Feats: Alertness, Far Shot, Run, Skill Focus (Climb), Toughness.

King/Queen of the Marsh
Terrain Type: Marsh.
Prerequisite Skill: Swim.
Terrain Element: Acid.
Bonus Feats: Alertness, Blind-Fight, Great Fortitude, Skill Focus (Swim), Toughness.

King/Queen of the Mountain
Terrain Type: Mountains.
Prerequisite Skill: Climb.
Terrain Element: Cold.
Bonus Feats: Alertness, Great Fortitude, Jump, Skill Focus (Climb), Toughness.

King/Queen of the Plains
Terrain Type: Plains.
Prerequisite Skill: Move Silently.
Terrain Element: Electricity.
Bonus Feats: Alertness, Far Shot, Point-Blank Shot, Run, Skill Focus (Move Silently).

King/Queen of the Sea
Terrain Type: Aquatic.
Prerequisite Skill: Swim.
Terrain Element: Cold.
Bonus Feats: Alertness, Blind-Fight, Exotic Weapon Proficiency (net), Silent Spell, Skill Focus (Swim).

King/Queen of the Skies
Terrain Type: Air.
Prerequisite Skill: Balance.
Terrain Element: Electricity.
Bonus Feats: Flyby Attack, Hover, Skill Focus (Balance), Snatch, Wingover.

King/Queen of the Underground
Terrain Type: Underground.
Prerequisite Skill: Escape Artist.
Terrain Element: Sonic.
Bonus Feats: Alertness, Blind-Fight, Extra Turning, Great Fortitude, Toughness.

OOZEMASTER

Seeping out of every crack and crevice in the dungeon is some foul, monochromatic substance that adventurers wish wasn't there. Just when they get around the yellow mold, green slime drips from the ceiling. Quite often, such abominations well up naturally, but occasionally they are placed by a more deliberate hand—that of the oozemaster.

The oozemaster is not a class for stable individuals. It involves relating one-on-one with things that relate to nothing at all. Unlike the animal lord's kindred creatures, the oozemaster's charges have nothing to say. No one has yet developed a *speak with ooze* spell—or if someone has, the oozes haven't responded. Given that oozemasters exude everything but confidence, most of them have few sentient friends and even fewer guests. Thus, they tend to gibber and talk to themselves a lot.

Characters of any spellcasting class can become oozemasters, though the class tends to be most appealing to druids, wizards, and—oddly—bards (who usually end up taking another direction before this one gets too creepy). Assassins, already masters of poison, find the benefits of this prestige class highly compatible with their line of work. Clerics, however, had better think about what their followers might say before taking this path. A cleric of Vecna's followers might think him clever for becoming an oozemaster, while followers of a cleric of Pelor might seek a new spiritual leader. Racially, half-orcs and gnomes are more suited to this class than elves and half-elves, most of whom consider themselves too refined for this basest of prestige classes. The drow, of course, are exceptions, since it was they who created this class in the first place. Certainly, the first oozemaster was a dark elf, though how this magic got out of the subterranean depths is a mystery best left unprobed.

Hit Die: d8.

Requirements

To qualify as an oozemaster, a character must fulfill the following criteria.

Skills: Alchemy 4 ranks, Swim 4 ranks.

Feats: Great Fortitude.

Spellcasting: Able to cast 3rd-level arcane or divine spells.

Class Skills

The oozemaster's class skills (and the key ability for each skill) are Alchemy (Int), Concentration (Con), Craft (any) (Int), Disguise (Cha), Heal (Wis), Knowledge (nature) (Int), Profession (any) (Wis), Spellcraft (Int), Swim (Str), and Wilderness Lore (Wis). See Chapter 4 of the *Player's Handbook* for skill descriptions.

Skill Points at Each Level: 4 + Int modifier.

TABLE 5–14: THE OOZEMASTER

Class Level	Base Attack Bonus	Fort Save	Ref Save	Will Save	Special	Spells per Day/Spells Known
1st	+0	+2	+0	+0	Minor oozy touch 1	
2nd	+1	+3	+0	+0	Charisma penalty –1, *oozy glob* 1/day, slithery face	+1 level of existing class
3rd	+2	+3	+1	+1	Minor oozy touch 2	
4th	+3	+4	+1	+1	Charisma penalty –2, *oozy glob* 2/day, malleability	+1 level of existing class
5th	+3	+4	+1	+1	Major oozy touch 1	
6th	+4	+5	+2	+2	Charisma penalty –3, *oozy glob* 3/day, indiscernible anatomy	+1 level of existing class
7th	+5	+5	+2	+2	Major oozy touch 2	
8th	+6	+6	+2	+2	Charisma penalty –4, *oozy glob* 4/day, *slime wave*	+1 level of existing class
9th	+6	+6	+3	+3	Major oozy touch 3	
10th	+7	+7	+3	+3	Charisma penalty –5, *oozy glob* 5/day, one with the ooze	+1 level of existing class

Class Features

The following are class features of the oozemaster prestige class.

Weapon and Armor Proficiency: Oozemasters gain no weapon or armor proficiencies.

Spells per Day/Spells Known: At 2nd level and every other oozemaster level thereafter, the character gains new spells per day (and spells known, if applicable) as if he had also gained a level in a spellcasting class to which he belonged before adding the prestige class. He does not, however, gain any other benefit a character of that class would have gained (additional *wild shape* options, metamagic or item creation feats, or the like). If the character had more than one spellcasting class before becoming an oozemaster, the player must decide to which class to add each oozemaster level for determining spells per day and spells known.

Minor Oozy Touch (Su): At 1st level, the oozemaster's hands can secrete a specific kind of ooze. Choose one kind of oozy touch from the table below. The character may, as a full attack action, make a melee touch attack that has the effect listed for that kind of ooze on the table below. The oozemaster can use this ability as often as desired. At 3rd level, he may choose one additional oozy minor oozy touch.

In addition, the oozemaster is immune to the effects of that particular kind of ooze, even in the form of oozy touch attacks from another oozemaster. Thus, an oozemaster with brown mold oozy touch is immune to the effects of all brown mold. This ability confers no special resistance to similar effects that do not stem from the character's selected kind of ooze, so the aforementioned oozemaster is still subject to cold subdual damage from other sources—such as cold weather.

Minor Oozy Touch Options

Kind	Damage/Effect
Brown mold	1d6 + oozemaster level points of cold subdual damage to flesh
Gray ooze	1d6 + oozemaster level points of acid damage to flesh, metal, or wood
Ochre jelly	1d4 points of stunning damage and 1d4 + oozemaster level points of acid damage to flesh only
Phosphorescent fungus	Touched area emits a soft violet glow as a light spell until the fungus is wiped off

Oozy Glob (**Sp**): The oozemaster can throw a glob of the same material as any oozy touch gained at a previous level, with a range increment of 10 feet. This is treated as a grenadelike weapon. He can throw one oozy glob per round. (A character attacks with a grenadelike weapon as a ranged touch attack. Direct hits deal direct hit damage as noted on the table above. All creatures within 5 feet suffer 1 point of the appropriate splash damage. See Grenadelike Weapon Attacks in Chapter 8 of the *Player's Handbook* for more details.) This ability is usable once per day at 2nd level. Thereafter, the oozemaster gains one additional use per day of this ability for every two oozemaster levels he acquires.

Slithery Face (Su): At 2nd level, the oozemaster learns to manipulate his facial features, gaining a competence bonus equal to his oozemaster level on Disguise checks.

Malleability (Su): At 4th level, the oozemaster can compress his body enough to squeeze through an inch-wide crack. He cannot expand inside a space that offers any resistance, such as an occupied suit of armor.

Major Oozy Touch (Su): At 5th, 7th, and 9th level, the oozemaster chooses a kind of major oozy touch from the table below, or from the choices in the Minor Oozy Touch Options table above. This ability is otherwise identical to minor oozy touch (above).

Major Oozy Touch Options

Kind	Damage/Effect
Black pudding	2d6 + oozemaster level points of acid damage to flesh, metal, wood, or stone
Gelatinous cube	Fort save (DC 15) or paralyzed for a number of rounds equal to 1d6 + oozemaster level
Green slime	1d6 temporary Constitution damage to flesh and 1d6 + oozemaster level points of acid damage to metal or wood
Yellow mold	2d4 points of temporary Constitution damage to flesh (DC 15 Fort save for half)

Indiscernible Anatomy (Su): At 6th level, the oozemaster's anatomy becomes difficult to discern. Treat all critical hits and sneak attacks against him as though he were wearing armor with the *light fortification* power.

Slime Wave (**Sp**): At 8th level, the oozemaster may use *slime wave* (see Chapter 6) once per day as the spell cast by a 13th-level druid.

One with the Ooze: At 10th level, the oozemaster is as slimy as the creatures he favors. His type changes to ooze for determining what effects and items can affect him. He gains the Blindsight feat (hearing-based version, see Chapter 2) and becomes immune to flanking, poison, sleep, paralysis, stunning, and all mind-influencing effects (charms, compulsions, phantasms, patterns, and morale effects). In addition, he is immune to *polymorph other*, but he retains any shapechanging ability he previously possessed.

SHIFTER

The shifter has no form that she calls her own. Instead, she clothes herself in whatever shape is most expedient at the time. While others base their identities largely on their external forms, the shifter actually comes closer to her true self through all her transformations. Of necessity, her sense of self is based not on her outward form, but on her soul, which is truly the only constant about her. It is the inner strength of that soul that enables her to take on any shape and remain herself within.

At first, the shifter can risk only humanoid forms and familiar animal shapes. As she grows more comfortable with her own true shapelessness, however, she can assume more outlandish forms. Eventually, she knows herself so well that she feels just as comfortable in the shape of a completely different creature type as she does in her own. At that point, her past—even her race—becomes irrelevant, since external form no longer matters to her.

TABLE 5–15: THE SHIFTER

Class Level	Base Attack Bonus	Fort Save	Ref Save	Will Save	Special
1st	+0	+2	+2	+0	*Greater wild shape* 1/day (Small or Medium-size, humanoid shape)
2nd	+1	+3	+3	+0	*Greater wild shape* (animal shape, monstrous humanoid shape)
3rd	+2	+3	+3	+1	*Greater wild shape* 3/day (Large or Tiny, beast shape, plant shape)
4th	+3	+4	+4	+1	*Greater wild shape* (giant shape, vermin shape)
5th	+3	+4	+4	+1	*Greater wild shape* 5/day (Diminutive, magical beast shape)
6th	+4	+5	+5	+2	Greater wild shape (aberration shape, ooze shape), supernatural ease
7th	+5	+5	+5	+2	Greater wild shape 7/day (Huge, dragon shape)
8th	+6	+6	+6	+2	Greater wild shape (undead shape, construct shape)
9th	+6	+6	+6	+3	Greater wild shape 9/day (Fine, elemental shape, outsider shape)
10th	+7	+7	+7	+3	Greater wild shape (Gargantuan), evershifting form

The shifter's path is ideal for a spellcaster of any race who has experienced shapeshifting and yearns for more of it. Such a character can be a great force for either good or ill in the world; an evil shifter in particular poses a terrible threat, for she can appear anywhere, in any form. The same opponents may face her again and again, in one shape after another, never realizing that they actually face a single, formless enemy.

Hit Die: d8.

Requirements

To become a shifter, a character must fulfill the following criteria.

Feats: Alertness, Endurance.

Spells: Able to cast 3rd-level spells.

Special: Alternate Form—ust either know *polymorph self* or have a natural alternate form, *alter self, polymorph self, shapechange,* or *wild shape* ability.

Class Skills

The shifter's class skills (and the key ability for each skill) are Animal Empathy (Cha, exclusive skill), Climb (Str), Concentration (Con), Craft (any) (Int), Diplomacy (Cha), Disguise (Cha), Handle Animal (Cha), Hide (Dex), Knowledge (nature) (Int), Listen (Wis), Spot (Wis), Swim (Str), and Wilderness Lore (Wis). See Chapter 4 of the *Player's Handbook* for skill descriptions.

Skill Points at Each Level: 4 + Int modifier.

Class Features

The following are class features of the shifter prestige class.

Weapon and Armor Proficiency: Shifters gain no weapon or armor proficiencies.

Greater Wild Shape (Sp): Beginning at 1st level, the shifter can take the form of another creature. *Greater wild shape* works like *wild shape,* with the following exceptions. As she rises in level, the shifter gains the ability to assume the forms of creatures with types other than animal (see Table 5–15 for details), though she cannot choose a form that normally has more Hit Dice than she herself does. She can designate at the time of the change which pieces of her equipment meld into her new form and which do not. Nonmelded equipment alters its size to match that of her new form, but retains its functionality. The shifter cannot, however, use any equipment unless she has either an appropriate appendage or a magical means of compensating for the lack of one. Any piece of equipment that is separated from her reverts to its original form.

At 1st level, the shifter is limited to humanoid forms of Small and Medium-size. Thereafter, she can use *greater wild shape* two more times per day for every two shifter levels she gains, and her range of available creature sizes and types increases as shown on Table 5–15. When she gains the ability to adopt an undead shape at 8th level, she may become incorporeal if she chooses the form of a creature with that subtype.

If the shifter already has the *wild shape* ability from another class, she may convert her uses per day of *wild shape* to uses per day of *greater wild shape* on a one-for-one basis. She may also mix and match the benefits of the two abilities as desired to gain the maximum advantage for any daily use. Thus, a Drd8/shifter1 has up to four uses per day of *greater wild shape,* and she could use the ability to become a Large humanoid (because an 8th-level druid can become a Large creature and a 1st-level shifter can adopt the form of a humanoid). In the same manner, a Drd8/Shifter2 could become a Large monstrous humanoid if she wished.

Supernatural Ease: At 6th level, the character's *greater wild shape* ability becomes supernatural rather than spell-like. It still requires a standard action and can be suppressed in an *antimagic field*, but its use no longer provokes attacks of opportunity and never requires a Concentration check.

Evershifting Form: At 10th level, the shifter has reached the pinnacle of her shapechanging abilities. From this point on, she can use *greater wild shape* once per round, as a move-equivalent action, as many times per day as she wishes. Her type changes to shapechanger for determining what effects and items can affect her, and she gains darkvision (60 feet), which remains in effect regardless of her form.

In addition, the shifter no longer suffers ability penalties for aging and is not subject to magical aging, though any aging penalties she may already have suffered remain in place. Bonuses still accrue, and the shifter still dies of old age when her time is up.

TAMER OF BEASTS

The ability to bond with animals opens up a new way of life for some druids and rangers. By exploring and strengthening their bonds with their animal companions, they can improve not only the creatures' lives, but their own as well.

Though a character who follows this path is called a tamer of beasts, this is perhaps a misnomer, since he does not truly master, tame, or domesticate his companions. Rather, through his magic and his overwhelming concern for his charges, he can make them tougher and more intelligent. Ultimately, he can even converse with them as equals.

This class appeals primarily to rangers and druids. A member of another class may feel some longing for the path of the tamer, but without first developing a deep relationship with an animal, it is impossible to embrace this prestige class. Tamers of beasts have been known among all races. Elves, half-elves, and gnomes are the most likely to take up this path because of their affinity for nature, and dwarves are the least likely. The philosophy of a tamer of beasts is compatible with any alignment.

Unlike most druids, tamers of beasts usually reside close to civilization. Some NPC tamers of beasts conceal their special relationships with animals and beasts by finding employment in a common circus or zoo. More typically, however, tamers of beasts adopt creatures that are threatened by growing populations of humanoids, protecting and shielding them from harm. If these creatures have suffered greatly at the hands of humanoids, tamers of beasts may also try to exact retribution.

Hit Die: d8.

Requirements

To become a tamer of beasts, a character must fulfill the following criteria.

Skills: Animal Empathy 10 ranks.
Feats: Skill Focus (Animal Empathy).
Spells: Able to cast *animal friendship*.

Class Skills

The tamer of beasts's class skills (and the key ability for each skill) are Animal Empathy (Cha, exclusive skill), Climb (Str), Concentration (Con), Craft (any) (Int), Diplomacy (Cha), Handle Animal (Cha), Heal (Wis),

TABLE 5–16: THE TAMER OF BEASTS

Class Level	Base Attack Bonus	Fort Save	Reflex Save	Will Save	Special	Spells per Day/Spells Known
1st	+0	+2	+2	+0	Animal mastery, Int 4	
2nd	+1	+3	+3	+0	Empathic link	
3rd	+2	+3	+3	+1	Blood bond, Int 6, natural armor +2	+1 level of existing class
4th	+3	+4	+4	+1	Animal senses (hearing, smell), speak with master	
5th	+3	+4	+4	+1	*Beast mastery*, Int 8	
6th	+4	+5	+5	+2	Natural armor +4, share saving throws	+1 level of existing class
7th	+5	+5	+5	+2	Animal senses (vision), Int 10, share spells	
8th	+6	+6	+6	+2	*Command creatures of kind*	
9th	+6	+6	+6	+3	Int 12, *magical beast mastery*, natural armor +6	+1 level of existing class
10th	+7	+7	+7	+3	Inspire greatness	

Hide (Dex), Intuit Direction (Wis), Knowledge (nature) (Int), Jump (Str), Listen (Wis), Ride (Dex), Scry (Int, exclusive skill), Spellcraft (Int), Spot (Wis), Swim (Str), and Wilderness Lore (Wis). See Chapter 4 of the *Player's Handbook* for skill descriptions.

Skill Points at Each Level: 4 + Int modifier.

Class Features

The following are class features of the tamer of beasts prestige class. All modifications and bonuses granted to the tamer's animal companions are immediately negated upon their release or the death of the tamer.

Weapon and Armor Proficiency: Tamers of beasts gain no proficiency with any weapon or armor.

Spells per Day/Spells Known: At 3rd, 6th, and 9th level, the tamer of beasts gains new spells per day (and spells known, if applicable) as if he had also gained a level in a spellcasting class to which he belonged before adding the prestige class. He does not, however, gain any other benefit a character of that class would have gained (additional *wild shape* options, metamagic or item creation feats, or the like). If the character had more than one spellcasting class before becoming a tamer of beasts, the player must decide to which class to add each tamer of beasts level for determining spells per day and spells known.

Animal Mastery: Beginning at 1st level, the tamer of beasts can have animal companions whose Hit Dice total no more than the sum of twice his tamer of beasts level plus twice his caster level for *animal friendship*. For example, a Drd7/tamer of beasts3 can have up to 20 Hit Dice of animal companions. No individual animal companion can have more Hit Dice than the tamer of beasts does.

Intelligence: Through constant exposure to the tamer of beasts, his animal companions become more intelligent than the average for their species. When the tamer of beasts is 1st level, the Intelligence score of each of his companions rises to 4, and the creature's type changes to magical beast. This minimum Intelligence score rises by 2 points for every two tamer of beasts levels the character gains thereafter. This improved Intelligence may allow the companion to follow more complex instructions than it could before. Also, the tamer of beasts can teach each companion three tricks per point of Intelligence it has (see the Animal Companions sidebar in Chapter 2 of the Dungeon Master's Guide and Chapter 2 of this book for more information on training animals).

Empathic Link (Su): At 2nd level, the tamer of beasts gains an empathic link that allows him to communicate telepathically with his companions to a maximum distance of one mile. The tamer of beasts and the companion can understand one another as if a *speak with animals* effect were in force. Of course, intelligence is still a factor in the content of such conversations, and misunderstandings on that basis are still possible.

Blood Bond: At 3rd level, each of the tamer of beast's companions gains a +2 bonus on all attack rolls, checks, and saves after witnessing any threat or harm to the tamer. This bonus lasts as long as the threat is immediate and apparent.

Natural Armor: Also when the tamer of beasts reaches 3rd level, each of his companions gains a +2 enhancement bonus to its natural armor. This bonus rises to +4 at 6th level and +6 at 9th level.

Animal Senses (Su): At 4th level, the tamer of beasts can hear through any designated companion's ears or smell through its nose. At 7th level, he can see through a companion's eyes. The tamer can activate his animal senses as a standard action, and he does not lose the ability to sense events around him by doing so.

Speak with Master (Ex): Also at 4th level, the tamer of beasts gains the ability to communicate verbally with his companions in a language of his own. Creatures other than his companions cannot understand this communication without magical aid.

Beast Mastery **(Sp):** At 5th level, the tamer of beasts can use the *animal friendship* spell to affect beasts in addition to animals, regardless of the target's Intelligence score. Beast companions count against the tamer's total allowed Hit Dice of companions just as animals do.

Share Saving Throws: When the tamer of beasts reaches 6th level, his companions can use either his base saves or their own, mixing and matching to gain the highest value for each.

Share Spells: At 7th level, the tamer of beasts may have any spell he casts on himself also affect one companion of his choice within 5 feet of him. A spell with a duration other than instantaneous stops affecting the companion if it moves farther than 5 feet away, and the effect is not reinstated even if that companion again comes within 5 feet of the character before the spell's duration expires. Additionally, the tamer may cast a spell with a target of "You" on a companion (as if the spell had a range of touch) instead of on himself. The tamer of beasts and the companion can share even spells that do not normally affect creatures of the companion's type.

Command Creatures of Kind **(Sp):** When the tamer of beasts reaches 8th level, his companions can use *command* as a spell-like ability at will against other creatures of their kind. This ability affects only creatures with fewer Hit Dice than that particular companion has. Each companion can use this ability once per day per two levels of the tamer, and the ability functions just like the spell *command* (for purposes of this spell, the companion can make itself understood).

Magical Beast Mastery **(Sp):** At 9th level, the tamer of beasts can use the *animal friendship* spell to affect magical beasts in addition to beasts and animals, regardless of the target's Intelligence. Magical beast companions count as double their own Hit Dice against the tamer's total allowed Hit Dice of companions. For example, a cockatrice with 5 Hit Dice accounts for 10 Hit Dice of companions.

Inspire Greatness (Su): At 10th level, the tamer of beasts can grant extra fighting ability to all his companions within 30 feet. An inspired companion gains +2 Hit Dice (d10s that grant temporary hit points), a +2 competence bonus on attacks, and a +1 competence bonus on Fortitude saves. Apply the companion's Constitution modifier, if any, to each bonus Hit Die. These extra Hit Dice count as regular Hit Dice for determining the effects of spells such as *sleep*. The tamer of beasts can inspire his companions once per day, and the effects last for 5 rounds. This is a supernatural, mind-affecting, enchantment ability.

TEMPEST

The tempest is the point of calm within a whirling barrier of deadly blades. Poets use colorful terms such as dancer to describe the movement of a tempest and her two blades, but mastery of this fighting style is not about dancing. Nor is it about impressing anyone—least of all poets. The tempest focuses on learning the ultimate secrets of two-weapon fighting for a single purpose—the destruction of her enemies.

Typically hardy individualists, tempests rarely learn their skills through any sort of formal training. Instead, they master their art though constant application of its disciplines and experimentation on their foes. Similarly, no matter how famous tempests become, it's rare for them to take on students. Their art, they say, is one that can be learned but never taught.

This prestige class is open to all classes and races. Though tempests are rare, every humanoid race has boasted at least a few. Elves make for nimble, clever tempests whose dexterity works to their advantage. Dwarves, perhaps because they favor heavy armor and heavy weapons, are the least likely characters to become tempests. Even members of the smaller races can find the tempest's path appealing.

Hit Die: d10.

Requirements

To qualify as a tempest, a character must fulfill the following criteria.

Base Attack Bonus: +9.

Feats: Ambidexterity, Dodge, Mobility, Spring Attack, Two-Weapon Fighting, and Weapon Finesse (any) or Weapon Focus (any).

Class Skills

The tempest's class skills (and the key ability for each skill) are Climb (Str), Intimidate (Cha), Jump (Str), Listen (Wis), Ride (Dex), and Wilderness Lore (Wis). See Chapter 4 of the *Player's Handbook* for skill descriptions.

Skill Points at Each Level: 2 + Int modifier.

Class Features

The following are class features of the tempest prestige class.

Weapon and Armor Proficiency: Tempests gain no weapon or armor proficiencies.

Improved Two-Weapon Fighting: Beginning at 1st level, a tempest can fight with two weapons as if she had the Improved Two-Weapon Fighting feat when she is wearing light armor or no armor. She loses this ability when fighting in medium or heavy armor, or when using a double weapon (such as a two-bladed sword).

Off-Hand Parry: At 2nd level, the tempest gains Off-Hand Parry as a bonus feat. As she gains tempest levels, her AC bonus from this feat increases, rising to +4 at 4th level and to +6 at 6th level.

Greater Two-Weapon Fighting: At 5th level, a tempest can fight with two weapons as if she had the Greater Two-Weapon Fighting feat when she is wearing light armor or no armor. She loses this ability when fighting in medium or heavy armor, or when using a double weapon (such as a two-bladed sword).

Absolute Ambidexterity: Beginning at 8th level, the tempest's attack penalties for fighting with two weapons lessen by 2 when she is wearing light armor or no armor. Thus, if she fights with a light weapon in her off hand, she suffers no penalties on her attack rolls for

TABLE 5–17: THE TEMPEST

Class Level	Base Attack Bonus	Fort Save	Ref Save	Will Save	Special
1st	+1	+2	+0	+0	Improved Two-Weapon Fighting
2nd	+2	+3	+0	+0	Off-Hand Parry +2
3rd	+3	+3	+1	+1	
4th	+4	+4	+1	+1	Off-Hand Parry +4
5th	+5	+4	+1	+1	Greater Two-Weapon Fighting
6th	+6	+5	+2	+2	
7th	+7	+5	+2	+2	Off-Hand Parry +6
8th	+8	+6	+2	+2	Absolute ambidexterity
9th	+9	+6	+3	+3	
10th	+10	+7	+3	+3	Supreme two-weapon fighting

fighting with two weapons. (If the off-hand weapon is not light, she suffers a –2 penalty on attack rolls with both her primary hand and her off hand.)

Supreme Two-Weapon Fighting: At 10th level, a tempest gains an additional attack with her off-hand weapon when she is wearing light armor or no armor. In addition to the three attacks she already has each round with her off-hand weapon (for Improved Two-Weapon Fighting and Greater Two-Weapon Fighting) at penalties of 0, –5, and –10, respectively, she is also entitled to a fourth attack with her off-hand weapon at a –15 penalty (see Table 8–2: Two-Weapon Fighting Penalties in the *Player's Handbook*). She loses this special ability when fighting in medium or heavy armor, or when using a double weapon (such as a two-bladed sword).

VERDANT LORD

Saying the verdant lord has a green thumb is like calling a red dragon a creature with a slight affinity for fire. The verdant lord is the final defender of the forest. He has left behind the druid's search for global understanding of nature's secrets to focus all his energies on the world's plant life.

Elven and half-elven druids are the most likely characters to embrace the role of the verdant lord. Druids of other races, rangers, and the occasional priest of Obad-Hai or Ehlonna have also been known to adopt this prestige class. It's almost impossible for characters without such ties to become verdant lords because they have neither the interest in nor the required understanding of seeds, saplings, and trees.

Since most verdant lords have little use for civilization, they tend to be loners, watching the years pass by from their groves. Adventuring verdant lords are rare, but those who do exist are marvelous to behold. They tend to take their gardens with them, often bringing several plant creatures, such as animated trees and treants, along on adventures. Verdant lords tend to be soft-spoken, easygoing individuals—right up until someone lights a torch and threatens living plants.

Hit Die: d8.

Requirements

To qualify as a verdant lord, a character must fulfill the following criteria.

Alignment: Any nonevil.

Skills: Profession (herbalist) 8 ranks, Wilderness Lore 8 ranks.

Feats: Plant Control, Plant Defiance.
Spells: Able to cast *control plants*.

Class Skills

The verdant lord's class skills (and the key ability for each skill) are Animal Empathy (Cha), Climb (Str), Concentration (Con), Craft (any) (Int), Diplomacy (Cha), Disguise (Cha), Handle Animal (Cha), Heal (Wis), Hide (Dex), Intuit Direction (Wis), Knowledge (nature) (Int), Listen (Wis), Scry (Int), Spellcraft (Int), Swim (Str), and Wilderness Lore (Wis). See Chapter 4 of the *Player's Handbook* for skill descriptions.

Skill Points at Each Level: 4 + Int modifier.

Class Features

The following are class features of the verdant lord prestige class.

TABLE 5–18: THE VERDANT LORD

Class Level	Base Attack Bonus	Fort Save	Reflex Save	Will Save	Special	Spells per Day/Spells Known
1st	+1	+2	+0	+2	Create Infusion	+1 level of existing class
2nd	+2	+3	+0	+3	Expert infusion, sun sustenance	+1 level of existing class
3rd	+3	+3	+1	+3	Spontaneity	+1 level of existing class
4th	+4	+4	+1	+4	Plant facility	+1 level of existing class
5th	+5	+4	+1	+4	Fast healing	+1 level of existing class
6th	+6	+5	+2	+5	*Treant wild shape*	+1 level of existing class
7th	+7	+5	+2	+5		+1 level of existing class
8th	+8	+6	+2	+6	*Animate tree*	+1 level of existing class
9th	+9	+6	+3	+6		+1 level of existing class
10th	+10	+7	+3	+7	Gaea's embrace	+1 level of existing class

Weapon and Armor Proficiency: Verdant lords gain no weapon or armor proficiencies.

Spells per Day/Spells Known: At each verdant lord level, the character gains new spells per day (and spells known, if applicable) as if he had also gained a level in a spellcasting class to which he belonged before adding the prestige class. He does not, however, gain any other benefit a character of that class would have gained (additional *wild shape* options, metamagic or item creation feats, or the like). If the character had more than one spellcasting class before becoming a verdant lord, the player must decide to which class to add each verdant lord level for determining spells per day and spells known.

Create Infusion: At 1st level, the verdant lord gains Create Infusion as a bonus feat.

Expert Infusion: At 2nd level, the character can automatically identify the spell contained in an infusion and the caster level of that spell (see Infusions in Chapter 3). He also gains a bonus equal to his verdant lord level on both Profession (herbalist) checks and Wilderness Lore checks related to plants, including the use of this skill to forage for herbs.

Sun Sustenance (Ex): Also at 2nd level, the verdant lord gains the ability to draw energy from the sun. As long as he spends at least 4 hours of the day outdoors, he can draw sustenance from the sun itself, and thus he requires no food that day. He still thirsts, however, and needs the standard amount of water to survive.

Spontaneity: Beginning at 3rd level, the verdant lord can channel stored spell energy into certain healing spells that he hasn't prepared ahead of time. This works like the cleric's spontaneous casting ability, with the following exceptions. He can "lose" a prepared spell to cast any *regenerate* spell of the same level or lower (a *regenerate* spell is any one with "regenerate" in its name; these spells are presented in Chapter 6). For example, a verdant lord who has prepared *faerie fire* (a 1st-level spell) may lose that spell to cast *regenerate light wounds* (also a 1st-level spell) instead. Domain spells, if the character has access to them, cannot be converted into *regenerate* spells.

Plant Facility: At 4th level, the verdant lord can rebuke or command plants with Plant Control as if he were three levels higher than the actual caster level he uses to determine the benefits of that feat. This means that he can also command 3 additional HD of plant creatures.

Fast Healing: At 5th level, the verdant lord gains Fast Healing as a bonus feat.

Treant Wild Shape (Sp): Beginning at 6th level, the verdant lord can use *wild shape* to take the form of a treant and back again once per day. This ability otherwise works like *wild shape*. Since a treant has a voice and manipulative appendages, the verdant lord can cast spells normally while in *treant wild shape*.

Animate Tree (Sp): At 8th level, a verdant lord can animate a tree within 180 feet of him once per day. It takes a full round for a tree to uproot itself; thereafter it has a speed of 30 feet and fights as a treant with respect to attacks and damage. The animated tree gains a number of bonus Hit Dice equal to the number of verdant lord levels the character possesses. Though its Intelligence score is only 2 while animated, the tree automatically understands the verdant lord's commands. The character can return the animated tree to its normal state at will, and it automatically returns to its normal state if it dies or if the verdant lord who animated it is incapacitated or moves out of range. Once the tree returns to its normal state by any means, the verdant lord cannot animate another tree for 24 hours.

Gaea's Embrace: At 10th level, the verdant lord permanently becomes a plant creature, though all forms of *wild shape* that the character could previously use remain available to him. His type changes to plant, and as a result he gains low-light vision, is immune to poison, sleep, paralysis, stunning, and polymorphing, and is not subject to critical hits or mind-influencing effects (charms, compulsions, phantasms, patterns, or morale effects). He no longer suffers penalties for aging and cannot be magically aged. Any aging penalties he may already have suffered, however, remain in place. Bonuses still accrue, and the verdant lord still dies of old age when his time is up.

Organized Druids: The Order of the Verdant Grove
"You cannot decide to be pure, novice."
— An elder of the Order, to a young Vadania

The Order of the Verdant Grove is a loose organization of about one hundred seventy druids and verdant lords who share certain interests and are committed to gaining and disseminating information about nature. The organization doesn't have much of a hierarchy, and the typical member also owes allegiance to some other druid circle in his or her local area. Many druids have heard of the Order of the Verdant Grove, but they often assume it is the name of some regional druid circle.

An applicant for membership must be invited and sponsored by a current member, and all available members periodically vote on whether to admit the current applicants. Once accepted, the new member (called an initiate) undergoes a rite of acceptance during which he or she receives a hoop earring bearing a green orb. Not only does this allow members to identify one another, but it is also a *pearl of power* (1st-level). The initiate is expected to make a donation that covers the cost of creating this talisman.

What makes the order different from other organizations is that its members intentionally spread themselves out over the world. A few are just as tied to a single sacred grove or woodland as any other druid or verdant lord would be, but most are travelers. They may be active adventurers out to address wrongs in the world or scholars in search of information that they can share with fellow members.

In this sense, the Order of the Verdant Grove is the closest thing druids have to a ring of spies. Of course, most of the information that its members acquire and disseminate within the organization would bore a typical spy to tears. They share information about their explorations of distant lands, discoveries of new creatures (animals and beasts), and of previously unknown wonders of the natural world. They also share knowledge of new spells and magic items that have come into use. Members of the Order of the Verdant Grove are encouraged to share whatever information they discover, but they are required to report on new druid communities, *standing stones*, or druid circles that they find. The Order of the Verdant Grove must occasionally act as a messenger service between independent druid circles in times of regional or greater crisis, so it's important for its members to know where the druids of the world can be found.

The origins of the order hearken back to a day when a druid circle broke apart following a war against a wizard cabal and its demonic servants. Many members of the original group became verdant lords—perhaps from a desire to form a deeper and more personal bond with nature after being dragged into a fight against outsiders. Thus, they tended to be somewhat reclusive. Now verdant lords have become rare, and they are found only among the older members of the organization. The druids and the verdant lords in the order do not compete—they share too much to become embroiled in petty rivalries.

WATCH DETECTIVE

When thieves and murderers strike in the night, citizens always wonder whether anyone can track down the perpetrators and set things straight. When the watch detective is on the case, they can rest easy.

The watch detective specializes in solving mysteries. Using a battery of clue-ferreting skills and abilities, he evaluates and discards possibilities until only one remains—the truth. The Rule of Evidence to which he ascribes (see sidebar) restrains him from using his gifts to gain the truth through unfair means, demanding that he focus only on tangible facts as proof. Of course, once the watch detective solves the mystery, it's likely that the guilty party won't want to be brought to justice. Thus, it's also important for the watch detective to know the techniques of combat.

Fighters and warriors make up the bulk of any city watch force, but watch detectives often begin their careers as rangers or rogues. The vast majority of the rangers who opt for this prestige class are urban rangers (see Chapter 1). Wizards, sorcerers, clerics, and bards make especially good watch detectives when they can qualify for the class, though they may find that the Rule of Evidence hampers their ability to get at the truth. Elves find this lifestyle especially gratifying because it celebrates the mind in a not-too-subtle show of intellectual superiority. Gnomes and halflings have the inquisitive streak necessary for this career, and they have established many an effective city watch force in lands

where their size would otherwise be a detriment.
Hit Die: d8.

Requirements

To become a watch detective, a character must fulfill the following criteria.
Alignment: Any nonevil.
Skills: Gather Information 4 ranks, Knowledge (any) 4 ranks, Search 8 ranks.
Feats: Track.
Special: The watch detective must honor the Rule of Evidence (see sidebar). If he abandons this code, he loses all special abilities of the prestige class until he retrains for six months under a local authority.

Class Skills

The watch detective's class skills (and the key ability for each skill) are Appraise (Int), Bluff (Cha), Climb (Str), Craft (any) (Int), Diplomacy (Cha), Disable Device (Dex), Disguise (Cha), Forgery (Dex), Gather Information (Cha), Heal (Wis), Hide (Dex), Innuendo (Wis), Intimidate (Cha), Intuit Direction (Wis), Jump (Str), Knowledge (any) (Int), Listen (Wis), Move Silently (Dex), Open Lock (Dex), Profession (Wis), Ride (Dex), Search (Int), Sense Motive (Wis), Spot (Wis), Swim (Str), and Use Rope (Dex). See Chapter 4 of the *Player's Handbook* for skill descriptions.

Skill Points at Each Level: 6 + Int modifier.

Class Features

The following are class features of the watch detective prestige class.
Weapon and Armor Proficiency: Watch detectives are proficient with light armor and simple weapons.
City Watch Training: At 1st level, the watch detective gains a +2 insight bonus on all Listen, Search, Sense Motive, and Spot checks.
Expertise: At 2nd level, the character gains the Expertise feat, regardless of his Intelligence score.

TABLE 5–19: THE WATCH DETECTIVE

Class Level	Base Attack Bonus	Fort Save	Ref Save	Will Save	Special
1st	+0	+0	+2	+2	City watch training
2nd	+1	+0	+3	+3	Expertise, obsessive specialty, profile
3rd	+2	+1	+3	+3	Cooperative interrogation, superior disarming
4th	+3	+1	+4	+4	*Deductive augury* 1/day, skill synergy
5th	+3	+1	+4	+4	No subdual penalty, sense secret doors
6th	+4	+2	+5	+5	*Locate object*
7th	+5	+2	+5	+5	*Deductive augury* 2/day, improved subdual
8th	+6	+2	+6	+6	Forensics
9th	+6	+3	+6	+6	*Discern lies, locate creature*
10th	+7	+3	+7	+7	*Deductive augury* 3/day, instant knowledge

Obsessive Specialty: When the watch detective reaches 2nd level, he obsessively seeks knowledge about a particular topic. Choose one Knowledge skill for his specialty. The character thereafter gains a bonus equal to his watch detective level on all Knowledge checks of this sort.

Profile (Ex): Also at 2nd level, the watch detective may compose an image of someone accused of a crime. By making a successful Gather Information check (DC 15) when talking with a witness to a crime, the watch detective can gain a roughly accurate mental picture of the perpetrator, even if the witness did not see him or her. The character may, if desired, try to commit this image to paper using the Craft (painting) skill. Either a verbal or a visual depiction grants a +2 insight bonus on any further Gather Information checks made when dealing with witnesses to that crime or persons acquainted with the perpetrator.

Cooperative Interrogation: At 3rd level, when the watch detective succeeds in a Bluff check against someone, he automatically grants any one other person a +4 circumstance bonus on one Intimidate check against that same target for 1 round. When the watch detective succeeds in an Intimidate check, he can give a similar +4 circumstance bonus on someone else's Bluff check. (Two watch inspectors can support each other with this maneuver for many rounds.)

Superior Disarming: At 3rd level, the watch detective is always considered armed when making a disarm attempt, and he gains a +4 bonus on any attack roll made to disarm an opponent.

Deductive Augury (Sp): The watch detective may ask for a hint to a mystery, puzzle, or trap. As a standard action, the player makes an assertion that can be true or untrue (such as "The half-orc did it" or "If I pull the red lever, the door will open"). The DM makes a secret percentile roll (chance of success = 70% + 1% per watch inspector level). If the roll is successful, the Dungeon Master gives the player a correct "true" or "untrue" answer to the assertion, though no reason need be given for why the response is correct. If the roll fails, the DM provides no information. The Dungeon Master is always free to determine that the watch detective doesn't have enough information to make an educated guess, but in this case the attempt doesn't count

against the allowed uses per day of the ability. The watch detective can use this ability once per day at 4th level. Thereafter, he gains one extra use per day for every three additional watch detective levels gained.

Skill Synergy: At 4th level, the watch detective may choose one of the following skill combinations: Bluff-Gather Information, Bluff-Diplomacy, Climb-Move Silently, Diplomacy-Gather Information, Disguise-Gather Information, Gather Information-Sense Motive, Hide-Move Silently, Listen-Read Lips, Listen-Spot, Sense Motive-Spot, Spot-Disable Device, Spot-Open Lock, or Spot-Search. If he has at least 5 ranks in both of the selected skills, he gains a +2 synergy bonus on checks involving both.

No Subdual Penalty (Ex): At 5th level, the watch detective can deal subdual damage with a weapon that deals normal damage without suffering a –4 penalty on the attack.

Sense Secret Doors (Ex): A 5th-level or higher watch detective who merely passes within 5 feet of a secret or concealed door is entitled to a Search check to notice it as if he were actively looking for it. An elven watch detective gains a +2 insight bonus on any Search check made to find a secret or concealed door.

Locate Object (Sp): At 6th level, the watch detective can produce an effect identical to that of a *locate object* spell cast by a sorcerer of his watch detective level.

Improved Subdual (Ex): At 7th level, the watch detective adds his Intelligence bonus on the subdual damage he deals whenever he makes an attack that can cause subdual damage only.

Forensics (Su): With a successful Search check (DC 20), an 8th-level or higher watch detective can discern the cause of death of any corpse he examines. Given time, he may take 20 on this roll. Success indicates that he knows what killed the person, the size and approximate strength of any attacker responsible, and any other key information the DM wishes to impart.

Discern Lies (Sp): At 9th level, the watch detective can produce an effect identical to that of a *discern lies* spell cast by a sorcerer of his watch detective level. This ability is usable once per day.

Locate Creature (Sp): At 9th level, the watch detective can produce an effect identical to that of a *locate creature* spell cast by a sorcerer of his watch detective level. This ability is usable once per day.

Instant Knowledge (Su): Once per day, a 10th-level watch detective may make an Intelligence check (DC 20). He may not take 10 or take 20 on this check. If successful, he gains a +10 insight bonus on one Knowledge check of any category. If he has no ranks in that particular Knowledge skill, he may make the check untrained.

WINDRIDER

The windrider is a specialist in mounted combat, but hers is no ordinary mount. The creature she rides is at least unusual and often rare—sometimes even bizarre. Although an experienced windrider can ride anything that runs, swims, or flies, the typical member of this prestige class settles on one particular kind of mount as a personal favorite.

Some windriders are no more than swaggering, arrogant adventurers looking for a good fight. Perhaps their pride is justified, considering the creatures they've turned into mounts. Many, however, are just as happy to sit back and tell stories of how they got their mounts and the adventures they've had since, no matter who buys the ale. The typical windrider cheerfully shares her knowledge about her various mounts with those who seek to ride similar creatures.

Since the skills they develop vary as widely as the abilities and natures of their mounts, windriders are a very independent bunch. Thus, they rarely form or belong to close-knit groups. Even a paladin windrider tends to be something of a knight-errant.

All races have produced windriders, though the class is particularly popular with humans and giants. Rangers, paladins, fighters, and barbarians all make excellent windriders because they can easily accumulate the prerequisites.

Hit Die: d10.

Requirements

To become a windrider, a character must fulfill the following criteria.

Base Attack Bonus: +5.

Skills: Handle Animal 8 ranks, Knowledge (nature) 6 ranks, Ride 8 ranks.

Feats: Mounted Combat.

Special: Must have a mount.

Class Skills

The windrider's class skills (and the key ability for each skill) are Balance (Dex), Concentration (Con), Craft (any) (Int), Diplomacy (Cha), Handle Animal (Cha), Heal (Wis), Jump (Str), Knowledge (nature), Profession (any) (Wis), and Ride (Dex). See Chapter 4 of the *Player's Handbook* for skill descriptions.

Skill Points at Each Level: 2 + Int modifier.

Class Features

The following are class features of the windrider prestige class. For the abilities described below, a mount is a creature that fits the criteria in the What's a Mount? section below.

Weapon and Armor Proficiency: Windriders are proficient with all simple and martial weapons, all types of armor, and shields.

Spells per Day: A windrider can cast a small number of divine spells. Her spells are based on Wisdom, so casting any given spell requires a Wisdom score of at least 10 + the spell's level. The DC for saving throws against these spells is 10 + spell level + the windrider's Wisdom modifier. When the table indicates that the windrider is entitled to 0 spells of a given level (such as 0 1st-level spells at 1st level), she gets only those bonus spells that her Wisdom score allows. A windrider prepares and casts spells just like a druid does, but she must choose them from the spell list, below.

Appraise Mount (Ex): At 1st level, a windrider can compare two mounts of the same kind and tell at a glance which one is superior (stronger, faster, more intelligent, better stamina, and so on). If desired, the windrider can also conduct a point-by-point comparison of two mounts. By spending 1 round examining both, she can determine which has the higher score in any single ability of her choice. After a second round of study, a windrider familiar with that kind of creature can also determine whether each mount's score in that ability is average, above average, or below average for the species. After a third round of study, the windrider can tell how extreme that ability score is—that is, whether the modifier it generates is more than 4 points higher or lower than the average for that species. The appraise mount ability never produces a numerical rating; DMs must describe the windrider's findings.

TABLE 5–20: THE WINDRIDER

Class Level	Base Attack Bonus	Fort Save	Ref Save	Will Save	Special	Spells per Day			
						1st	2nd	3rd	4th
1st	+1	+2	+0	+2	Appraise mount, chosen mount, empathic link, mount proficiency 4 HD	0	—	—	—
2nd	+2	+3	+0	+3	Mount assistance, mount feat 1	1	—	—	—
3rd	+3	+3	+1	+3	Bonus feat, mount healing	1	0	—	—
4th	+4	+4	+1	+4	Mount proficiency 8 HD	1	1	—	—
5th	+5	+4	+1	+4	Mount feat 2, mount friendship	1	1	0	—
6th	+6	+5	+2	+5	Mount proficiency 12 HD	1	1	1	—
7th	+7	+5	+2	+5	Bonus feat, mount link	2	1	1	0
8th	+8	+6	+2	+6	Mount proficiency 16 HD	2	1	1	1
9th	+9	+6	+3	+6	Mount feat 3, mount luck	2	2	1	1
10th	+10	+7	+3	+7	Mount proficiency (all)	2	2	2	1

Chosen Mount: The windrider may designate any one mount she has previously ridden as her chosen mount. This creature may not be a bonded companion (such as a familiar, paladin's mount, or animal companion) to anyone else at the time, and if its Intelligence score is 3 or higher, it must also agree to this relationship. The windrider can use any means desired to obtain this agreement—the Diplomacy skill, bribery, or even magical persuasion—but the creature must be willing.

The windrider must spend a minimum of three days training her chosen mount before any benefits accrue. Thereafter, the creature gains the advantages listed on Table 5–21 based on the windrider's level. The creature retains its own type and gains no abilities other than those listed, though it is considered a bonded companion for the *unbond* ability (see the blighter prestige class earlier in this chapter).

TABLE 5–21: THE WINDRIDER'S MOUNT

Windrider Level	Bonus Hit Dice	Natural Armor Bonus	Strength Adjustment
1–3	+2	+4	+2
4–6	+4	+6	+2
7–9	+6	+8	+4
10	+8	+10	+4

Windrider Level: The character's windrider levels only. If the mount suffers a level drain, treat the creature as the mount of a lower-level windrider.

Bonus Hit Dice: These are extra eight-sided (d8) Hit Dice, each of which provides a Constitution modifier, as normal. Remember that extra Hit Dice also improve the mount's base attack and base save bonuses.

Natural Armor: The amount by which the creature's natural armor bonus is increased.

Strength Adjustment: Add this figure to the mount's Strength score.

The windrider may have only one chosen mount at a time, and either party may sever this relationship at any time without penalty. Once it ends, the mount loses the benefits it gained according to Table 5–21. If the chosen mount is a paladin's warhorse, the rules in the Paladin's Mount sidebar in the *Player's Handbook* supersede those given here.

Empathic Link (Su): The windrider has an empathic link with her chosen mount. This ability works like the empathic link that a paladin has with her mount (see Paladin in Chapter 3 of the *Player's Handbook*).

Mount Proficiency: At 1st level, the windrider gains a +2 competence bonus on any check to avoid being unseated while riding her chosen mount. In addition, she can ride any mount with 4 Hit Dice or less at the full benefit of her Ride skill, suffering neither the –2 penalty for riding similar mounts nor the –5 penalty for riding dissimilar mounts. The Hit Dice of the mounts to which this latter benefit applies increase with windrider level: 8 Hit Dice at 4th level, 12 Hit Dice at 6th level, 16 Hit Dice at 8th level, and any mount at 10th level.

Mount Assistance (Ex): At 2nd level, the windrider can assist any mount she is riding in one of two ways per use of the ability. First, she can use the cooperation and aid another rules (Chapter 4 and Chapter 8 respectively of the *Player's Handbook*) to provide a +4 bonus

(double the usual amount) to her mount's Armor Class or on any single attack roll or any skill or ability check the mount attempts. Alternatively, she can provide her mount a +10 competence bonus to speed for 1 full round. Mount assistance is usable once per round and requires a standard action.

Mount Feat: At 2nd level, a windrider can grant her chosen mount one bonus feat from the Mount Feats list, below. This feat does not count against the creature's normal feat capacity, though it must still meet all prerequisites for it, as noted in the appropriate feat description in this book or Chapter 5 of the *Player's Handbook*. To grant a bonus feat, the windrider must spend one month training the mount. The windrider can bestow a second bonus feat on the same mount at 5th level, and a third at 9th level. These additional bonus feats require the same training time as the first. The windrider can train only one mount at a time.

Bonus Feat: At 3rd and again at 7th level, a windrider may take a bonus feat from the windrider bonus feats list below. This feat does not count against the windrider's normal feat capacity, though she must still meet all prerequisites for it, as noted in the appropriate feat description in this book or Chapter 5 of the *Player's Handbook*.

Mount Healing (Ex): At 3rd level, A windrider gains a +4 competence bonus on any Heal checks she makes on a creature of the same species as her current mount and a +2 bonus on any Heal checks made on other creatures capable of serving her as mounts (see sidebar).

Mount Friendship: At 5th level, the windrider gains a +4 circumstance bonus on Animal Empathy and Diplo-

TABLE 5–22: HANDLE ANIMAL DCs FOR TRAINING MOUNTS

Creature Is . . .	Example	Task Counts as . . .	Handle Animal DC
Domestic animal of a kind typically used for riding	Horse	Teach an animal tasks	15
Domestic animal of a kind not typically used for riding	Dog	Teach an animal unusual tasks	20
Wild animal	Tiger	Train a wild animal	20 + creature's HD
Beast	Tyrannosaurus	Train a beast	25 + creature's HD
Any other creature of Intelligence 2 or lower*	Carrion crawler	Train a beast	25 + creature's HD

*Windrider only

macy checks when dealing with creatures of the same species as her current mount and a +2 bonus when dealing with any other creatures capable of serving her as mounts (see sidebar).

Mount Link (Su): At 7th level, the windrider can establish an empathic link (see above) with any mount that she rides for at least 1 hour, as long as its Intelligence score is at least 1. She can maintain only one such link at a time with a mount other than her chosen one.

Mount Luck (Su): At 9th level, the windrider can, as a free action, confer a luck bonus equivalent to her Charisma bonus on the saving throw of any mount within 60 feet with which she has an empathic link.

Windrider Bonus Feats List

The following bonus feats are available to mounts and windriders.

Mount Feats: Alertness, Blind-Fight, Combat Reflexes, Dodge, Dragon's Toughness**, Dwarf's Toughness**, Endurance, Flyby Attack**, Giant's Toughness**, Great Fortitude, Hover**, Improved Critical*, Improved Flight**, Improved Initiative, Iron Will, Lightning Reflexes, Multiattack**, Power Attack, Run, Snatch**, Toughness**, Weapon Finesse*, Weapon Focus*, Wingover**.

Windrider Feats: Ambidexterity, Blind-Fight, Combat Reflexes, Dodge, Exotic Weapon Proficiency, Expertise, Improved Critical*, Improved Initiative, Improved Unarmed Strike, Mounted Combat, Point Blank Shot, Power Attack, Quick Draw, Weapon Finesse*, Weapon Focus*.

*This feat may be taken more than once, but for a different kind of weapon each time.

**Described in Chapter 2 of this book.

Windrider Spell List

Windriders choose their spells from the following list.

1st Level—*alarm, animal trick†, calm animals, detect poison, endure elements, know direction, remove fear, resistance, speak with animals.*

2nd Level—*bottle of smoke†, delay poison, endurance, resist elements, magic fang, mage armor, nature's favor†, protection from arrows, shield other.*

3rd Level—*heal mount, neutralize poison, pass without trace, phantom steed, protection from elements.*

4th Level—*freedom of movement, greater magic fang, greater magic weapon, repel vermin.*

†New spell described in Chapter 6 of this book.

Ex-Windriders

A windrider who intentionally mistreats any mount she has ridden loses all windrider prestige class abilities, and her chosen mount immediately terminates that relationship. Until she atones (see the *atonement* spell description in the *Player's Handbook*), creatures of the same species as her last chosen mount treat her with enmity, which manifests as a –4 racial penalty on interactions with creatures of the same species as that mount and a –2 racial penalty on interactions with any other creature capable of serving her as a mount.

What's a Mount?

You can't just hop on and ride any creature, even if you have the Ride skill for that creature type. A mount must have all the following characteristics.

- Be able and willing to carry its rider in a typical fashion. (A camel trained with the Handle Animal skill to bear a rider is able and willing. A tiger might be able but not willing. A giant might be willing but not truly able. An intelligent creature whose alignment differs significantly from yours is unlikely to be willing.)
- Be at least one size category larger than you. Also, a flying mount can carry no more than its maximum light load aloft. (This is a change from the *Monster Manual*, which says that a flying creature's carrying capacity is equal to its medium load limit.)
- Have a CR no higher than your character level –3. If the mount can fly, its CR can be no higher than your character level –4.

Any animal or beast can be trained to bear a rider with the Handle Animal skill, as described in the appropriate skill description in the *Player's Handbook*. In addition, the windrider can use this skill to train a creature of any other type that has an Intelligence score of 2 or below to bear a rider. The category of the task and its Handle Animal DC are as given on Table 5–22.

Any creature not of the animal type counts as a beast for this check, regardless of its actual type. Any of these forms of training requires two months, as noted in the skill description.

Any creature with an Intelligence score of 3 or higher needs no Handle Animal check to learn how to bear a rider. If it is willing to serve as a mount, it can determine for itself how it must move to manage the additional weight, how to interpret its rider's directional commands, and so forth. It does, however, require at least one week of training with a rider before it can perform as a mount.

> ### Other Mount Feats
> The DM might decide to make additional feats available to mounts. The feats given in the windrider class description are from the core books and this book. You might consider the following as well:
>
> From *Sword and Fist*: Blindsight 5-foot Radius, Close Quarters Fighting, Dirty Fighting, Dual Strike, Improved Overrun, Power Lunge.
>
> From *Defenders of the Faith*: Extra Smiting.
>
> From *Song and Silence*: Dash, Fleet of Foot.

CHAPTER 6: SPELLS

"What is natural magic? What makes druids stand above those mired in civilized trinket-worship? Certainly natural magic is the ability to bend the universe to serve your will, but even a mason can force stone to serve his needs. Certainly natural magic is the power to do what others cannot, but any aristocrat will tell you he can do what other men cannot. No, natural magic is more than this. It is the command of the ineffable, of the earth, of the spirit, and of the elements—the command of all this through a focused mind and soul."

—Vadania

A druid is a healer with mastery over weather, plants, and animals. The water you drink, the food on your table, even the air you breathe—all these are subject to the druid's power. A neophyte druid can find the lost members of a herd (*detect animals or plants*), repair damaged pots and clothes (*mending*), and soothe a wild animal (*calm animals*). Yet, unlike the typical good cleric, she is more than just a civil servant. Before long, she can repel her enemies with spells such as *heat metal, produce flame,* and *summon nature's ally.*

As a druid grows in power, her mastery of the natural world increases. She can speak with, and soon control, animals and even plants. Foes foolish enough to cross her path may find themselves poisoned, diseased, or plagued with swarms of insects. Meanwhile, she can walk bravely through the harshest of environments and easily resist magical attacks of cold and fire. Then, at 7th level, the druid gains something that the cleric never does. With *reincarnate,* the druid can offer anyone a new lease on life. Even the aged can be reborn into a young body through her power.

A druid at the height of her career knows little in the way of limitation. She can cure any ill (*heal*), alter the climate (*control weather*), and slay her foes in their tracks just by pointing (*finger of death*). The very earth trembles beneath her feet (*earthquake*). At this point, her divine spells are the most concrete manifestation of nature's power in the world.

This chapter includes more than fifty new spells for druids and rangers to cast. A few of these are also available to other spellcasters.

NEW DRUID SPELLS

0-Level Druid Spells
Animal Trick. Animal companion performs a trick.
Darkseed. Slow-kills plants.
Dawn. Awakens sleeping creatures.
Daze Animal. Animal loses one action.
Fire Eyes. You see through natural fire, smoke, and fog.
Scarecrow. Animal becomes shaken.

1st-Level Druid Spells
Camouflage. Grants +10 on Hide checks.
Hawkeye. Increases range increments.
Power Sight. Determines a creature's HD or level.
Regenerate Light Wounds. Target heals 1 hp/round.
Sandblast. Creates a brief sandstorm in an arc.
Wood Wose. Summon minor nature spirit.

2nd-Level Druid Spells
Adrenaline Surge. Grants each of your summoned creatures +4 Str.
Animal Reduction. Animal shrinks in size.
Body of the Sun. Fire and light extend 5 ft. from caster's body.
Briar Web. As *entangle,* but thorns deal damage each round.
Creeping Cold. Deals progressive damage from cold (+1d6/round).
Decomposition. Wounded creatures suffer 1 extra hp/round.
Green Blockade. Creates a wall of vegetable matter.
Might of the Oak. Grants +4 Str, –2 Dex.
Persistence of the Waves. Grants +4 Con, –2 Str.
Regenerate Moderate Wounds. Target heals 2 hp/round.
Speed of the Wind. Grants +4 Dex, –2 Con.

3rd-Level Druid Spells
Bottle of Smoke. Creates a steed made of smoke.
Countermoon. Stops lycanthropic shapechanging for 12 hours.
Embrace the Wild. The caster gains an animal's senses and skills.
False Bravado. Causes false barbarian rage.
Nature's Favor. Target animal gains attack and damage bonus of +1/two levels.
Regenerate Ring. One creature/two levels heals 1 hp/round.
Standing Wave. Transports across water.

4th-Level Druid Spells
Beget Bogun. Creates natural homunculus.
Blight. Deals 1d6/level to a plant creature, or blights a 100-ft. spread.
Feathers. *Polymorphs* willing creature into bird.
Forestfold. Grants +20 on Hide and Move Silently checks.
Languor. Causes short-term Strength loss and slowing.
Last Breath. Creature killed within 1 round returns to 0 hp.
Mass Calm. As *calm animals,* but affects any number of targets.
Miasma. Gas cloud suffocates target.
Regenerate Serious Wounds. Target heals 3 hp/round.
Waterball. Splash does subdual damage.

5th-Level Druid Spells
Big Sky. Sky spirits cause fear.
Cloak of the Sea. Bestows *water breathing, freedom of movement,* and *invisibility* in water.
Druid Grove. Trees store spells for 24 hours.
Kiss of Death. Creates reusable poison, delivered by touch attack.
Mass Trance. As *animal trance,* but affects any number of targets.
Regenerate Critical Wounds. Target heals 4 hp/round.

6th-Level Druid Spells

Contagious Touch. Infects one touched creature/round with chosen disease.

Greater Call Lightning. As *call lightning*, but produces twice as many bolts.

Mandragora. Deafens those who fail Will saves, grants *true seeing* to others.

Protection from All Elements. Reduces the effects of all elemental spells.

Regenerate Circle. One creature/two levels heals 3 hp/round.

7th-Level Druid Spells

Cloudwalkers. Clouds support creatures, allowing flight.

Greater Creeping Cold. As *creeping cold*, but has a higher damage cap.

Slime Wave. Creates a 15-ft. spread of green slime.

8th-Level Druid Spells

Mass Awaken. One animal or tree/three levels gains human intellect.

Speak with Anything. Allows conversation with any creature or object.

9th-Level Druid Spells

Epidemic. Infects subject with chosen disease, and subject can infect others.

Invulnerability to Elements. Grants immunity to energy damage.

Lookingglass. Connects two mirrored surfaces for *clairvoyance* and transport.

Nature's Avatar. Target animal gains +10 attack and damage bonus, *haste*, and +1d8 temporary hit points/level.

Thunderswarm. Deals 16d8 points of lightning damage, plus bursts.

True Reincarnate. As *reincarnate*, plus remains aren't needed and some choice of form exists.

NEW RANGER SPELLS

1st-Level Ranger Spells

Animal Trick. Target animal companion performs a trick.

Bloodhound. Grants extra checks when tracking.

Camouflage. Grants +10 on Hide checks.

Dawn. Awakens sleeping creatures.

Hawkeye. Increases range increments.

2nd-Level Ranger Spells

Bottle of Smoke. Creates a steed made of smoke.

Briar Web. As *entangle*, but thorns deal damage each round.

Nature's Favor. Target animal gains attack and damage bonus of +1/two levels.

3rd-Level Ranger Spells

Animal Reduction. Animal shrinks in size.

Detect Favored Enemy. Reveals favored enemies.

Embrace the Wild. The caster gains an animal's senses and skills.

Forestfold. Grants +20 on Hide and Move Silently checks.

NEW CLERIC SPELLS

1st-Level Cleric Spells

Regenerate Light Wounds. Target heals 1 hp/round.

3rd-Level Cleric Spells

Regenerate Moderate Wounds. Target heals 2 hp/round.

5th-Level Cleric Spells

Blight. Deals 1d6/level to a plant creature, or blights a 100-ft. spread.

Regenerate Serious Wounds. Target heals 3 hp/round.

6th-Level Cleric Spells

Regenerate Critical Wounds. Target heals 4 hp/round.

7th-Level Cleric Spells

Slime Wave. Creates a 15-ft. spread of green slime.

NEW SORCERER/WIZARD SPELLS

2nd-Level Sorcerer/Wizard Spells

Adrenaline Surge. Grants each of your summoned creatures +4 Str.

Body of the Sun. Fire and light extend 5 ft. from caster's body.

5th-Level Sorcerer/Wizard Spells

Cloak of the Sea. Bestows *water breathing*, *freedom of movement*, and *invisibility* in water.

More Spells For Adepts

The adept as presented in the DUNGEON MASTER'S Guide is primarily a spellcaster for tribal societies, especially bestial humanoids such as orcs and gnolls and giant species such as ogres. Several of the spells presented in this book and in other accessories are also appropriate for the adept. If you wish, you can add the following spells to the adept's spell list. The spells marked with an asterisk(*) are from *Defenders of the Faith*, and those marked with a dagger (†) are from *Tome and Blood*. The remaining spells are from this chapter.

0 Level—dawn

1st Level—hawkeye, lesser cold orb†, scarecrow

2nd Level—choke†, decomposition, owl's wisdom†

3rd Level—beastmask*, embrace the wild, enhance familiar†

4th Level—false bravado, languor, weather eye*

5th Level—big sky, ghostform†

NEW SPELLS

"Zyok was moving in on the little goblin girl when she snapped this talisman off her junklace. Next thing I saw, Zyok's skin was streaked with ice. His scar-paint smeared and twisted under the ice that kept shattering and growing . . . shattering and growing. But Zyok kept fighting. Now that goblin was really in for it! At least she would have been, 'cept Zyok's skin started bleeding . . . and bleeding, until I couldn't see where the blood ended and the ice began. That's when Zyok fell and the goblin won the Challenge. A goblin winning a Challenge! Phah!"

—A boyhood memory of Krusk,
seeing the effects of *creeping cold*

Adrenaline Surge

Transmutation
Level: Drd 2, Sor/Wiz 2
Components: V, S, DF
Casting Time: 1 action
Range: Close (25 ft. + 5 ft./2 levels)
Area: Your summoned creatures within a spherical emanation with a radius equal to the range, centered on you
Duration: 1 round/level
Saving Throw: Will negates (harmless)
Spell Resistance: Yes (harmless)

Each of your summoned creatures within the area receives a +4 enhancement bonus to Strength. This effect lasts until the spell ends or the creature leaves the area.

Animal Reduction

Transmutation
Level: Drd 2, Rgr 3
Components: V, S
Casting Time: 1 action
Range: Touch
Target: One willing animal of size Small, Medium-size, Large, or Huge
Duration: 1 hour/level
Saving Throw: Will negates
Spell Resistance: Yes

You reduce the target animal's size by one category. For example, a Large tiger affected by this spell becomes a Medium-size tiger. This decrease in size allows the animal to fit better into tight spaces, such as the typical dungeon room or subterranean passage. The size change also has a number of other effects, as given in the *Monster Manual* and summarized below. If this spell would cause any ability score to drop to 0 or below, that score instead becomes 1 while all other effects apply normally.

Huge to Large: The subject loses 8 points of Strength, 4 points of Constitution, and 3 points of natural armor, while gaining 2 points of Dexterity, a +1 bonus to AC, and a +1 bonus on attack rolls. Overall, this change results in a –3 penalty on melee attack rolls, a +2 bonus on ranged attack rolls, a –4 penalty on melee damage rolls, a –1 penalty to AC, and –2 hit points per Hit Die. The subject's face/reach becomes 5 feet by 10 feet/5 feet.

Large to Medium-Size: The subject loses 8 points of Strength, 4 points of Constitution, and 2 points of natural armor, while gaining 2 points of Dexterity, a +1 bonus to AC, and a +1 bonus on attack rolls. Overall, this change results in a –3 penalty on melee attack rolls, a +2 bonus on ranged attack rolls, a –4 penalty on melee damage rolls, no change to AC, and –2 hit points per Hit Die. The subject's reach becomes 5 feet by 5 feet/5 feet.

Medium-Size to Small: The subject loses 4 points of Strength and 2 points of Constitution, while gaining 2 points of Dexterity, a +1 bonus to AC, and a +1 bonus on attack rolls. Overall, this change results in a –1 penalty on melee attack rolls, a +2 bonus on ranged attack rolls, a –2 penalty on melee damage rolls, a +2 bonus to AC, and

–1 hit point per Hit Die. The subject's face/reach becomes 5 feet by 5 feet/5 feet.

Small to Tiny: The subject loses 4 points of Strength while gaining 2 points of Dexterity, a +1 bonus to AC, and a +1 bonus on attack rolls. Overall, this change results in a –1 penalty on melee attack rolls, a +2 bonus on ranged attack rolls, a –2 penalty on melee damage rolls, a +2 bonus to AC, and no change to hit points. The subject's face/reach becomes 2 1/2 feet by 2 1/2 feet/0 feet.

Animal Trick

Transmutation
Level: Drd 0, Rgr 1
Components: V, S, DF
Casting Time: 1 action
Range: Close (25 ft. + 5 ft./2 levels)
Target: One animal companion bonded to you by an *animal friendship* effect
Duration: Instantaneous
Saving Throw: Will negates
Spell Resistance: Yes

Your animal companion performs a trick of your choosing that it does not already know. This trick can be any of those listed in the Animal Companions sidebar in Chapter 2 of the DUNGEON MASTER'S *Guide* or in Chapter 2 of this book. The animal retains no knowledge of the trick after performing it.

Beget Bogun

Conjuration (Creation)
Level: Drd 1
Components: V, S, M, XP
Casting Time: 1 action
Range: Touch
Effect: Tiny construct
Duration: Instantaneous
Saving Throw: None
Spell Resistance: No

Beget bogun allows you to infuse living magic into a small mannequin that you have created from vegetable matter. This is the final spell in the process of creating a bogun. See the bogun's description for further details.

Material Component: The mannequin from which the bogun is created.

XP Cost: 25 XP.

BOGUN

Tiny Construct
Hit Dice: 2d10 (11 hp)
Initiative: +3
Speed: 20 ft., fly 50 ft. (good)
AC: 15 (+3 Dex, +2 size)
Attacks: Nettles +1 melee
Damage: Nettles 1d4–2 and poison
Face/Reach: 2 1/2 ft. by 2 1/2 ft./0 ft.
Special Attacks: Poison
Special Qualities: Construct traits
Saves: Fort +0, Ref +3, Will +1
Abilities: Str 7, Dex 16, Con —, Int 8, Wis 13, Cha 10

Climate/Terrain: Any (typically forest)
Organization: Solitary
Challenge Rating: 1
Treasure: None
Alignment: Any neutral (always the same as the creator)
Advancement: 3–6 HD (Tiny)

A bogun is a small nature servant created by a druid. Like a homunculus, it is an extension of its creator, sharing the same alignment and link to nature. A bogun does not fight particularly well, but it can perform any simple action, such as attacking, carrying a message, or opening a door or window. For the most part, a bogun simply carries out its creator's instructions. Because it is self-aware and somewhat willful, however, its behavior is not entirely predictable. On rare occasions (5% of the time), the bogun may refuse to perform a particular task. In that case, the creator must make a Diplomacy check (DC 11) to convince the creature to cooperate. Success means the bogun performs the task as requested; failure indicates that it either does exactly the opposite or refuses to do anything at all for one day (DM's option as to which).

A bogun cannot speak, but the process of creating one links it telepathically with its creator. It knows what its creator knows and can convey to him or her everything it sees and hears, up to a range of 500 yards. A bogun never travels beyond this range willingly, though it can be removed forcibly. In that case, it does everything in its power to regain contact with its creator.

An attack that destroys a bogun also deals its creator 2d10 points of damage. If the creator is slain, the bogun also dies, and its body collapses into a heap of rotting vegetation.

A bogun looks like a vaguely humanoid mound of compost. The creator determines its precise features, but the typical bogun stands about 18 inches tall and has a wingspan of about 2 feet. Its skin is covered with nettles and branches.

COMBAT

A bogun attacks by brushing against opponents with harsh nettles that deliver an irritating poison.

Poison (Ex): Nettles, Fort save (DC 11); initial and secondary damage 1d6 temporary Dex. The creator of a bogun is immune to its poison.

Construct Traits: Immune to mind-influencing effects, poison, disease, and similar effects. Not subject to critical hits, subdual damage, ability damage, energy drain, or death from massive damage. Although it is made of vegetable matter, a bogun is not a plant and is therefore is not subject to spells that affect only plants.

CONSTRUCTION

Unlike a homunculus, a bogun is created from natural materials available in any forest. Thus, there is no gold piece cost for its creation. All materials used become permanent parts of the bogun.

The creator must be at least 7th level and possess the Craft Wondrous Item feat to make a bogun. Before casting any spells, a physical form must be woven out of living (or once-living) vegetable matter to hold the magical energy. A bit of the creator's own body, such as a few strands of hair or a drop of blood, must also be incorporated into this crude mannequin. The creator may assemble the body personally or hire someone else to do it. Creating the mannequin requires a Craft (basketweaving or weaving) check (DC 12).

Once the body is finished, the creator must animate it through an extended magical ritual that requires a week to complete. The creator must labor for at least 8 hours each day in complete solitude in a forest grove; any interruption from another sentient creature undoes the magic. If the creator is personally weaving the creature's body, that process and the ritual can be performed together.

When not actively working on the ritual, the creator must rest and can perform no other activities except eating, sleeping, or talking. Missing even one day causes the process to fail. At that point, the ritual must be started anew, though the previously crafted body and the grove can be reused.

On the final day of the ritual, the creator must personally cast *control plants*, *wood shape*, and *beget bogun*. These spells can come from outside sources, such as scrolls, rather than being prepared, if the creator prefers.

Big Sky
Enchantment (Compulsion) [Fear, Mind-Affecting]
Level: Drd 5
Components: V, S, DF
Casting Time: 1 action

Range: 30 ft.
Area: You and all allies and enemies within a 30-ft.-radius emanation centered on you
Duration: 1 round/level
Saving Throw: Will negates (see text)
Spell Resistance: Yes

This spell creates the sensation that the sky is filled with invisible nature spirits and sussurating voices. This effect is a boon to you and your allies and a bane to your enemies. You gain a +2 morale bonus on attack rolls and a +4 morale bonus on saving throws against fear effects for the duration of the spell, as does each of your allies within the area. Each of your enemies within the area who fails a Will save behaves as if affected by a *fear* spell. Each round, every affected enemy gets a new Will save to shake off the effects of this spell. An enemy who makes a successful save need not make any more saving throws for the duration of the spell. Creatures immune to fear are immune to both aspects of this spell.

Blight

Necromancy
Level: Clr 5, Drd 4
Components: V, S, DF
Casting Time: 1 action
Range: See text
Area or Target: See text
Duration: Instantaneous
Saving Throw: See text
Spell Resistance: Yes

This spell has two versions. To cast either version, you must touch a plant and breathe on it.

Blight Area: When you center this spell on a single normal plant, all normal plants within a 100-foot spread (including the one on which the spell was centered) immediately die. Flowers wilt, leaves fall to the ground, and foliage withers. This spell has no effect on the soil, so new growth can replace the dead plants. This effect allows no saving throw.

Blight Plant Creature: When targeted on a single mobile or intelligent plant, such as a shambling mound or a treant, this spell deals 1d6 points of damage per caster level, to a maximum of 15d6. The plant receives a Fortitude save for half damage.

Bloodhound

Divination
Level: Rgr 1
Components: V, S
Casting Time: 1 action
Range: Personal
Target: You
Duration: 1 hour/level

If you fail a Wilderness Lore check to track a creature while this spell functions, you can immediately attempt another roll against the same DC to establish the trail. If the reroll fails, you must search for the trail for 30 minutes (if outdoors) or 5 minutes (if indoors) before trying again.

Body of the Sun

Transmutation [Fire]
Level: Drd 2, Sor/Wiz 2
Components: V, S, DF
Casting Time: 1 action
Range: 5 ft.
Area: 5-ft.-radius emanation centered on you
Duration: 1 round/level

By drawing on the power of the sun, you cause your body to emanate fire. This fire extends 5 feet in all directions from your body, illuminating the area and doing 1d4+1 points of fire damage (Reflex save for half) to any creature it touches except you.

Bottle of Smoke

Conjuration (Creation)
Level: Drd 4, Rgr 3
Components: V, S, F
Casting Time: 10 minutes
Range: Touch
Effect: One smoky, horselike creature
Duration: 1 hour/level
Saving Throw: None
Spell Resistance: No

You use a fire source to create a plume of smoke, which you capture in a special bottle you're holding. If the bottle is thereafter opened before the spell duration expires, the smoke emerges to form a vaguely horselike creature made of wisps of smoke. It makes no sound, and anything that touches it simply passes through it.

To mount this smoke horse, the would-be rider must make a successful Ride check (DC 10) while holding the bottle in one hand. Anyone attempting to mount without the bottle simply passes through the horse's form. Letting go of the bottle after mounting causes the rider to fall through the horse's smoky form; he or she cannot thereafter remount without the intact bottle in hand. If the bottle is broken, the spell ends immediately and the rider (if mounted) falls to the ground.

The smoke horse has a speed of 20 feet per caster level, to a maximum of 240 feet. It can send smoke billowing out behind it at the rider's behest, leaving behind a bank of smoke 5 feet wide and 20 feet high as it moves. A wind that is at least severe (31+ mph), or magical wind of any kind, disperses the horse (and any smoke it has produced) instantly. Otherwise, the bank of smoke lasts 10 minutes, starting on the turn it was laid down. Starting or stopping the smoke trail is a free action. The mount and the smoke trail it produces give one-half concealment (20% miss chance) to anyone behind them.

The mount is immune to all damage and other attacks because material objects and spells simply pass through it. It cannot attack.

The rider can return the smoke horse to the bottle, and thus pause the spell, at any time by simply uncorking it (a move-equivalent action) and stoppering it again (another move-equivalent action) in the next round after the horse is inside. If the bottle is reopened later, the spell reactivates with its remaining duration intact.

An entangled creature can try to break free and move at half normal speed by using a full-round action to make a Strength check or Escape Artist check (DC 20). A nonentangled creature can move through the area at half speed, taking damage as described above. Each round nonentangled creatures remain in the area, the plants attempt to entangle them.

The plants provide one-quarter cover for every 5 feet of substance between a creature in the area and an opponent—one-half for 10 feet of *briar web*, three-quarters for 15 feet, and total cover for 20 feet or more.

The DM may alter the effects of the spell somewhat, based on the nature of the available plants.

Camouflage

Transmutation
Level: Drd 1, Rgr 1
Components: V, S, M
Casting Time: 1 action
Range: Personal
Target: You
Duration: 10 minutes/level

You change your coloring to match your environment, gaining a +10 competence bonus on Hide checks.

Material Component: Mud painted on your face.

Cloak of the Sea

Transmutation
Level: Drd 5, Sor/Wiz 5
Components: V, S, DF
Casting Time: 1 action
Range: Touch
Target: Creature touched that is in contact with water
Duration: 1 hour/level (D)
Saving Throw: Will negates (harmless)
Spell Resistance: Yes (harmless)

The subject retains his or her form, but appears to be composed of water. While underwater, the subject functions as if affected by *blur, freedom of movement,* and *water breathing* and doesn't suffer subdual damage from water pressure or hypothermia for the duration of the spell. Outside (or even partially outside) of water, the subject gains none of these advantages except *water breathing.* He or she may leave and reenter water without ending the spell.

Cloudwalkers

Transmutation
Level: Drd 7
Components: V, S, DF
Casting Time: 1 action
Range: Close (25 ft. + 5 ft./2 levels)
Targets: One creature/level, no two of which can be more than 30 ft. apart
Duration: 1 hour/level (D)
Saving Throw: Reflex negates (harmless)
Spell Resistance: Yes (harmless)

You create gaseous pads of cloudstuff on the subjects' feet, allowing them to walk on the clouds. These pads

Regardless of how much duration remains unused, the spell ceases functioning one day after it is cast. If dispelled at any time while the bottle is corked, the spell ends.

Focus: An ornate, corked bottle worth at least 50 gp.

Briar Web

Transmutation
Level: Drd 2, Rgr 2
Components: V, S, DF
Casting Time: 1 action
Range: Medium (100 ft. + 10 ft./level)
Area: Plants in a 40-ft.-radius spread
Duration: 1 minute/level
Saving Throw: See text
Spell Resistance: No

This spell causes grasses, weeds, bushes, and even trees to grow thorns and then wrap, twist, and entwine about creatures in the area, holding them fast. Creatures that stand still are entangled but experience no other effects and take no damage. A creature attempting an action (attack, cast a spell with a somatic component, move, or the like) takes thorn damage of 1d4 points +1 additional point per caster level and must make a successful Reflex save or be entangled (−2 penalty on attack rolls, −4 penalty to effective Dexterity, and unable to move). Anyone trying to cast a spell within the area must also make a Concentration check (DC 15 + spell level + damage taken) or lose the spell.

allow each subject to move straight up or down at a speed of up to 30 feet or laterally with a fly speed of 60 feet (perfect), as desired. (Lateral movement is possible only for a subject who is already at least 90 feet off the ground.) To touch the earth again, a subject must use a standard action to shake off the cloudstuff, which ends the spell for that creature. You may dismiss the spell, but only for all subjects at once—an act that can have significant consequences for subjects already in the air.

Contagious Touch

Necromancy
Level: Drd 6
Components: V, S
Casting Time: 1 action
Range: Personal
Target: You
Duration: 1 round/level
Saving Throw: Fortitude negates
Spell Resistance: Yes

Upon casting this spell, you must choose one disease from this list: blinding sickness, cackle fever, filth fever, mindfire, red ache, the shakes, or slimy doom (see Disease in Chapter 3 of the DUNGEON MASTER's Guide for descriptions). Any living creature you hit with a melee touch attack during the spell's duration is affected as though by the contagion spell, immediately contracting the disease you have selected unless it makes a successful Fortitude save. You cannot infect more than one creature per round.

Countermoon

Abjuration
Level: Drd 3
Components: V, S, F
Casting Time: 1 action
Range: Close (25 ft. + 5 ft./2 levels)
Target: One lycanthrope
Duration: 12 hours
Saving Throw: Will negates (D)
Spell Resistance: Yes

This spell stops a lycanthrope from changing form, preventing both voluntary shapechanging via the alternate form ability and involuntary shapechanging because of lycanthropy. The subject retains whatever form he or she had when the spell was cast for the duration; even death does not cause reversion to normal form until the spell ends. Natural lycanthropes gain a +4 competence bonus on the saving throw against this spell.
   Material Component: Hair, scale, or other castoff from the creature to be affected.

Creeping Cold

Transmutation [Cold]
Level: Drd 2
Components: V, S, F
Casting Time: 1 action
Range: Close (25 ft. + 5 ft./2 levels)
Target: One creature

Duration: 3 rounds
Saving Throw: Fortitude half
Spell Resistance: Yes

You turn the subject's sweat to ice, creating blisters as the ice forms on and inside the skin. The spell deals 1d6 cumulative points of cold damage per round it is in effect (that is, 1d6 on the 1st round, 2d6 on the second, and 3d6 on the third). Only one save is allowed against the spell; if successful, it halves the damage each round.
   Focus: A small glass or pottery vessel worth at least 25 gp filled with ice, snow, or water.

Darkseed

Transmutation
Level: Drd 0
Components: V, DF
Casting Time: 1 action
Range: Close (25 ft. + 5 ft/2 levels)
Target: One normal plant or plant creature
Duration: 1 day
Saving Throw: Reflex negates
Spell Resistance: Yes

If the target fails its Reflex save, it takes 1 point of damage when the spell is cast and another every hour while it is in effect. Hardness is ignored for damage from *darkseed*. It would take weeks to kill a large tree with successive applications of this spell, but a small plant would die in a matter of hours. *Darkseed* does not affect plant creatures with Wisdom and Charisma scores.

Dawn

Abjuration
Level: Drd 0, Rgr 1
Components: V
Casting Time: 1 action
Range: Personal
Target: All creatures within a 15-ft.-radius burst centered on you
Duration: Instantaneous
Saving Throw: Fortitude negates (harmless)
Spell Resistance: Yes

All sleeping creatures in the area awaken. Those who are unconscious because of subdual damage wake up and become staggered (see Subdual Damage in Chapter 8 of the *Player's Handbook*). This spell does not affect dying creatures.

Daze Animal

Enchantment [Compulsion, Mind-Affecting]
Level: Drd 0
Components: V, S, DF
Casting Time: 1 action
Components: V, S
Range: Close (25 ft. + 5 ft./2 levels)
Target: One Medium-size or smaller animal with less than 5 HD
Duration: 1 round
Saving Throw: Will negates
Spell Resistance: Yes

This enchantment clouds the target animal's mind. The subject is not stunned, so attackers get no special advantage against it, but it cannot move or attack.

Decomposition
Necromancy
Level: Drd 2
Components: V, S, DF
Casting Time: 1 action
Range: 50 ft.
Area: All enemies within a 50-ft.-radius emanation centered on you
Duration: 1 round/level
Saving Throw: None
Spell Resistance: Yes

Whenever an enemy within the area suffers normal (not subdual) damage, that wound festers for an additional 1 point of damage per round thereafter for the duration of the spell. A successful Heal check (DC 15) or the application of any *cure* spell or other healing magic (*heal, healing circle,* and so on) stops the festering. Only one wound festers at a time; additional wounds suffered while the first is still festering are not subject to this effect. Once festering has been stopped, however, any new wound suffered while the subject is within the area (before the spell expires) begins the process anew.

For example, a subject who takes 6 points of damage from an attack while within the area of a *decomposition* spell suffers 1 point of damage from festering the next round, and another 1 point on the round after that. On the following round, that subject receives 4 points of healing from a *cure light wounds* spell, so the festering stops and the subject takes no festering damage that round. The next round, the subject remains within the emanation and takes another 3 points of damage in battle. The festering begins again, inflicting 1 point of festering damage on the next round.

Detect Favored Enemy
Divination
Level: Rgr 3
Components: V, S, DF
Casting Time: 1 action
Range: Long (400 ft. + 40 ft./level)
Area: Quarter circle emanating from you to the extreme of the range
Duration: Concentration, up to 10 minutes/level (D)
Saving Throw: None
Spell Resistance: No

You can sense the presence of a favored enemy. The amount of information revealed depends on how long you study a particular area.
1st Round: Presence or absence of a favored enemy in the area.
2nd Round: Types of favored enemies in the area and the number of each type.
3rd Round: The location and HD of each individual present, as though revealed by a *power sight* effect.
Note: Each round you can turn to detect things in a new area. The spell can penetrate barriers, but 1 foot of

stone, 1 inch of common metal, a thin sheet of lead, or 3 feet of wood or dirt blocks it.

Druid Grove
Transmutation
Level: Drd 5
Components: V, S
Casting Time: At least 10 minutes (see text)
Range: Close (25 ft. + 5 ft/2 levels)
Target: One or more trees
Duration: 1 day/level or until discharged
Saving Throw: None
Spell Resistance: No

By casting *druid grove*, you reshape a living tree so that it can contain a spell. Thereafter, you can access this stored spell at any time, as if the tree were a very large, immobile scroll.

In conjunction with *druid grove*, you can cast druid spells totaling no more than one-third of your caster level (rounded down, maximum 6th). Instead of taking effect, these companion spells are stored in trees within the area. Each tree can hold only one spell. *Druid grove* and the companion spells must all be cast during the same uninterrupted ritual. The 10-minute casting time noted above is the minimum for the entire ritual; if any of the companion spells take longer than 10 minutes to cast, use the actual total casting time instead.

By touching the tree that contains a companion spell (a standard action), you can activate that spell instantaneously. You must make any decisions about its effect (such as targeting and direction) upon touching the tree.

You may have only one *druid grove* in effect at a time. If you cast a second *druid grove* before the first expires or is fully discharged, the first is dispelled.

A tree affected by *druid grove* detects as magical, but the detection process does not harm the tree in any way.

Embrace the Wild
Transmutation
Level: Drd 3, Rgr 3
Components: V, F
Casting Time: 1 action
Range: Personal
Target: You
Duration: 10 minutes/level

This spell allows you to adopt the nature and some abilities of a wild animal. You retain your own form, but you gain the natural and extraordinary senses of the creature you choose, as well as its skill ranks (though these do not stack with any ranks you already have in the same skills), for the duration of the spell. Thus, depending on your choice of animal, you could gain blindsight, scent, and ranks in Listen, Spot, or other skills. *Embrace the wild* does not grant you the animal's natural attacks, methods of locomotion, feats, or nonsensory extraordinary abilities, such as trample or improved grab.

Focus: Hide, skin, or feathers of the selected animal, or an item or component of its lair. You must have obtained the focus from the animal yourself.

Epidemic

Necromancy
Level: Drd 9
Components: V, S
Casting Time: 1 action
Range: Touch
Target: Living creature touched
Duration: Instantaneous
Saving Throw: Fortitude negates
Spell Resistance: Yes

Upon casting this spell, you must choose one disease from this list: blinding sickness, cackle fever, filth fever, mindfire, red ache, the shakes, or slimy doom (see Disease in Chapter 3 of the DUNGEON MASTER'S *Guide* for descriptions). The touched creature contracts the disease you have selected immediately (no incubation period) unless it makes a successful Fortitude save.

Unlike a creature affected by *contagion*, the subject of an *epidemic* spell becomes a powerful vector for spreading the disease. As long as the subject is afflicted with the disease, any living creature (except the caster) within 30 feet of him or her must make a Fortitude save or immediately contract the disease, regardless of its usual incubation period or method of transmission. Anyone infected in this manner also becomes a vector for the disease and can spread it in the same manner.

The save DC drops by 1 each day after the spell is cast, regardless of when any particular creature contracted it. A creature that makes a successful Fortitude save against this particular *epidemic* cannot contract that disease by any means for one day. Thereafter, coming within 30 feet of an infected creature requires another save, with the same consequences for failure or success.

You are immune to any infection that originates from your own casting.

False Bravado

Enchantment (Compulsion) [Mind-Affecting]
Level: Drd 3
Components: V, S, F
Casting Time: 1 action
Range: Close (25 ft. + 5 ft./2 levels)
Target: One humanoid
Duration: 3 rounds + the subject's Constitution modifier
Saving Throw: Will negates
Spell Resistance: Yes

False bravado causes the subject to grow overconfident, believing that he or she has gained the full effects of a barbarian's rage (Constitution and Strength bonuses as well as improved Will saves). In fact, however, the affected creature incurs all the penalties of a barbarian's rage but gains none of its advantages. The subject suffers a –2 penalty to AC and cannot use skills or abilities that require patience and concentration, such as moving silently or casting spells. At the end of the spell's duration, the creature is fatigued (–2 penalties to Strength and Dexterity, unable to charge or run) for the rest of that encounter.

Focus: A small mirror with a sigil of bravery painted upon it, worth at least 25 gp.

Feathers

Transmutation
Level: Drd 4
Components: V, S, DF
Casting Time: 1 action
Range: Close (25 ft. + 5 ft./2 levels)
Targets: One willing creatures/level
Duration: 1 hour/level (D)
Saving Throw: None (see text)
Spell Resistance: Yes (harmless)

This spell functions like *polymorph other*, except that you *polymorph* each subject into a feathered animal of Small size or smaller (your choice of species, but all subjects take the same form). Any subject may choose to resume his or her normal form (as a full-round action); doing so ends the spell for that individual alone. Otherwise, all subjects remain in the bird form until the spell expires or you dismiss it, restoring all affected creatures to normal form.

Fire Eyes

Transmutation
Level: Drd 0
Components: V, DF
Casting Time: 1 action
Range: Touch
Target: Creature touched
Duration: 10 minutes/level
Saving Throw: Will negates (harmless)
Spell Resistance: Yes (harmless)

Fire eyes grants the subject the ability to see through normal smoke, fire, and fog as if they weren't there. While the spell functions, other creatures do not gain concealment from these effects with respect to the subject. This spell does not enable a subject to see through magical fog, such as *obscuring mist* and *fog cloud*.

Forestfold

Transmutation
Level: Drd 4, Rgr 3

This spell grants you a +20 competence bonus on Hide and Move Silently checks. It is otherwise the same as *camouflage*.

Greater Call Lightning

Evocation [Electricity]
Level: Drd 6
Components: V, S
Casting Time: 10 minutes, +1 action per bolt called
Range: Long (400 ft. + 40 ft./level)
Effect: See text
Duration: 10 minutes/level
Saving Throw: Reflex half
Spell Resistance: Yes

This spell is similar to *call lightning*, except that you may call down bolts every 5 minutes. To cast *greater call lightning*, you must be in a stormy area—a rain shower, a tornado (including a whirlwind formed by a djinn or air elemental of 7 HD or more), clouds and wind, or even hot and cloudy conditions will do. While you are in such an area, you can call down one bolt of lightning every 5 minutes. You need not do so immediately upon casting—other actions, even spellcasting, can be performed at any time during the spell's duration. However, you must use a standard action to concentrate on the spell when you call each bolt.

Each bolt of lightning flashes down in a vertical stroke, striking any target point you designate that is within range (measured from your position at the time). It takes the shortest possible unobstructed path between a nearby cloud and the target point. Any creature within a 10-foot radius of the bolt's path or the point where it strikes is affected. Each bolt deals 1d10 points of electrical damage per caster level (maximum 15d10).

Greater call lightning is usable only outdoors; it does not function indoors, underground, or underwater. The spell ends if you leave the stormy area.

Greater Creeping Cold
Transmutation [Cold]
Level: Drd 7
Duration: See text

This spell is the same as *creeping cold*, but it adds a fourth round to the duration, during which it deals 4d6 points of damage. If the caster is at least 15th level, it adds a fifth round at 5d6 points of damage. If the caster is at least 20th level, it adds a sixth round at 6d6 points of damage.

Green Blockade
Conjuration (Creation)
Level: Drd 2
Components: V, S, DF
Casting Time: 1 action
Range: Close (25 ft. + 5 ft./2 levels)
Effect: 20-ft.-long, 1-ft.-thick wall of vegetation
Duration: 1 round/level
Saving Throw: None
Spell Resistance: No

You raise a barrier of plant life before you. Any creature trying to pass through this blockade must succeed at a Strength check (DC 15) to do so; success ends its movement on the other side of the wall. Fire burns away the blockade in 1 round, or creatures with appropriate implements can chop through it in 1 minute.

Hawkeye
Transmutation
Level: Drd 1, Rgr 1
Components: V
Casting Time: 1 action
Range: Personal
Target: You
Duration: 10 minutes/level

This spell gives you the ability to see accurately at long distances. Your range increment for projectile weapons increases by 50%, and you gain a +5 competence bonus on all Spot checks.

Invulnerability to Elements
Abjuration
Level: Drd 9
Components: V, S, DF
Casting Time: 1 action
Range: Touch
Target: Creature touched
Duration: 10 minutes/level
Saving Throw: None
Spell Resistance: Yes

As *protection from all elements*, but the target creature becomes immune to damage from acid, cold, electricity, fire, and sonic damage while the spell is in effect.

Kiss of Death
Necromancy
Level: Drd 5
Components: V, S, DF
Casting Time: 1 action
Range: Personal
Target: You
Duration: 1 round/level
Saving Throw: Fortitude negates (see text)
Spell Resistance: Yes (see text)

Your teeth and tongue become coated with a fast-acting, virulent poison. Each round, you may make a melee touch attack to deliver the poison via a kiss. The poison deals 1d10 points of temporary Constitution damage immediately and another 1d10 points of temporary Constitution damage 1 minute later. Each instance of damage can be negated by a Fortitude save (DC 10 + one-half caster level + caster's Wisdom modifier). If you fail to overcome a creature's spell resistance, both primary and secondary damage are negated, but only for that attack. If you use this attack against that creature again while the spell is in effect, you can try again to overcome its spell resistance.

Languor
Transmutation
Level: Drd 4
Components: V, S
Casting Time: 1 action
Range: Close (25 ft. + 5 ft./2 levels)
Effect: Ray
Duration: 1 round/level
Saving Throw: Will negates
Spell Resistance: Yes

This spell causes creatures it hits to become weak and slow. A subject who fails a Will save is *slowed* as the spell and suffers a cumulative enhancement penalty to Strength equal to 1d6–1 per two caster levels (minimum additional penalty of 0, maximum of –10) each round. If the subject's Strength drops below 1, it is helpless. This spell does not counter *haste* nor it is countered by it, but a *hasted* creature can be brought to normal speed by *languor*, and a creature affected by *languor* can be brought to normal speed by *haste*.

Last Breath

Necromancy
Level: Drd 4
Components: V, S
Casting Time: 1 action
Range: Touch
Target: Dead creature touched
Duration: Instantaneous
Saving Throw: None (see text)
Spell Resistance: Yes (harmless)

With this spell, you can return a dead creature to 0 hit points, provided it died within the last round. You suffer 1d4 points of damage per Hit Die of the creature affected, and your spell resistance cannot overcome this damage.

The subject's soul must be free and willing to return (see Bringing Back the Dead in Chapter 10 of the *Player's Handbook*). If the subject's soul is not willing to return, the spell does not work; therefore, a subject who wants to return receives no saving throw.

Last breath cures enough damage to bring the subject's current hit points to 0. Any ability scores damaged to 0 or below are raised to 1. Normal poison and normal disease are cured, but magical diseases and curses are not undone. The spell closes mortal wounds and repairs lethal damage of most kinds, but missing body parts are still missing when the creature returns to life. None of the dead creature's equipment or possessions are affected in any way by this spell.

Coming back from the dead is an ordeal. The subject loses one level when it returns to life, just as if it had lost a level to an energy-draining creature. This level loss cannot be repaired by any spell. A subject who was previously 1st level loses 1 point of Constitution instead. A character who died with spells prepared has a 50% chance of losing any given spell upon being raised, in addition to losing spells for losing a level. A spellcasting creature that doesn't prepare spells (such as a sorcerer) has a 50% chance of losing any given unused spell slot as if it had been used to cast a spell, in addition to losing spell slots for losing a level.

Last breath has no effect on a creature that has been dead for more than 1 round. A creature that died from a death effect can't be raised by this spell, nor can constructs, elementals, outsiders, and undead creatures. *Last breath* cannot bring back a creature who has died of old age.

Lookingglass

Transmutation
Level: Drd 9
Components: V, S, DF
Casting Time: 1 hour
Range: Medium (100 ft. + 10 ft./level)
Target: A reflective surface at least as big as a Medium-size creature
Duration: 1 day/level
Saving Throw: See text
Spell Resistance: Yes

When you cast this spell, you create one end of a path between two natural mirrored surfaces, such as pools of water or clear lakes. If you cast a second *lookingglass* spell on a similar surface before the duration of the first expires, you can look through it as if you were using *clairvoyance*. Within 1 minute/level of casting the second *lookingglass*, you and up to one other creature/level may step through as if affected by *teleport without error*. This spell doesn't provide any ability to survive in the location of either *lookingglass*, so if you cast it the first spell on a lake, your allies had better be able to swim. If the spell duration of the first *lookingglass* spell elapses before you can complete the path with a second casting, the first spell is useless.

Mandragora

Enchantment (Compulsion) [Mind-Affecting]
Level: Drd 6
Components: V, S, M
Casting Time: 1 action
Range: 15 ft.
Effect: All creatures in a 15-ft. radius
Duration: 1 round/level
Saving Throw: Will negates
Spell Resistance: Yes

With this spell, you can trigger the insightful and baleful magic of a mandrake root. When you pull it from its dark container, you and all other creatures within 15 feet must make a Will save against its scream. Those who succeed gain a *true seeing* effect; those who fail behave as though affected by *confusion*. Both effects last until the spell ends.

Material Component: A mandrake root worth at least 100 gp in a secure container with the same value.

Mass Awaken

Transmutation
Level: Drd 8
Components: V, S, F, XP
Casting Time: One day
Range: Medium (100 ft. + 10 ft./level)
Target: One animal or tree/three levels, no two of which may be more than 30 ft. apart
Duration: Instantaneous
Saving Throw: See text
Spell Resistance: Yes

You awaken one or more trees or animals to humanlike sentience. All *awakened* creatures must be of the same kind. To succeed, you must make a successful Will save (DC 10 + the HD of the highest-HD target, or the HD the highest target tree has once *awakened*, whichever is greater). Failure indicates that the spell fails for all targets.

The *awakened* animal or tree is friendly toward you. You have no special empathy or connection with it, but it serves you in specific tasks or endeavors if you communicate your desires to it.

An *awakened* tree has characteristics as if it were an animated object (see the *Monster Manual*), except that its Intelligence, Wisdom, and Charisma scores are all

3d6. *Awakened* plants gain the ability to move their limbs, roots, vines, creepers, and so forth, and they have senses similar to a human's. An *awakened* animal has 3d6 Intelligence, a +1d3 bonus to Charisma, and +2 HD.

An *awakened* tree or animal can speak one language that you know, plus one additional language that you know per point of Intelligence bonus (if any).

XP Cost: 250 XP per creature awakened.

Mass Calm

Enchantment [Compulsion, Mind-Affecting]
Level: Drd 4
Components: V, S
Casting Time: 1 action
Range: Close (25 ft. + 5 ft./2 levels)
Target: Any number of animals, beasts, and magical beasts with Intelligence 1 or 2, no two of which can be more than 30 ft. apart
Duration: 1 minute/level
Saving Throw: Will negates (see text)
Spell Resistance: Yes

This spell soothes and quiets the subjects, rendering them docile and harmless. Animals trained to attack or guard, dire animals, legendary animals, beasts, and magical beasts are entitled to saving throws against this effect; normal animals are not. (A druid could calm a normal bear or wolf with little trouble, but it's more difficult to affect a winter wolf, a bulette, or a trained guard dog.)

The subjects remain where they are and do not attack or flee. They are not helpless, so they defend themselves normally if attacked. Any threat (fire, a hungry predator, or an imminent attack, for example) breaks the spell on the threatened creatures.

Mass Trance

Enchantment [Compulsion, Mind-Affecting]
Level: Drd 5
Components: V, S
Casting Time: 1 action
Range: Close (25 ft. + 5 ft./2 levels)
Target: Any number of animals, beasts, and magical beasts with Intelligence 1 or 2, no two of which may be more than 30 ft. apart
Duration: Concentration
Saving Throw: Will negates (see text)
Spell Resistance: Yes

Your swaying motions and music (or singing, or chanting) compel the subjects to do nothing but watch you. Animals trained to attack or guard, dire animals, legendary animals, beasts, and magical beasts are entitled to saving throws; normal animals are not. An affected creature can be struck (with a +2 bonus on the attack roll, as if it were stunned), but such an action breaks the spell on that creature.

Miasma

Evocation
Level: Drd 4
Components: V, S, DF
Casting Time: 1 action
Range: Medium (100 ft. + 10 ft./level)
Target: One living creature
Duration: 5 rounds/level
Saving Throw: See text
Spell Resistance: Yes

By filling the subject's mouth and throat with unbreathable gas, you prevent him or her from doing much more than coughing and spitting. The subject can hold his or her breath for 2 rounds per point of Constitution but must make a Constitution check (DC 10 +1 per previous success) each round thereafter to continue doing so. Failure on any such check (or voluntary resumption of breathing) causes the subject to fall unconscious (0 hp). On the next round, the subject drops to −1 hit points and is dying; on the third round, he or she suffocates (see Suffocation in Chapter 3 of the DUNGEON MASTER's *Guide*).

Might of the Oak

Transmutation
Level: Drd 2
Components: V, S, DF
Casting Time: 1 action
Range: Touch
Target: Living creature touched
Duration: 10 minutes/level
Saving Throw: Will negates
Spell Resistance: Yes

This spell grants the quiet strength of a massive oak tree. The subject gains a +4 enhancement bonus to Strength and suffers a −2 enhancement penalty to Dexterity.

Nature's Avatar

Evocation
Level: Drd 9
Components: V, S, DF
Casting Time: 1 action
Range: Touch
Target: Animal touched
Duration: 1 minute/level
Saving Throw: Will negates (harmless)
Spell Resistance: Yes (harmless)

You infuse the subject with the spirit of nature. The affected creature gains a +10 morale bonus on attack and damage rolls and 1d8 temporary hit points per caster level, plus the effects of *haste*.

Nature's Favor

Evocation
Level: Drd 3, Rgr 2
Components: V, S, DF
Casting Time: 1 action
Range: Touch
Target: Animal touched
Duration: 5 rounds/level
Saving Throw: Will negates (harmless)
Spell Resistance: Yes (harmless)

By calling on the power of nature, you grant the target animal a +1 luck bonus on attack and damage rolls for every two caster levels you possess.

Persistence of the Waves

Transmutation
Level: Drd 2
Components: V, S, DF
Casting Time: 1 action
Range: Touch
Target: Living creature touched
Duration: 10 minutes/level
Saving Throw: Will negates
Spell Resistance: Yes

This spell bestows the smooth indomitability of waves crashing on a shore. The subject gains a +4 enhancement bonus to Constitution and suffers a −2 enhancement penalty to Strength.

Power Sight

Divination
Level: Drd 1
Components: V, S
Casting Time: 1 action
Range: Close (25 ft. + 5 ft./2 levels)
Target or Area: One creature
Duration: Instantaneous
Saving Throw: None
Spell Resistance: No

You determine the number of Hit Dice (including those from class levels) a creature currently has. If the creature has both monster Hit Dice and class levels, *power sight* reveals only the total. You cannot determine what class levels a creature has, and negative levels do not count against its HD. For example, both a 10-HD creature and a 10th-level character with 4 negative levels appear as 10-HD creatures.

Protection from All Elements

Abjuration
Level: Drd 6
Components: V, S, DF
Casting Time: 1 action
Range: Touch
Target: Creature touched
Duration: 10 minutes/level or until discharged
Saving Throw: None
Spell Resistance: Yes

The subject becomes invulnerable to acid, cold, electricity, fire, and sonic damage. The spell absorbs damage the subject would otherwise take from all the above energy types, regardless of whether the source of damage is natural or magical. This protection also extends to the subject's equipment. When the spell has absorbed a total of 12 points of damage per caster level dealt by any combination of the above energy types, it is discharged.

Protection from all elements absorbs only damage. The subject could still suffer unfortunate side effects, such as drowning in acid (since drowning damage comes from lack of oxygen) or becoming encased in ice.

The effects of this spell do not stack with those of *protection from elements*, *endure elements*, or *resist elements*. If a creature is warded by *protection from all elements* and any of these other spells, *protection from all elements* absorbs damage until it is discharged.

Regenerate Circle

Conjuration (Healing)
Level: Drd 6

This spell is the same as *regenerate ring*, except that it grants fast healing at the rate of 3 hit points per round.

Regenerate Critical Wounds

Conjuration (Healing)
Level: Clr 6, Drd 5

This spell is the same as *regenerate light wounds*, except that it grants fast healing at the rate of 4 hit points per round.

Regenerate Light Wounds

Conjuration (Healing)
Level: Clr 1, Drd 1
Components: V, S
Casting Time: 1 action
Range: Touch
Target: Living creature touched
Duration: 10 rounds + 1 round/level
Saving Throw: Will negates (harmless)
Spell Resistance: Yes (harmless)

With a touch of your hand, you boost the subject's life energy, granting him or her the fast healing ability for the duration of the spell. This healing applies only to damage sustained during the spell's duration, not to that from previous injuries. The subject heals 1 hit point per round of such damage until the spell ends and is automatically stabilized if he or she begins dying from hit point loss during that time. *Regenerate light wounds* does not restore hit points lost from starvation, thirst, or suffocation, nor does it allow a creature to regrow or attach lost body parts.

The effects of multiple *regenerate* spells do not stack; only the highest-level effect applies. Applying a second *regenerate* spell of equal level extends the first spell's duration by the full duration of the second spell.

Regenerate Moderate Wounds
Conjuration (Healing)
Level: Clr 3, Drd 2

This spell is the same as *regenerate light wounds*, except that it grants fast healing at the rate of 2 hit points per round.

Regenerate Ring
Conjuration (Healing)
Level: Drd 3
Components: V, S
Casting Time: 1 action
Range: 20 ft.
Target: One creature/two levels, no two of which can be more than 30 ft. apart
Duration: 10 rounds + 1 round/two levels
Saving Throw: Will negates (harmless)
Spell Resistance: Yes (harmless)

You invoke healing energy over a group of creatures, granting each the fast healing ability for the duration of the spell. This healing applies only to damage sustained during the spell's duration, not to that from previous injuries. Each subject heals 1 hit point per round of such damage until the spell ends and is automatically stabilized if he or she begins dying from hit point loss during that time. *Regenerate ring* does not restore hit points lost from starvation, thirst, or suffocation, nor does it allow a creature to regrow or attach lost body parts.

The effects of multiple *regenerate* spells do not stack; only the highest-level effect applies. Applying a second *regenerate* spell of equal level extends the first spell's duration by the full duration of the second spell.

Regenerate Serious Wounds
Conjuration (Healing)
Level: Clr 5, Drd 4

This spell is the same as *regenerate light wounds*, except that it grants fast healing at the rate of 3 hit points per round.

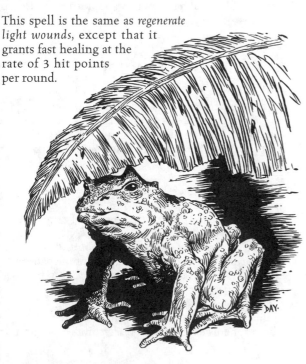

Sandblast
Evocation
Level: Drd 1
Components: V, S, DF
Casting Time: 1 action
Range: 10 ft.
Area: Semicircular burst of sand 10 ft. long, centered on your hands
Duration: Instantaneous
Saving Throw: Reflex half
Spell Resistance: Yes

You fire a hail of hot sand from your fingers, dealing 1d6 points of subdual damage to creatures in the arc. (See the illustration in the *burning hands* spell description in the *Player's Handbook* for details of the arc.) Any creature that fails its Reflex save is also stunned for 1 round.

Scarecrow
Necromancy [Fear, Mind-Affecting]
Level: Drd 0
Components: V, S
Casting Time: 1 action
Range: Close (25 ft. + 5 ft/2 levels)
Target: One animal
Duration: 1 round/level
Saving Throw: Will negates
Spell Resistance: Yes

The subject becomes shaken, suffering a –2 morale penalty on attack rolls, saves, and checks for the duration of the spell.

Slime Wave
Conjuration (Summoning)
Level: Clr 7, Drd 7
Components: V, S, M
Casting Time: 1 action
Range: Close (25 ft. + 5 ft./2 levels)
Area: 15-ft.-radius spread
Duration: 1 round/level
Saving Throw: Reflex negates
Spell Resistance: No

You create a wave of green slime that begins at the range you choose and violently spreads to the limit of the area. The wave splashes and splatters as it passes; some slime clings to any wall or ceiling. Each creature in the area that fails its Reflex save is covered with one patch of green slime for every 5 feet of its face.

Green slime devours flesh and organic materials on contact, and even dissolves metal. A patch of green slime deals 1d6 points of temporary Constitution damage per round while it devours flesh. Against wood or metal, green slime deals 2d6 points of damage per round, ignoring the hardness of metal but not that of wood. It does not harm stone.

On the first round of contact, the slime can be scraped off a creature (most likely destroying the scraping device), but after that it must be frozen, burned, or cut away (applying damage to the victim as well). Extreme cold or heat, sunlight, or a *remove disease* spell destroys the green slime. Unlike normal green slime, the slime created by this spell gradually evaporates, disappearing by the end of the duration.

Material Component: A few drops of stagnant pond water.

Speak with Anything
Divination
Level: Drd 8
Components: V, S
Casting Time: 10 minutes
Range: Personal
Target: You
Duration: 1 minute/level

This spell grants you the effects of *speak with animals*, *speak with plants*, and *tongues*, enabling you to communicate with any living creature, including unintelligent ones such as normal plants. You can ask questions of and receive answers from any creatures, although the spell doesn't make them any more friendly or cooperative than normal. You can make yourself understood as far as your voice carries.

You also gain the ability to speak with stone, metal, earth, water, or any other solid or semisolid object or terrain feature as though under the influence of *stone tell*. Any such object or terrain feature can relate to you who or what has touched it, as well as what is covered or concealed behind or under it, providing complete descriptions as requested. However, an object's perspective, perception, and knowledge may prevent it from providing the details you are looking for (DM's discretion).

This spell does not include a *speak with dead* effect, so you cannot access the past memories of dead creatures.

Though you understand every creature and object, you may speak only one language (or rough equivalent) at a time.

Speed of the Wind
Transmutation
Level: Drd 2
Components: V, S
Casting Time: 1 action
Range: Touch
Target: Living creature touched
Duration: 10 minutes/level
Saving Throw: Will negates
Spell Resistance: Yes

With this spell, you can grant the ephemeral quickness of a sudden breeze. The subject gains a +4 enhancement bonus to Dexterity and a −2 enhancement penalty to Constitution.

Standing Wave
Transmutation
Level: Drd 3
Components: V, S, DF
Casting Time: 1 action
Range: Close (25 ft. + 5 ft/2 levels)
Target: Waves under a creature or object within range
Duration: 10 minutes/level
Saving Throw: Reflex negates
Spell Resistance: Yes

You command the waters to lift a creature or object and propel it forward. An object so lifted may contain creatures or other objects. What the wave can lift depends on your caster level.

Caster Level	Size of Creature or Object
5th	Up to Medium-size
7th	Large
9th	Huge
11th	Gargantuan
13th	Colossal

Standing wave moves the lifted creature or object in a straight line at a speed of 60 feet over water. The spell dissipates when the wave contacts land, lowering its burden harmlessly to shore.

Thunderswarm
Evocation [Electricity]
Level: Drd 9
Components: V, S
Casting Time: 1 action
Range: Long (400 ft. + 40 ft./level)
Area: Pattern of lightning spreads similar to a *fireball* (see text)
Duration: Instantaneous
Saving Throw: None or Reflex half (see text)
Spell Resistance: Yes

Like the arcane spell *meteor swarm*, *thunderswarm* evokes blasts similar to those of the spell *fireball*, except that this spell creates balls of lightning. When you cast it, either four large (2-foot-diameter) spheres or eight small (1-foot-diameter) spheres spring from your outstretched hand and streak in a straight line to the spot you designate. Each sphere leaves a trail of sparks behind it.

Any creature in the straight-line path of these spheres is struck by each one and takes a total of 16d6 points of electricity damage (no save). The spheres dissipate after dealing this damage.

If the spheres reach their destination, each bursts like an electrical *fireball* in a spread. The patterns of their detonation and damage dealt to creatures in the area depend on the size of the spheres, as follows. (See the *meteor swarm* spell description in the *Player's Handbook* for details on the patterns.)

Large Spheres: Each large sphere has a 15-foot-radius spread and deals 4d8 points of electricity damage. The four spheres explode with their points of origin forming either a large diamond or a large box pattern (your choice) around the spell's central point of origin. The blasts are 20 feet apart along the sides of the pattern, creating overlapping areas of the spell's effect and exposing the center to all four blasts.

Small Spheres: Each small sphere has a 7 1/2-foot-radius spread and deals 2d6 points of electricity damage. These spheres explode with their points of origin form-

ing either a box-within-a-diamond pattern or a diamond-within-a-box pattern around the spell's central point of origin. Each of the pattern's outer sides measures 20 feet long. All four areas overlap in the center of the pattern, and two or three areas overlap in various peripheral sections.

A creature caught in one of the blasts may attempt a Reflex save for half damage. Creatures struck by multiple blasts must save against each blast separately. Any creature that fails a save is stunned for 1d4 rounds in addition to taking full damage.

True Reincarnate

Transmutation
Level: Drd 9
Components: V, S, DF, XP
Casting Time: 10 minutes
Range: Touch
Target: Dead creature touched
Duration: Instantaneous
Saving Throw: None (see text)
Spell Resistance: Yes (harmless)

This spell is the same as *reincarnate*, except that the druid can reincarnate a creature that has been dead up to 10 years per caster level. *True reincarnate* can even bring back a subject whose body has been wholly destroyed, provided that you unambiguously identify that creature in some fashion (reciting the deceased's time and place of birth or death is the most common method).

Upon completion of this spell, the subject has a new body, and all physical ills and afflictions are repaired. Refer to the description and the table for the *reincarnate* spell (in the *Player's Handbook*) to determine the subject's new incarnation. When rolling to determine the new form, roll twice; the returning creature can select from either of the two forms indicated.

The subject suffers neither loss of level (or Constitution point) nor loss of any prepared spells or spell slots.

You can reincarnate someone killed by a death effect or someone who has been turned into an undead creature and then destroyed, as well as someone killed by hit point loss.

XP Cost: 1,000 XP.

Waterball

Evocation
Level: Drd 4
Components: V, S, M
Casting Time: 1 action
Range: Long (400 ft. + 40 ft./level)
Area: 20-ft.-radius spread
Duration: Instantaneous
Saving Throw: Reflex half
Spell Resistance: Yes

A *waterball* is a spherical burst of water that looks like a blue *fireball*. As with a *fireball*, you point your finger and determine the range (distance and height) at which the

waterball is to burst. A blue, pea-sized bead streaks from the pointing digit and, unless it impacts upon a material body or solid barrier prior to attaining the prescribed range, blossoms into the *waterball* at that point. (An early impact results in an early detonation.) If you attempt to send the bead through a narrow passage, such as an arrow slit, you must "hit" the opening with a ranged touch attack, or else the bead strikes the barrier and detonates prematurely. (See the *fireball* spell description in the *Player's Handbook* for details of the blast pattern.)

When it detonates, the *waterball* deals 1d6 points of subdual damage per caster level (maximum 10d6). An affected creature can make a Reflex save for half damage. Since the damage is subdual rather than energy, it is subject to damage resistance.

Objects take no damage unless they have a hardness of 0, in which case they take full damage. If the damage caused to an interposing barrier shatters or breaks through it, the *waterball* may continue beyond it if the area permits; otherwise it stops at the barrier just as any other spell effect does.

Material Component: A full waterskin that you burst when casting the spell.

Wood Wose

Conjuration (Creation)
Level: Drd 1
Components: V, S, DF
Casting Time: 1 action
Range: Close (25 ft. + 5 ft./2 levels)
Effect: One nature servant
Duration: 1 hour/level
Saving Throw: None
Spell Resistance: No

A *wood wose* is a translucent, green nature spirit that you can command to perform simple natural tasks. It can build a campfire, gather herbs, feed an animal companion, catch a fish, or perform any other simple task that doesn't involve knowledge of technology. It cannot, for example, open a latched chest, since it doesn't know how a latch works.

The wose can perform only one activity at a time, but it repeats the same activity if told to do so. Thus, if you commanded it to gather leaves, it would continue to do so while you turned your attention elsewhere, as long as you remained within range.

The wose has an effective Strength score of 2, so it can lift 20 pounds or drag 100 pounds. It can trigger traps, but the 20 pounds of force it can exert is not enough to activate most pressure plates. Its speed is 15 feet in any direction, even up.

A *wood wose* cannot attack in any way; it is never allowed an attack roll or a saving throw. It cannot be killed, but it dissipates if it takes 6 points of damage from area attacks. If you attempt to send the wose beyond the spell's range (measured from your current position), it ceases to exist.